D1044693

HELL FOLLOWED

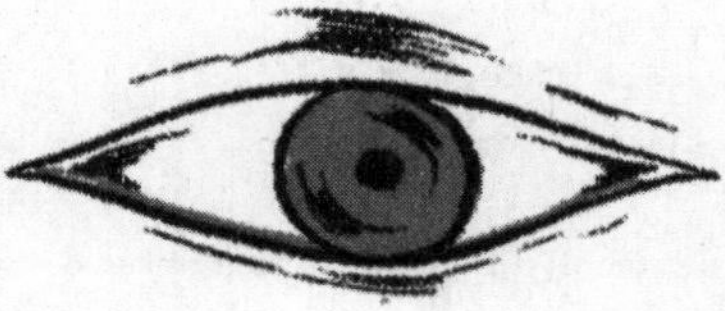

WITH US

Published by Peachtree Teen
An imprint of PEACHTREE PUBLISHING COMPANY INC.
1700 Chattahoochee Avenue
Atlanta, Georgia 30318-2112
PeachtreeBooks.com

Text © 2022 by Andrew Joseph White
Cover image © 2022 by Evangeline Gallagher

All rights reserved. No part of this publication may be reproduced, stored in a retrieval system, or transmitted in any form or by any means—electronic, mechanical, photocopy, recording, or any other—except for brief quotations in printed reviews, without the prior permission of the publisher.

Edited by Ashley Hearn
Design and composition by Lily Steele
Cover design by Melia Parsloe

Printed and bound in April 2022 at Lake Book Manufacturing, Melrose Park, IL, USA.
Jacket printed in April 2022 at Phoenix Color, Hagerstown, MD, USA.
10 9 8 7 6 5 4 3

ISBN: 978-1-68263-324-3

Cataloging-in-Publication Data is available from the Library of Congress.

HELL FOLLOWED WITH US

ANDREW JOSEPH WHITE

PEACHTREE
Teen

For the kids who sharpen
*their teeth and **bite***

—A. J. W.

LETTER FROM THE AUTHOR

If you set a fire, you're going to inhale some smoke. I'm all for setting fires and burning whatever will catch flame, but I encourage you to be careful when you pour the kerosene.

This book contains depictions of graphic violence, transphobia, domestic and religious abuse, self-injury, and attempted suicide.

Hell Followed with Us is a book about survival. It is a book about queer kids at the end of the world trying to live long enough to grow up. It is a book about the terrible things that people do in the name of belief and privilege. So if any of the topics above will burn you, I respect your decision to step away. Actually, I admire you—I've never been so careful.

But if you've stepped even closer, close enough that you can feel the heat on your cheeks . . .

I wrote this book for a few reasons: Because I wanted more stories about boys like me. Because I was angry. Because I still am. But mainly, I wanted to show queer kids that they can walk through hell and come out alive. Maybe not in one piece, maybe forever changed, but alive and worthy of love all the same.

That's what you'll find here. Terrible things, survival, love, and a future worth fighting for.

Sharpen your teeth, take up your fire, and let's do this.

Yours,

ANDREW

And thus the LORD spoke to us—
for again we have failed Him, again He regrets His creations, so again the earth must flood! And we have done His holy work, amen!

—High Reverend Father Ian Clevenger, before releasing the Flood virus on Times Square

Be not afraid.

—Joshua 1:9, King James version

BENJAMIN

CHAPTER 1

You will return to the earth for out of it you were taken;
for from dust you were made and to dust you will return.

—Angel prayer

Here's the thing about being raised an Angel: You don't process grief.

Grief is a sin. Loss is God's design, and to mourn the dead is to insult His vision. To despair at His will is sacrilege. How dare you betray His plan by grieving what was always His to take? Unfaithful, disgusting heretic, you should be hung from the wall so the nonbelievers will know what's coming for them. Romans 6:23—*for the wages of sin is death.*

So the image of Dad's body burns into the folds of my brain, writes itself between the grooves of my fingerprints, and I swallow it down until I choke. Angels cut out the parts of us that remember how to cry until we can't. We learn to mask the grief, to pack it away for later, later, *later*, until eventually we just die.

The way I see it, I don't have to worry. If the Angels get their way, all this grief will be His problem soon enough. And if they don't—

God, please don't—

I'm running. Dad's blood is in my mouth. Brother Hutch shot him once in the chest to stop him and once in the head to kill him. Brother Hutch calls for me, "We can do this the easy way, we really can!" The other Angels sweep the riverfront, shining white in the blazing February sun, moving slow and sure through the streets. They don't have to be quick. They know they'll catch me eventually.

One sixteen-year-old boy against a death squad of Angels? I'm doomed.

I crash to a stop behind a stone pillar by the riverbank and double over to gasp for air. My hair sticks to my forehead in a slurry of sweat and blood—Dad's blood—drying on my face and hands. My lungs burn. I can't tell if the roaring in my ears is my heartbeat or the river.

Dad's gone. He's dead, he's dead, he's dead.

"Please, God," I whisper before I can stop myself. What makes me think He's going to answer me now? "Please give me something, anything—"

"Sister Woodside!" Brother Hutch cries. "Your mother is worried about you! She wants her daughter to come home."

The first thing Dad told me—when Mom said I'd see the Lord's plan for my womanhood eventually, that she'd carve it into me if she had to—he told me I'm a man, and I fought for it, and nobody can take that from me.

Open your eyes. Breathe. Pull it together, Benji, pull it together.

The death squads haven't gotten me yet.

I can finish what Dad started.

I can get out of Acheson, Pennsylvania.

I peek from behind the pillar to look down the street. The riverfront district was probably beautiful before Judgment Day. Before the Flood hit. Now, ivy climbs up glass skyscrapers and cars rust in parking-lot graveyards. Lawns and gardens have gone wild, smothering everything they can reach. Flowers bloom in February. It's one of the few good months for flowers. They'll die of thirst by April.

But I don't see any Angels. Not yet.

Brother Hutch shouts to the heavens, "We don't want to hurt you, we don't."

The only way in or out of southern Acheson is the bridge—the one bridge the Angels didn't destroy on Judgment Day. It's just half a block from me. With the death squads closing in and the bridge guards called away to join the hunt, this is my only shot.

I was supposed to do this with Dad. We were supposed to leave Acheson together. We were supposed to make it to Acresfield County *together*. Now he's a corpse in the lawn of a crumbling hotel, brains soaking into the dirt, returning to earth for out of it he was taken.

I can't finish what we started if I stand here begging God for things to be different. It won't bring him back.

Breathe.

Run.

I've been running for days but not like this. Not with my legs screaming and my sneakers pounding the sidewalk in time with my heartbeat. I pretend Dad is right behind me, that I can't hear him because I'm breathing too hard, that I can mistake him for a blur in the windows across the street.

I make it to the mouth of the bridge. I don't stop, just dive between the wreckage of cars choking the entrance. The bridge shines silver, suspension towers dangling thick metal wires from bank to bank. It belongs to the Angels now. A banner flutters high above me: *GOD LOVES YOU.* Corpses dangle from the wires, yellow-pink organs hanging from their stomachs to obscure their nakedness, like Adam and Eve ashamed of their bodies.

One of the bodies is twisted, the leg held at a broken angle, and I can't tell if the Angels did that or the Flood did. The Flood is cruel. It'll do some terrible things to a body.

Not that I need another reminder.

This is a long bridge. I can almost convince myself that Dad is waiting on the other side, holding our backpacks, demanding, *What took you so long?* I'll crash into him, and we'll run until we're away from Acheson, so far away from every Angel camp and colony that they'll never find us again. Dad and I memorized a map of every outpost in the surrounding states and every major stronghold in North America. We'll be okay. We'll be okay.

"There!"

I shouldn't look, I *shouldn't.*

I do.

I know the Angel behind me is Brother Hutch because his robes are splattered with Dad's blood. His rifle hangs from a strap over his shoulder. He's close enough that I can make out the bruises on his knuckles, the stains on his face mask.

Masks keep the Flood out, but I haven't worn one for a while. I can't get infected twice.

"Sister Woodside," Brother Hutch says, and the other Angels emerge from the shadows, the ruins, the back-streets, and I don't stand still a moment longer.

The second thing Dad told me—when we finally escaped, listening for the scream of monsters and the beat of boots against the ground—was that if the Angels want to get their hands on me, I have to make them suffer for it.

I still taste his blood.

I vault the Jersey barriers at the Angel checkpoint and hit the ground hard on the other side. There are lawn chairs back here, a Bible, and a few bottles of water. The road is full of broken glass. The bodies sway.

Run.

I dreamed about what it would be like on the other side of the bridge. Dad and I could head north and find a place to make it through the summer. Sure, there would be Angels, because there would always be Angels until the last nonbeliever was dead, but we would have all the earth to avoid them. Maybe we would meet someone: a handsome nonbeliever who would fall for me when I soaked his hands in warm water and bandaged his wounds. He would be sweet and a little brash and queer as hell, and he wouldn't mess up my pronouns when he saw my chest for the first time. Sometimes he was blond, like my fiancé. Most of the time, he wasn't.

Stop. Don't think about him. Don't think about Theo. None of it matters anyway, because none of it will ever happen. The Flood will break me like it breaks everything else, and I need to keep the monster away from the Angels. I need to get out, I need to get away, I need to—

An Angel whistles, and the whistle is met with a scream.

Between the cars ahead of me, a tangle of limbs unfolds, and it shrieks and howls with all the pain of Hell, the weeping and gnashing of teeth. A creature made of corpses and the Flood—sharpened ribs lining its back in a row of spines, eyeballs blinking between sinew, muscles so swollen they split the skin—rises from the wreckage. Claws the size of arm bones curl around a truck cab and crumple it.

I stop running. No. No, no, *no. NO.*

Not a Grace. Not when I'm so close.

What had once been a person's face opens from the bottom of its jaw, up between the eyes and back to the nape of its neck, showing teeth smeared black with Flood rot.

I faintly register the sound of boots and shouting, but that doesn't matter. The only thing that matters is the monster towering above me, dripping decay and blocking the only way out.

The third thing Dad told me—when he realized what I could do, when I reached out to a Grace and begged it to kill every Angel it could find; when I stood in a sea of gore, a beast curled around me.

He told me to be good.

To never become the monster the Angels want me to be, for evil begets evil begets evil.

The sound of boots slows and stops. My legs fail me. I stumble to the ground, pressing my palms to the burning road.

Be good. Make them suffer. Being good means being quiet, obedient, turning away from the virus's power the same way Eve should have turned away from the apple. Making them suffer means seizing the Grace and taking the Angels down with me in a blaze of flesh and fury.

I could stop this. I could whisper across this street and make the Angels regret ever laying their hands on me.

I almost reach out for the Grace.

But.

Dad died holding my face—his blood smeared down my tongue, across my cheeks, matted in my hair—and begging me to be good.

He's not waiting for me. I can't keep running like this. I am so, so tired.

Good wins out.

"I'll be good. I'll be good, I'll be good." I say it out loud like that will make failure feel any better, as if my insides aren't screaming to burn the Angels in hellfire, as if there's *any* way I could obey all of Dad's words at once. "I'll be good, O Lord, lend me Your strength, lead and guide me—"

Hot liquid trickles over my chin, and I wipe my mouth. My fingers come away black and red.

A pair of heavy boots appears in the corner of my vision, wreathed by stained white robes. I stare at my hand, the horizon, the rising sun.

Is this really what He wants? Is this really His plan?

Brother Hutch says, "I'm sorry," and he almost sounds like he means it.

I make an awful keening sound deep in my throat. It's the closest I've come to crying in years. Past Brother Hutch and past the Grace, the river rushes, perfect blue and clear and clean; the mountains of Acresfield County shine with green and gold; the black wings of carrion birds glimmer in the morning sun.

I pretend Dad is out there. I tell him I was good and to go on without me. I tell him I'll meet up with him eventually, one day, maybe, I promise.

Brother Hutch says, "It's time to come home."

Chapter 2

What do Angels believe? As true believers, our priority is to serve the LORD. We know salvation comes in service to God, in carrying out His final command. We call ourselves ANGELS to proclaim our truth in servitude.

—The Angelic Movement official website

It's time to come home.

Brother Hutch holds out his hand to me. The hand that clasped Mom's in prayer, the hand that pulled the trigger on Dad.

Home means going back to New Nazareth. Back to Theo, back to Mom. Every Angel in New Nazareth will fall to their knees and beg for my blessings. Theo will take me back as his betrothed, like he didn't spit at me and call me a lying, ungrateful bitch. Mom will kiss my cheeks, pretending she doesn't notice my boys' clothes and short hair, and then she'll slam me in an isolation cell until the Flood turns me into a monster.

Into Seraph. Into a six-winged beast burning with holy fire, leading Graces and the Flood to war, carving a path to Heaven through the bodies of nonbelievers.

I don't take his hand.

I don't want to go home.

My stomach seizes, and I vomit onto the road. It's yellow, red, and black; sour and hot all the way up my throat. Around me—*click*, *click*, *clack*, a choir of safeties coming off. But the Angels won't shoot. They won't kill me. Imagine what the faithful would do to the soldier that did. He'd be crucified. He'd be cut open, and he would die watching maggots squirming in his intestines.

"Hey!" Brother Hutch snaps at the soldiers. "Stand down, *now*!"

I heave again. Nothing comes up except acid. Brother Hutch hums softly, and it's such a kind sound, it's terrifying.

"There we go," he murmurs. He rubs small circles between my shoulders. "It's okay."

My words come out in an unsteady wheeze, bubbling with saliva. "Don't touch me."

"All right," Brother Hutch says. "I understand. I heard what your father called you. Ben, was it? I'll call you Ben if that's what you want. Your mom is worried about you, Ben. She wants to make sure you come home."

Mom's not worried about *me*. She's worried about salvation.

I say, "Rot in Hell."

That does it. Brother Hutch snarls and hauls me up—not enough to stand or even get onto my knees, just enough to look him in the eyes. His bloodshot, beady eyes.

"How about a deal?" he says. I try to pull back, but he holds me tight. "I'll give you a choice. You can come with us the easy way, or we can take you by force. You can come to your senses, or I can break your legs." He's smiling. It makes his face shine in the ugliest way. A mask can never hide that. "It's up to you. How do you want to do this?"

There's something on his cheekbone. A splatter, strangely soft and pink. A little piece of meat.

A little piece of Dad.

I spit in his face.

Brother Hutch howls. Watery Flood rot—saliva mixed with my own putrefying insides—drips into his eyes before he can wipe it away, and I'm backhanded so hard my vision explodes with sparks. My hearing dissolves into a high-pitched squeal. I barely catch myself before my head hits the road.

"It's not contagious," a bridge guard says, yanking Brother Hutch's hands away from his face. "It isn't contagious, brother, Sister Kipling said—"

I'm kicked onto my back. Hot asphalt burns through my shirt. Loose gravel digs into my shoulder blades. The heel of a boot pins me to the road and grinds into my stomach like it's trying to snuff out a cigarette butt.

I know the man standing on me. The scar across his nose, his small eyes, the wrinkles digging into his forehead.

"Steve," I whisper, as if using his actual name instead of "Brother Collins" will make one of the Lord's holy murderers any kinder. "Steven. It's me. You know me."

We met, when I was eleven and he was twenty-one, because we came to New Nazareth around the same time. I remember when he got his death-squad markings: wings carved into his back, feathers from his shoulders to right where the ribs end. Theo stared at the raw tattoos the way little boys look at soldiers coming home from war. I stared at them the way little girls look at that one uncle their sisters tell them to stay away from.

Steven lets up, just a bit, and I think it might have worked, but he's wrestling me up and pinning my head against his chest. He smells so much like sweat, I almost taste it.

A *flick*, and there's a knife to my throat. A thick one, with a black blade glinting in the sun.

"You want to be a boy so bad," Steven says. "I think we can start cutting shit off. That's how it works, right?"

I can't get the word out. I shake my head. *No.*

"That's what I thought. So be a good girl and do what he says."

I'm sorry, Dad. I'm sorry.

I say, "Okay."

Brother Hutch picks up the Bible from the bridge

checkpoint as Steven gets me into a set of whites and hooks a mask around my ears—a flimsy fabric mask worn only beyond the walls of New Nazareth, where we step beyond God's protection. "*Whore,*" Steven whispers, glaring at my bulky denim shorts before they're smothered by robes. The bridge guards take their places behind the Jersey barriers, waiting for nonbelievers to string up and Angel messengers from distant camps to let through. The soldier by the Grace gently coaxes it out from behind the cars, and its virus-melted body shivers in the humid breeze coming off the water.

"Lord," Brother Hutch cries, raising his free hand as if reaching for the bodies swinging overhead. Everyone joins him but me. "Lord, how I praise You; how great You are in Your never-ending mercifulness, to bring our blessed Seraph back to us!"

I will be good. I will be good. I will be good. I will keep Seraph hidden, locked up in my chest, whatever it takes to make sure the Angels never get the weapon they made of me.

But I'm just so tired of running.

The death squad takes me away from the bridge, away from Acresfield County, and leads me through the streets of Acheson toward New Nazareth. I ask if I can clean myself, but they refuse, so Dad's blood is still on my face, hair, and hands. *Get off.* I smear it down my sleeves, but it's settled into the lines of my fingers and the creases of my palms. I want to stick my hands in boiling water. *Get off, get off, get off.*

Steven grabs my shoulder and shakes me. "Shut the fuck up."

I wince. That sort of language would never be allowed inside the New Nazareth walls. Not even if you don't say it out loud. Mom said God would know anyway.

Besides the soldiers and the Grace dragging itself along with us, the only things we see all morning are abandoned cars and empty buildings. The world is only two years gone, so everything is almost exactly how it used to be: clusters of stickers clinging to bus shelters, weeds springing up between cracks in the sidewalk, trees outgrowing their dirt squares in the concrete. A corpse hangs from a flagpole, and massive letters on the building behind it scream *REPENT, SINNER*.

That's the way it works now. Everybody is dying, and it's just a matter of what kills you. Whether it's Angels or the Flood or heatstroke or good old sepsis.

For most of humanity, it was the Flood. Theo's mom was martyred on Judgment Day, and he grieved her in the only way he was allowed: by learning everything. How the virus burned through billions, missionaries like his mom carrying it to every major city in the world. How it either kills you when a new set of ribs grow through your lungs or how an unlucky few survive long enough to find salvation as a Grace. How the death squads infect themselves with a taste of the Flood at their initiation ritual, walking the fine line between taking a step closer to God and succumbing to the sickness . . .

How Seraph is a balance of the Flood's need to devour and its need to survive—ravenous enough to turn me into a monster, patient enough to do it right. Because Sister Kipling made the Flood powerful, and she made Seraph perfect.

She made *me* perfect.

The Grace rumbles, shaking like a horse twitching away flies. I come up to its hunched-over chest, maybe. When its mouth is closed, I can see remnants of the person—people—it used to be. Human teeth between serrated fangs. The remains of a button nose.

Brother Hutch catches me staring. I avert my eyes, but it's not enough. He slows down to match my stride. In front of us, two soldiers peer at a map, murmuring about previous ambushes and new paths through the city.

Acheson has been devouring Angels lately.

"Isn't it amazing?" Brother Hutch croons, spreading his fingers toward the Grace. "This new life they've been given? How merciful of our Lord to allow them to be born again, to become warriors in our fight for His plan. Just like you."

Just like me. This is what I was chosen for. For the virus to turn me into a monster that will lead the Angels to Heaven.

That will wipe humanity from the earth once and for all, just like God demanded.

A little after noon, the youngest of the squad calls for a rest. We're on a wide street lined with restaurants and hipster offices sporting strange logos. Some were abandoned long before Judgment Day, thanks to skyrocketing inflation, rent prices, and everything, really. Water-conservation flyers and open calls for protest peel off brick walls, next to eviction notices and *Going Out of Business* signs. I haven't seen any bodies or Angel propaganda for a few blocks. This must be a new path.

"I need a drink," the youngest soldier whines. I've been trying to place him the whole walk, but I keep coming up blank. Whose brother is he, whose son? "My feet hurt."

Steven shoves a water bottle against his chest. "Then drink. Stop complaining."

I wouldn't take a break either, if I were escorting my only sure shot at eternal life. But Brother Hutch says, "He's right." Steven's eye twitches above his mask. "There's no point in wearing ourselves down. We're still an hour out from Reformation."

Reformation? He means Reformation Faith Evangelical Church. Memories of the place come rushing back, and so does vomit in the back of my throat. I should have seen this coming. Reformation is halfway between the bridge and New Nazareth; it's the perfect place to rest in this beast of a city, and if I walk into that building, I am going to lose it. If I walk into *any* church *ever* again—

“Sit,” Brother Hutch says. “Eat, rest. All of you.”

“Thank God,” says the youngest, who immediately slumps against the hood of a bullet-scarred sedan. The others roll their eyes at him. He’s scrawny and strange, not that much older than me. Probably just graduated from training, his wings still aching, assigned to a squad that happened to get the most important task in the world. If he’s as new as I think, I’m surprised somebody hasn’t smacked him hard on the back yet, right where the tattoos are still painful. Theo used to complain about that all the time, back when he still had squadmates to complain about. Granted, I’m too big a deal for that kind of roughhousing.

If Theo hadn’t been exiled from the death squads, that could be him right there. My betrothed, staring at me with a mask and a gun.

One soldier points at the road. The Grace folds itself up and sits, shuddering all the way down. There’s enough gray matter left in the heads of Graces that they can be whipped into following basic commands—sit, stay, kill. Steven doesn’t give me the dignity of following orders. He just forces me down to the curb. The others trade packages of food and their map, praying over their meals and clustering in the shade. The rookie squabbles for the map and jerks it out of someone’s hands with a triumphant snort.

I weave my bloody fingers together and press my lips to my knuckles like I’m praying too. If we’re going to stop, I’m going to take advantage of it. There has to be a way out. If

I can put some distance between me and the Angels, any distance, I can lose them again. There's an old café behind us, and the glass door is shattered, revealing a path through a seating area with chic little tables, right to a back door labeled *Emergency Exit*.

If I distract them long enough, I could do it.

By the sedan, the rookie says, "We're *really* close to where Salvation disappeared."

Everyone stops. Unease settles like a fog.

I heard something about that a while ago. Squad Salvation went out to sweep a possible camp of nonbelievers last month and never came back. Mom held a service on the chapel lawn for them, lifting her hands to help them to their destined place with Jesus, *the gift of eternal life now and in Heaven forever.* Not a funeral, though. Angels never hold funerals.

Brother Hutch takes the map. "We shouldn't be," he says. "We're nowhere near the northeastern quarter, we should be fine. We should be . . ."

The Grace snuffles.

"We are," Brother Hutch says. "Aren't we?"

Another soldier crowds in. "I thought we were taking the long way around."

"I thought we were too," Brother Hutch says. "Maybe we got turned around by the courthouse."

CRACK.

A wound blooms across Steven's throat, like someone aimed for center mass and botched it, tearing his neck into a mess of meat and severed arteries. He stays upright for a second, gurgling, before he falls.

We walked right into an ambush.

The Grace screams, long and loud and high. It clatters to its feet, and its mouth opens into a hole of teeth and spit, swinging toward the office building across the street. I jam myself against the sedan for cover. Brother Hutch slides into place next to me, cradling his rifle to his chest.

CRACK. The rookie stumbles in silence, eyes bugging. *CRACK.* He's dead.

The Angels scatter. Some jump through the broken window of the storefront next door, some duck behind the pickup parked in front of the sedan. Steven's body stares at me, mouth open, a halo of blood spreading around his head.

"Where are they?" Brother Hutch snaps.

"There!" someone shouts back, pointing to the top of the office building.

Up there, backlit by the sun, a smudge of black—and it's gone. Brother Hutch pulls me down and hisses, "*Stay.*"

Brother Hutch shatters.

It's not a clean shot. The bullet nicks his eye and takes out a piece of his skull, blowing it open. I jerk back, slamming against the curb. Brother Hutch is gone. The man who watched with a gentle smile while Mom cleaned my scraped knee, the man who congratulated Theo and me on our betrothal and wished us a happy marriage through holy war, he's gone. His body sags. There are brains on the sedan. There are brains on *me.*

Dad's shattered skull. His blood in my mouth.

If they want their monster, make them suffer for it.

I'm on my feet. Away from the sedan, up the café stairs, through the shattered glass door. I tear off the robes and yank down the mask. I just have to get to the back door. I can lose them. I can make it if I just—

There's movement behind the coffee bar.

A boy in black points a rifle at my chest.

Chapter 3

The Angels describe themselves as an interdenominational Protestant movement founded in 2025 by Ian Clevenger, pastor and conservative Virginia state senator. However, they are described by critics as "evangelical eco-fascists" and a Christian terrorist group.

—What is 'Eco-Facism' Anyway? The Angelic Movement Explained

If the boy in black pulls the trigger, he'll kill me. I picture it, mapping each detail from Dad's body to mine. One shot to the chest to drop me, a second to the head to finish the job. His face, *my* face, caving around the bullet, sucked in toward the black hole of our eyes.

It would keep Seraph out of the Angels' hands. If I were dead.

Wouldn't it?

"Wait! I'm not with them!" I'm begging the same way I pray, before I can stop myself. "*Please* don't shoot. Please."

The boy gestures with the barrel of the gun. "Explain the whites."

The whites, my robes; the robes I'm holding. I drop them to the floor like they're burning me. "It's not what it looks like, they—they kidnapped me. They made me wear them."

Angels don't kidnap people. They just kill.

Neither of us move. Every inch of the boy is smothered in black: gloves, belt, heavy laced boots. Even his mask is black, made with a thick fabric hiding everything below his eyes. The photo negative of an Angel, a perfect copy of the shadow on the office building across the street.

Is he going to shoot me?

A heartbeat.

Two. Three.

He fires.

There is no splitting of the sky this time, just a shriek as the world erupts into ringing. Heat scorches the edge of my ear, and blood trickles down my jaw, and *he shot me, oh God, he SHOT ME.*

Something heavy hits the floor. The boy grabs my arm—*"Down!"* I think he says, I *can't hear him*—and yanks me behind the coffee bar.

We collapse against trash cans, plastic bags, and wash buckets. It smells like dust and dead roaches. I push myself away until my back hits the cabinets. The ringing starts to fade.

"Christ," I say, and cringe, like Mom's palm is going to crack against my cheek. But it doesn't. The boy just watches me. He's white as an Angel under his black clothes, and there's a half-confused crinkle between his brows like he isn't sure what he's seeing.

"You're bleeding," he says.

I touch my ear. My fingertips come away red.

"There's been a lot of that today," I say, because otherwise I'm going to break down screaming behind a display case of moldy pastry remains.

He tears open a package of napkins. "Here." He shoves a handful my way. I press them to my ear, and it stings but only a little bit. "You're fine."

"You *shot* me."

He says, "There was an Angel."

I peek out from behind the counter. Lying on the floor, eyes wide like this is all just some strange surprise, is a soldier. One of the ones I didn't recognize, with a simple wedding ring on his left hand. There's Brother Hutch too, slumped against the sedan. The line of fire matches up perfectly.

I pull back. "Who are you?"

"Nick."

With that, Nick pushes me away and rests his rifle on the counter, trying to find a decent angle. It's no use. His field of vision will be garbage no matter where he sets up. There's no way he can get a good look at the street with the sedan and the cluttered windows.

He couldn't have chosen this spot. I'm the pampered child of a church leader, and even I know you don't hold a position alone. Especially not a bad position.

"Uh," I say, "I'm Benji."

He doesn't say, *Is that a girl's name?* Or, *Like the dog from that old movie?* His finger just taps on the trigger guard. *Tp tp tp.* A heartbeat.

"How many are there?" he asks.

I do some quick subtraction: Brother Hutch, Steven, the rookie, the wedding band. "There are three now. Plus the Grace."

"Three," Nick says. What's going on out there? All the sounds blur into a roar. "Only Angels call them Graces."

Oh. *For by grace you have been saved through faith; but by the grace of God; His grace is a gift, grace upon grace.*

Shakily, I manage, "They do?"

Tp tp tp. "They do."

"I . . ." I swallow hard. "I didn't know that."

That's it. I'm dead. He's going to take that gun and—

He says, "Get up."

"What?"

He pulls me up beside him. I drop the napkins. The counter comes to my nose, and I can't see anything but dead bodies and the sedan. Maybe a sliver of the office building.

"Do you know where anybody is?" Nick asks. *Tp tp tp.* "I need you to tell me."

"There's, uh, some in the store next door. And by the

pickup truck, but that's, you know." I gesture weakly to the side. "All the way over there."

"Would we be able to see them from the window seat?"

The window seat, all the way across the café. "I guess? I don't know—"

I don't get to finish. With the screaming of metal and glass, the Grace slams out from the office building, contorting its body spiderlike through the doors.

There's a person in its mouth. A boy. It's pulling him, thrashing, down the front stairs.

Nick's tapping stops.

This is nothing I haven't seen before. This is nothing I haven't *done* before. I've whispered against a Grace's neck and turned the Flood against the Angels, but sick still wells in the back of my throat. This is what my power looks like. This is why the Angels made me a monster.

Bullets slam into the Grace's back, blowing apart what's left of its face, but it keeps moving. It drags the boy into the street, lifts him high like it's showing off a kill, and bites all the way down.

The sound is thick and wet. Like a soggy branch snapping underfoot. Pieces of bone glint in the sun. The boy does not make any noise at all as he drops to the ground, his severed leg dangling from the Grace's mouth.

An Angel cries, "*The Lord is good!*" and Nick says, "Cover your ears."

I don't hesitate. I clamp my hands tight, but it's still so *loud*. A burst of three bullets: one hits the sedan, the other nicks the Grace's shoulder, and the other hits it right in what once had been the jaw. None do anything. Gore splatters the road, but the Grace just brings its giant, clawed foot down.

Onto the boy's chest.

His body gives instantly. Dozens of bones crack at once. There's a chorus beyond the ringing in my ears—the death squad howling praise and holy words like dogs.

The Grace will hunt down every one of Nick's people and slaughter them. Nobody stands a chance against a Grace, the ones built into perfect blessings of war. Unless you get a bullet through what's left of its brain or take off enough limbs that it can't come after you anymore, there's nothing anyone can do.

Except Seraph. Except me.

No. No, *no.* I promised I wouldn't. Evil begets evil begets evil; giving into Seraph is what the Angels want; *I promised I would be good.* I *can't.*

Dad told me to keep the monster hidden as long as I could—chain it between my ribs, to never accept what the Angels did to me. But if I sit back and watch them die, how can I call myself good at all? I wouldn't be ending lives; I'd be saving them. Turning away from Seraph isn't *good* if it means leaving people to be devoured.

And I won't let the Angels get their hands on me.

I whisper, "Stop."

I don't have to say it out loud, but if I don't say it at least to myself, it feels like I'm throwing my mind to the ether and letting it fall. Mom always said I should pray out loud because it lets God know I'm not ashamed of my love for Him.

I say it again, softer, so small there's no sound, but it's *there.* "Stop."

Stop.

STOP.

The Grace stops.

The boy's leg falls out of its mouth. Piles of skin and knotted muscle twitch in fear. In confusion. In pain.

If I whisper one more word, the Grace will turn on the Angels with the scream of burning sinners, a choir of voices swallowed whole by the Flood. It will break their spines and crush their skulls the same way it killed that boy.

It would be so easy.

"What—" Nick starts.

I say, "Take the shot."

Nick needs nothing else. He yanks the gun to his shoulder and lines it up—between two shards of glass clinging to the windowpane, above the sedan, into the gaping maw of the Grace's mouth, where it will hit the brain and turn it off like a light.

One day, somebody is going to think the same thing about me.

In the half a second between Nick deciding on the shot and reaching for the trigger, it dawns. This is my future. I've seen the failed Seraph trials. I've seen martyrs pull off their skin, desperate, afraid, *aware.*

That's going to be me, and there's nothing I can do.

CRACK.

It's a perfect shot. One bullet. Instantaneous. Not like Dad, where I watched him bleed out from a gaping wound and pressed my hands to the raw meat of his chest, as if I could have ever helped. This borders on merciful. The Grace stumbles, almost as if it's tripped, and falls in a jumble of limbs.

I did it. I actually did it. It worked.

It *hurts.*

I fall and hit the cabinet. Pain burns down like I swallowed hellfire, and my black liquefied guts come out of my mouth, and they're dripping onto my lips. I press my hands to my mouth because those are my insides, those are my *insides* coming out, and maybe if I hold them in, they'll go back to normal, if I just—

There's a noise. My vision is a narrow blurry point, or maybe my eyes are just squeezed shut. Something's touching me, and I want it to *stop.* Another noise. I think it's a voice. The Flood rot is bitter and way too sweet, the way a corpse smells sweet in the summer sun, and someone is saying my name. *Lord, I kneel before You a sinner, have mercy, have mercy.*

"Up here," Nick says. "Benji. Up here. Focus on me."

Benji. That's my name, the name I picked. Nick catches me by the shoulders and presses napkins against my face the way you'd clean a fussy baby.

"Look at me." When he's done, he pulls my mask up over my nose. "Keep that there, no matter what. Am I clear?"

The pain has settled into a throbbing ache like a bad period cramp. Bad, *really* bad, but nothing I haven't felt before. Nothing I haven't survived before.

"Clear," I say.

A shout: *"Nick!"*

"No matter what," Nick repeats and stands. "Aisha! Here!"

For a moment, the world is quiet. No gunfire. No screaming. Just footsteps on concrete. The cautious tweeting of birds.

A Black girl with tear streaks down her face steps into the café. I see her through the pastry case. Her black outfit is dirty at the knees, and her knuckles are raw. She sees Nick, stops, and jabs a trembling finger at him.

"You," she whimpers, "were supposed to *stay with us.*"

It's been so long since I've seen somebody cry. Her voice hitches, and tears hesitate at the corner of her eyes before finally falling, soaking the edge of her mask.

"You said you'd be right behind us," she says. "You *said.*"

"I'm okay," Nick says, impossibly calm. "You and Faith made it without me."

"Fuck you!" The girl—Aisha—stamps her foot. "We thought you were dead too!"

Nick says nothing. Aisha's lashes flutter pitifully as the tears come faster.

"I'm sorry," she sobs. She can't be any older than me. Her fingers still have a little bit of baby fat below the knuckle. "I'm sorry, I just . . . I need to find the others."

"They can handle themselves."

"No, I need to."

"Okay. When you find Faith, bring her back here."

Aisha's bloodshot eyes go wide. "What's wrong? I can't handle anything else being wrong, I can't."

"Nothing else is wrong. Just bring her back."

Aisha hiccups and leaves. As soon as she's gone, Nick is back on the floor with me, his hands keeping me upright.

"Listen to me closely," he says. "Do not call them Graces. Do not call it Judgment Day. And do not take this mask off. Okay?"

I say, "Okay."

Nick says, "Breathe."

A few minutes later, Aisha comes back with another girl in tow. Faith. She's a white shaved-head butch, taller than any of us and a few years older. Aisha's pinkie is hooked through hers.

"Was told you wanted me," Faith says, voice hoarse.

"You okay?" Nick asks.

"Oh," she says, "of course not."

When they round the counter, they freeze.

Faith sums it up. *"Shit."* She crouches, tilting her head. "Hey, bud. What's your name?"

When I can't answer, Nick cuts in. "This is Benji." Not my deadname. Not Sister Woodside. My real name. "Help me get them up."

The girls bring me to my feet as Nick deftly moves my jacket to hide the black stains on my shirt. One of my knees gives out, and I slump against Faith's chest.

Aisha's voice cracks when she speaks. "All right, we got you."

I manage, "Sorry."

"Don't be sorry," Faith says. "It's okay."

"The Angels are gone," Nick says. He's so close, I could rest my head on him if I wanted. I want to. I'm so tired. "You're safe now. I promise."

There's a look in his eyes that's nothing like the girls'. Like he's found something he'd lost for years.

Like I'm the final piece of some terrible puzzle.

Chapter 4

REJECT FEAR AND HYPOCRISY. FIND PURPOSE AND LOVE ON THE PATH OF THE LORD—JOIN HIM IN HIS GRACE AND WALK THE PATH OF ETERNAL LIFE. FIND SALVATION IN HIS PLAN!

—The Angelic Movement recruitment poster

What I remember:

Aisha and Faith holding me steady. One asks Nick if there's any chance I'm infected. He shakes his head even though there's a splatter of Flood rot on his sleeve.

A sunburned boy balancing Brother Hutch's head in his hands, cutting off his left ear with a knife. He does the same thing to Steven but can't walk by the boy smeared into the road. Bones stick out of him like monuments.

Nick standing by the Grace in silence. Finally, he

wrenches out a tooth, prying it free with a knife of his own. My tongue running along my canines as I wonder how long it'll be until my mouth looks just like that.

All of us standing together, perfect strangers on the battlefield, and it's almost like my prayers have been answered, amen—but I don't believe it for a second.

I wake up on the floor. I recognize that much immediately: the crick in my neck, the carpet that's never plush enough to disguise the concrete underneath. I bury my face in my arms and groan.

"Finally, a sign of life," says someone beside me. "You awake?"

"No." I want to ask where I am, but it doesn't matter. Anywhere is better than New Nazareth. I could wake up in a cell, and as long as it wasn't Angels on the other side of the bars, I'd be better off than I was.

"No?" says the voice. "Damn, all right."

After a minute, I sit up by propping myself against the desk behind me. The room looks like an office. Books are scattered in piles on messy shelves. Papers are on every available surface. Certifications, newspaper clippings, and photos hang on the walls, their glass frames dull like they haven't been cleaned since Judgment Day.

As interesting as this is, though, I feel like *shit*. And so does the person in the chair across the room, if their scars and grief-reddened eyes have anything to say about it. The right side of their face is destroyed with pockmarks. One eye doesn't open all the way. *Latinx, scarred face,* and *painted nails* don't combine into a person I recognize. "Who . . . ?"

"Shit, we gotta do introductions." The stranger leans back, fingers lacing together as if to distract from the obvious tears. "Name's Salvador. I was with the group that found you, though I didn't get to say hi before you passed out. Got stuck on babysitting duty—no offense—to make sure you didn't lose your shit when you woke up." I'm too tired for that. I've lost it enough for one day. "So yeah, nice to finally meet you. Xe/xem pronouns."

Right, Salvador was the one who pulled the sunburned boy away from the body. The memory is hazy, though. There's a fog in my brain I'm too tired to claw through. I recognize everything that's happened today from a distance, like the color's been bleached out by the sun. Dad's blood under my nails is the only evidence that he died today. That he died a few *hours* ago.

Salvador watches me warily.

"Yeah," I say. "Cool. Xe/xem." I go through the rest of the set: xe, xem, xyr, xemself. I read about neopronouns in a book Dad smuggled from the burn pile of confiscated items at New Nazareth. He brought up the book again our second night in the city, just a few days ago, when we sat in a dead stranger's bathroom and cut off two feet of my hair with sewing scissors. He apologized with every snip, certain he was ruining it. By the end, I was sitting in a pile of red-brown scraps and running my hands through my choppy, shaggy, awkward *boy* hair.

I need to stop thinking about Dad. So I say, "Are you trans?"

Salvador blinks. "Uh."

"Wait, no." I can't just ask people if they're trans. "I shouldn't have . . ."

"No, it's fine," Salvador says. "I mean, yeah, of course. I'm super trans. Like, an honestly heretical amount of trans. Why?"

I've never met another trans person before. Can I say that? Would it give me away as an Angel?

I decide on, "It's been a while."

"Then you're going to lose your mind when I tell you this is an LGBTQ+ youth center."

Xe's right. "A *what*?"

Salvador gestures to the office. "This is the Acheson LGBTQ+ Center. Kind of like the YMCA but even gayer somehow. We call it the ALC for short." *Alck,* xe pronounces it, like it's some sort of medicine or maybe a hard liquor. An entire building, just for people like us? "It's not much, and we've had to make a few adjustments"—xe nods to the boarded-up window beside xyr head—"but it's home."

A pause.

"Granted," xe mutters, "today's been shit. So."

"I'm sorry about your friend."

"Yeah. Me too." Xe tugs at one long curl of hair falling out from behind xyr headband and changes the subject. "Nick said you'd been kidnapped."

"It's, uh, it's a long story."

"I mean, I figured," Salvador says. "Angels don't kidnap people."

They don't. They string up the heretics and cut them open. Maybe they make it painless if the nonbelievers come willingly. Hell, I remember a reverend praying to a newborn child before their parents drowned them in the river, repenting for bringing a sinner into the world without the church's blessing. There is no need for new flesh.

Not with the Flood. Not with Seraph.

"I thought that too," I say.

"Well, terrorists are terrorists, I guess. What I'm getting at is that Nick wants to talk to you. He's picked up some kinda scent, and he's not gonna let up until he figures it out, so you might as well get it over with. Think you can manage?"

Manage? I can manage a hell of a lot—whether it's a smart idea is another thing entirely. "No better time than now."

"Thought so." Salvador gets up with a stretch. "Be right back. And don't try anything funny. Cormac is outside, and he has an itchy trigger finger."

That almost sounds like a threat, but before I say anything else, Salvador is gone.

So. An LGBTQ+ center. I stand, bracing myself on the desk. I've spent a lot of time in Sister Kipling's office over the past few months, staring at the sparse decorations to avoid looking at the prophet of Armageddon, the woman who created the Flood. Sister Kipling had a crucifix above her door, framed diplomas above the desk, and *WALK HIS PATH, FIND SALVATION, RETURN TO EARTH* painted across the back wall.

This office is completely different. There's a rainbow flag behind the office chair, a biography of a trans-rights leader on the bookshelf. One of the newspaper clippings is from all the way back in 2015, celebrating the legalization of gay marriage in the United States. I can't picture 2015. I don't think Mom and Dad had even met.

Every picture shows a world I left behind when I was eleven. A world the Angels *destroyed* when I was fourteen. A world I don't know at all.

I'm staring at a photo—people with their fists in the air, screaming with rage and power—when the door opens again. I shove my hands into my pockets. Back straight, chin up, like Mom is checking my posture at church.

Salvador comes in with two people: Nick and a stranger. Nick takes a spot by the door like a guard dog, arms crossed. His hood is down, and his combat mask has been traded in for a pale gray one that goes well with his overgrown black hair. Bobby pins are jammed near his temples and forehead to keep loose strands out of his face.

He's—he's *cute*. His dark eyes, sharp brows, the distant but curious tilt of his head . . .

I dig my thumbnail into my finger, where my engagement ring used to be. I am still betrothed to Theo. I held his hand in front of the church and prayed for the world we were going to build together in Jesus's name. I promised to bring glory as God's fiery sword; Theo promised to fight beside me. We were perfect together.

To think like this about anyone else is wrong. No matter what Theo did to me that night.

The stranger says, "Hey, Sal," so impossibly soft, like Salvador might crumple if xe hears anything other than a whisper. "You doing all right?"

"As all right as I can be," Salvador says unconvincingly, "with everything."

"If it's not too much trouble, can you go check on Alex? Please? I haven't seen them in a while, and I'm worried."

Salvador disappears through the heavy wooden doors, and it's down to three.

The stranger is a doe-eyed and delicate Black girl with deep brown skin dewy in the warmth of the office and long, braided twists decorated with thin golden bands. There isn't a shred of black in her clothing. I can't imagine it on her, not with the flowers on her mask and salvaged pastel eyeshadow.

"You have blood on you," she says.

I pick at a bit of it that's crusted on my jaw. "I get that a lot."

"We'll have to get you a bath, and some extra clothes, and . . ." She groans. "I'm so sorry. Today's been hell, I can't think straight. I'm Erin, and I use she/her pronouns. Sal told me you were excited to meet another trans person, so I hope meeting a second makes your day a little better."

She's trans. *She's trans too.* "What name and pronouns do you want me to use for you?"

I can say whatever I want. And that's what she'll call me. No questions asked.

"Benji, short for Benjamin. He/him." It tastes so sweet that it almost wipes the memory of blood off my tongue. I would have smiled if I didn't have more important things to worry about. I collect myself. "Are you in charge?"

"I wouldn't say I'm in charge," Erin says. "We don't really do 'in charge' here."

Nick says, "We do."

"Well, *you* do. But I don't. It doesn't seem right." Erin brings one of her braids around her front and starts picking at the ends. "Everyone thinks I'm in charge because I volunteered here before That Day, not because I was elected or anything. I'm more of an organizer? I like to think everybody is in charge a little bit—"

"Erin," Nick says.

"Sorry." Erin sighs. "We are the closest thing the ALC has to someone in charge, yes."

Nick says, "And we have a deal for you."

Shit.

Erin balks. "I wanted to ease into that."

"No use." Nick steps away from the door. I counter with a half step back. "Either he accepts or he doesn't. How we say it doesn't matter."

I cut in. "Accept *what*?"

Nick holds out a tri-folded document from his jacket.

The red wax seal is broken, but I would know it anywhere: folded wings at rest.

The Angels.

Another half step, and I hit the bookshelf. I check Nick and Erin for weapons. "Where did you get that?"

"A messenger," Nick says, which translates to, *I killed an Angel and looted their body.* "Open it."

"It's okay," Erin says. "Go ahead. I promise."

Deep breaths. It's fine. No matter what this is, it can't be worse than what the Angels want.

Right?

"Fine," I say. "Okay. I'll open it. If you back up."

Nick takes a respectful step away, and Erin ducks her head.

In blocky, typewritten letters, it reads:

NEW NAZARETH CHURCH OF GRACE
Church of the Angel, Church of the LORD
Reverend Mother Veronica Woodside of New Nazareth speaks:

True believers of God's word rejoice! The time has come. The LORD has blessed us with grace beyond our comprehension, a miracle beyond us all; eternal life is within our grasp. For we have found our way to SERAPH through—

My deadname.

My deadname is right there on the paper. It's only been a week since I last heard it, but it still feels like a knife to the chest. And it's on the official announcement of my recognition as the true Seraph. Copies of this announcement left New Nazareth in the bags of messengers who broadcasted it to camps across the world. News would reach colonies on almost every continent, soldiers embedded in the ruins of every country, and what a joyous day it would be. Now every Angel knows that after nineteen failed trials, nineteen false Seraphs, I will finally lead them to Heaven.

Except my name is Benji, and they don't have me anymore.

I whisper, "What do you want from me?"

"So you are Seraph, then," Nick says.

Erin looks away from us both.

I stammer. "You weren't sure?"

"I wasn't," Nick says. "You could've been a failed trial who escaped. You could've been a sick kid who just got lucky."

Tricky *bastard*.

"Hey." Erin leans forward a bit to catch my eye. I lean away in turn. "We're not going to hurt you. The ALC was built to help queer teenagers, and that's what it's always done. It's just that the specifics have changed in the past few years." She folds the document closed in my hands. "We want to help you escape."

What? No. That can't be—that can't—

"But we need to figure out how to do it," she says. "We have two ideas, and all you have to do is tell us which one you like best. Okay?"

Nothing is ever this easy. There has to be a catch.

But what if they're telling the truth? Not everyone is as cruel as the Angels. Dad wasn't. Theo wasn't, for a time. Kind people exist. I know that.

I can take a chance on this.

"Tell me."

Erin lights up—a switch is flipped, her face beaming despite the fog of death hanging over her. "The first option is that Nick and the others will get you out of Acheson and into Acresfield County. The path will suck, and you'll have to stick it out on your own at the end, but we know a place where you can cross in the suburbs outside the city." I stare at her, awestruck. "You get out of the city, and we won't have to worry about a giant monster stalking around in a few weeks. It's a win for everybody."

I imagine the weight taken off her shoulders, knowing Seraph is far away from her and the ALC. That the Angels will never get their hands on me, and her friends can go back to preparing for the deadly heat and droughts of the upcoming summer instead of worrying about monsters like me.

And it's what Dad wanted. I could just *do it*. Take their help and meet up with his memory in the farmland like I promised.

But could I really manage the whole world alone?

Without him?

Quietly, I ask, "And option two?"

Erin's brows pull up, just a little, into something like worry, and Nick says, "What have the Angels done to you?"

"What?"

The truth is, the real question is, what *haven't* they done? Mom snarling in the living room when I was little, threatening to press kidnapping charges if Dad tried to take me away again. Glittering wounds gouged into Theo's back, shallow like tide pools, as his father held up Angel wings he'd been deemed unworthy of. The smell of mass graves and shit. Watching the world wink out of existence, community by community, family by family, when no one on Earth deserved a fate that cruel and lonely.

Nick reaches into his jacket again, and this time, he takes out a folded knife as black as his uniform, as black as rich earth.

He presses a small lever, and the blade springs out with a snap. An Angel knife, the same kind Steven held to my throat. Just like, I realize, the ALC's guns are Angel guns. Stolen from their dead bodies and turned against them.

He says, "Because you could join us."

The Angel killers.

I'll be good, I'll be good, I'll be good.

"Take their greatest weapon," Nick says, "and make them pay. You'll escape by making sure there's no one left to chase you. You'll make them suffer for what they did to you."

Make them suffer.

On the surface, there's no way to do that *and* be good. They're commandments at each other's throats. But I found more good in helping Nick—in whispering to the Grace—than I ever could if I kept Seraph hidden.

Maybe, if I join the ALC, I can do both.

Nick holds the knife out to me, the blade between his dirty, bruised fingers. He trusts me. Even after seeing the letter, even knowing what I'll become.

I take the handle.

It feels like there's something writhing in my gut and erupting into screaming fury. Six wings outstretched and crying HOLY, HOLY, HOLY.

It feels like a chance to be *anything* but what the Angels made me.

Chapter 5

Today we learned what God has asked his followers to do. We learned the truth of the righteous path. Will you follow it too, as your parents have done? Will you find love and eternal life? Or will you rot on the wall and in the fields with the rest of the sinners?

—Sister Mackenzie's Sunday school lesson

Erin offers to show me around the ALC, and Nick gives a half-assed excuse for why he can't come along and disappears.

"He's . . . ," Erin offers, the scrunched expression under her floral mask telling me she's stepping carefully. "He's got a lot on his plate right now. Stay here, okay? I'll get you some water and a change of clothes."

She asks what underclothes I use, and I turn red as I ask for boxers and a sports bra.

In exchange, I get a bucket of murky water, a rag, and an outfit a size too big.

"The water's safe," she assures me. "Just used a little, is all."

By the time I'm done washing myself, the water is disgusting. I stare at it for too long, because now that all Dad's blood is gone, I'm realizing I no longer have anything to remember him by.

Erin gathers me when I'm done changing, noting my freshly washed hair and clean face with a soft tilt of her head. "Looking better already." I'm glad I *look* better. I had to resist the urge to rinse my mouth with the blood water, as if that would get out the taste of the Flood. "Ready?"

Walking into the ALC is like walking into a funeral home.

The boy's death has gotten into the walls and under the floorboards of this place. He lurks behind faded pride flags and flyers advertising STD tests and water-restriction protocols. He's even made his way between the wires of an ugly ham radio sitting in a back corner of the lobby. Teenagers and young adults of every shape and size have huddled together, refusing to look up. One mends cloth face masks in silence. Another slumps by a barred front door, resting their forehead against the wall.

"Most of us were here on That Day," Erin whispers, and I make note of the proper term to use. She shows me around the gaunt kitchen and food pantry. "We had a great summer program for at-risk teens. So when everything happened, a lot of kids just didn't leave."

She takes me to the chalkboard near the barred front door, where people volunteer for chores like cleaning, cooking, and guard duty. There are about forty names. One section is separated: the Watch. I recognize all the names written there. Nick, Aisha, Faith, Cormac, Salvador, and a fresh smudge. Cormac must be the sunburned redhead I remember cutting off ears. The smudge is the dead boy.

"I could've gone home, I guess," Erin says, gesturing for me to follow. "But I was too worried about everyone, so I stayed behind. You can see how well that went. At least it's easier to transition when the rest of the world is gone?" Someone steps aside to let us down a narrow hall, eyes downcast. Erin's voice is quiet with sadness. "I mean, all the hormones are either expired or spoiled, but at least there are no transphobic relatives to worry about anymore."

I don't want to think about hormones. Even if they weren't years too old or baked by the summer heat, I won't be in this body long enough for it to matter.

"How did you all survive?" I ask instead. The Angels made it as long as they have through sheer numbers, strict travel protocols, and culling people at the first sign of infection. The ALC doesn't seem to have enough people or supplies to pull that off.

"Well, some of us didn't. But if I had to guess, it's some combination of . . . I don't know. Timing? Location? Sadaf's parents were doctors, and Aisha's were doomsday preppers, so that helped. And luck, maybe? There's got to be some credit due for being scared kids who locked ourselves in and waited for adults to come save us, even if they never did." She shakes her head as we get to the storeroom. "Whatever it was, things got easier when Nick picked up the slack. He can be rude in making sure people stay safe, but he's good at what he does. Anyway, here are the pads and tampons if you need them. Just try to be stingy, okay?"

My face flushes. I really don't want to think about being on my period and having to deal with Seraph at the same time. Shedding my insides out one orifice is more than enough. "Okay."

Our last stop is the gym, which has been rebuilt into dozens of one-room apartments the size of closets. Sheets stand in for doors. A few femmes linger in the narrow pathways, and they watch me the way deer pick up their heads when they think a wolf might be nearby.

One "apartment" at the back of the gym is mine. It's much smaller than my dorm at New Nazareth, but it's perfect.

"Nick and I think it's best to let you get some rest before you make your final decision," Erin says while I push aside the sheet. Even though I took Nick's knife, it's not a done deal. "So take it easy, okay?"

"Thank you," I say, even though it isn't nearly enough for what they've done. "Really."

Erin pauses for a moment, then says, "Trevor's funeral will be in a few days. I don't want to push, and you don't have to if you don't want, but I think it'd mean a lot to his partner if everyone came. Just to show their support."

Trevor. The boy's name, the boy with bones like monuments. I turn it over in my head. Such a normal name, normal like Steven's and everyone else's.

"I'll be there," I promise.

If grief gets caught in my body like it's tangled up with burrs, the least I can do is support the people who can actually feel something. The least I can do is help the people who are helping me. That's what it means to be good.

I don't mean to lose the rest of the day, but as soon as my body recognizes I'm safe, it shuts down on me. No guns, no Graces, and my brain is out like a light. I barely have time to pull the curtain door of my apartment closed. If I was on the fence about trusting the ALC before, my body has made the call for me. And my body has also made the call to whisper as I press the heels of my hands into my eyes and topple onto the mattress: *Thank you, God, thank you.*

Before I know it, I'm waking up the next morning, disoriented and dry mouthed. There is no cross on the wall watching me sleep, no Bible waiting for me to open my eyes. The strange pattern on my sheets is penguins and polar bears. I roll onto my back and stare at bare plywood.

Penguins and polar bears. Have all the animals of Earth been doing better without us? Two years isn't nearly enough for Earth to recover. Even late spring can be deadly hot, and I haven't seen snow since I was really little, even though

Dad told me it used to snow in Pennsylvania every year. But the world must have gotten at least a bit better, right?

What a terrible thing to wonder. That's Mom in my head, all the Sunday school lessons, all the preachers at the pulpit, finding reasons for why the slaughter of nine billion people was God's righteous plan.

I put on my shoes and push aside the curtain.

Outside the apartment, early-morning sun comes in through small windows at the gym ceiling. In the narrow path between rooms, I'm just someone else getting ready for the day—one of all the people stretching, leaning over the tops of their rooms to whisper to a friend, groggily wandering out to the lobby. More pride flags hang from the walls and drawings are tacked next to torn-out pages of books and other tokens, necklaces and charm bracelets and all sorts of things held up to ward off evil.

More than anything, the ALC is quiet. *Good morning* and *wake up, asshole* and *go get the job before someone takes it* are all whispers, from raspy to gentle and everything in between, but never loud. As if Angels are pressing their ears to the outside, waiting to strike if they hear the smallest sound.

Following a voice's advice, I go out to the chalkboard. Forty names wait for the day's chores, with the Watch in the corner. A boy picks up a piece of chalk from the bottom of the board and jots his name down for maintenance duty. *Sarmat*, he spells out and hands it to me.

I need to do something. Make up for the ALC taking me in. Or give my hands something to do to keep them from shaking, give my head something to focus on besides the rot trickling between my fingers.

I scrape my name down under cleaning duty.

Benji.

It's the first time I've written it. That's me. That's *me*. I savor it until the person behind me clears their throat. I pass the chalk along.

I skip breakfast—I'm not hungry, and I don't want to bother anyone by asking what the food protocols are here—and end up in the kitchen with a rag and a small bucket of soapy water. Gray water; no good for drinking. The kitchen is bright with glaring paint colors, trying and failing to liven up a Spartan room. A few people in the back huddle around plates of scavenged food.

By the sink, Faith makes coffee on a battery-operated heating coil. My head spins at the scent. I haven't smelled coffee since Mom brought us to New Nazareth. It's so sweet and strong, I can almost taste it.

I set my bucket down on the counter and lean against the sink—it's not a sink that works, since there's no running water, but still. Faith looks over with a start.

"Scared me for a second there," she says, rubbing the bags under her eyes. Even though she has more muscle than most people and half a foot on me, she looks small. "You're so quiet. Benji, right?"

"Yeah. I just wanted to . . ." How am I supposed to word this? "Thank you for what you guys did yesterday. I'm really sorry about your friend."

"People die," Faith says roughly. "He knew what he was getting into when he joined." Her throat tenses as she turns back to the coffee, watching it brew. "You want some? This is for Aisha, but I think I made too much. She'll be pissed if I waste it."

"I'll try it."

Faith raises an eyebrow. "You've never had coffee before?"

"No? Should I have?"

"Hmm. Maybe not. You're, like, what? Fourteen?"

Fourteen was probably just her being polite. I could be mistaken for twelve on a bad day. Dad used to say my baby face would serve me well when I grew up, so I consider it a waste. "Sixteen, actually."

"I'm teasing," Faith says. "Give it a shot."

When the coffee's done, she gives me a swallow's worth in a mug. It smells amazing, but it's so dark, it's almost black. I remember it being a nice, warm brown in movies.

I carefully pull down my mask and bring it to my lips.

Oh *no*. I cough and splutter. A few heads turn. "This tastes like dirt!"

For the first time, Faith manages a laugh and takes a handful of brightly colored sugar packets from the drawer beside me. There aren't many left. "Yeah, it's awful. That's why you don't drink it plain. You want sugar? I think we can spare some."

"No, thank you. I think you've put me off it forever."

"More for the rest of us. Actually, have you seen Aisha? I don't want this to get cold . . ."

Faith leans against the wall to wait, and I start scrubbing the counters. It's relaxing: sweeping, cleaning up, doing things with my hands. In New Nazareth, it never mattered that I was the only child of Reverend Mother Woodside—I still had to do chores like everybody else. There's something about menial work that lets your brain go quiet, something satisfying in the way your arms and feet ache afterward. Something to be proud of in looking across a clean room and knowing you've done your part.

Even then, I'm watching Faith from the corner of my eye, the shaved stubble of her head and the scars above her low-cut tank top. That kind of outfit would get her torn to pieces in New Nazareth. There's so much freedom here. And *so* many different kinds of people too. I swear I've seen more nonwhite faces than white. I've spent the past five years of my life looking at so many shades of white people that I've been doing double takes, then gluing my eyes to my shoes, because that's rude.

What gets me most of all, though, is that everybody here is a nonbeliever. All of them. Not a single one believes in the Angelic Movement. Not a single one has given themselves to God in the exact way the Angels demand it. Every person is someone I've been taught to hate since I first stepped foot in New Nazareth. I checked Nick and Erin for weapons and demanded they back away, I've held tension in my shoulders so hard for the past few hours that they hurt—and the ALC has done nothing but offer me coffee and a place to sleep.

I'm an asshole. Thanks for the brain rot, Mom.

Truth is, I'm the person they should be worried about, not the other way around. I can't let anyone but Nick and Erin know what I used to be, because they'll want me dead, and I won't blame them. I have to figure out the rules for the ALC the way I figured out the rules for New Nazareth.

Rule one: Be careful with religion. Even if Faith is wearing cross earrings. Even if her name is *Faith*.

I really want to ask about the earrings. They're the first crosses I've seen in days besides the ones carved into the dead. After a second of scrubbing a stain off the countertop, I decide my best course of action is not to ask at all, but to point it out, no judgment implied.

"I like your earrings," I say.

Faith reaches up to touch them, eyes widening a bit in surprise. "What, these?"

Her hand jerks away.

"They don't mean anything," she says defensively. "I just thought they were pretty."

Her tone takes me off guard. "They are."

"They were my mom's. We stopped going to church when I was ten, anyway. It doesn't mean anything, really."

Her chest heaves. Her gaze won't meet mine.

"It's fine," I assure her. "Do people give you trouble for it? For the earrings, for going to church—"

"No. Nobody does. Sorry, I'm overreacting."

I put the rag back in the bucket. We're the only two on this side of the kitchen. For what it's worth, we might as well be alone.

So I say, "Can I ask if you believe in God?"

Faith blinks at me.

"It's not a trap," I say. "I swear."

She immediately falls into a ramble, like she's just been waiting for someone to ask. "I do, actually. And I'm still trying to figure out how I feel about that. Talking to friends—you know, Sadaf is Muslim, Salvador is Catholic, Carly is Jewish—to see if anything clicks. Or if I'm just going to have to deal with believing in the same kind of God those motherfuckers do." Even though I flinch at the sudden swear, her cheeks push up into her eyes, the way it happens when someone is actually, really smiling. "You know, the first time I brought it up to Sadaf, she couldn't stop laughing. I felt like an asshole. I guess what I'm saying is, I believe in something, and I don't know what to do with it, and maybe I don't actually believe in anything at all, and I just *want* to because I hate the idea of Trevor being faced with nothing."

A moment of silence. It's not awkward or anything. Just a second of respect for the dead.

"I'm sorry," Faith says again. "I don't mean to be so . . ."

"No, I get it."

"I've been thinking a lot about it. Since he. You know."

"I know."

Faith says, "What about you? What's going on in your head?"

Before I can answer, Aisha wanders into the kitchen, rubbing sleep from her eyes. Faith mouths *Sorry* and grabs a mug from the cabinet.

"I smell coffee," Aisha mumbles.

"That's because I made some." Faith pours a cup and sets it gently in Aisha's hands. "Take it easy today."

"You don't have to—"

"Please take the coffee."

"You can't act like nothing's wrong."

Faith's smile wavers, the light dropping from her eyes for just a second. "Please. Let me have this."

Aisha accepts the mug, bringing down her mask to take a slow, tentative sip, and her eyes close in exhaustion for just a moment, perfectly still like if she moves, she'll shatter into a million pieces. Under her mask, she's put on a pretty red lipstick that stains the rim of the mug.

Faith's question latches on with teeth. What's going on in my head? What do I believe? How much of it is *me*, and how much of it was *put* there?

I don't know.

Over the course of the day, a few other people introduce themselves, and I fumble through a parade of awkward conversations. One is with another trans guy, Calvin. When I turn down the offer of a chest binder—I've never really cared about flattening my chest—he scrunches up his nose like I smell bad and says he has something else to do.

The only person I manage to hold a decent conversation with is Sadaf, a Black hijabi girl with a medical textbook who asks me to visit her if I ever feel even slightly under the weather.

"Never hurts to be proactive," she says, smiling so wide her eyes close a little bit.

"What do you do if someone gets infected?" I ask.

She says, "I tell Nick. He takes care of it."

I do the math, trying to recall how long the other Seraph trials lasted. The time it took for the other martyrs to fall apart, for their skin to come off in their hands. Instead of the Flood's usual days, *hours*, Seraph has given me a precious few weeks. I can hide the vomiting and the pain, but by the end of February, there will be no hiding anything.

Nick said I would be okay. Erin said I would be okay. They promised. I know that.

Right?

Chapter 6

Our LORD's message is clear: Mankind has disappointed Him once again. We have been tempted beyond salvation and have become a plague upon His earth. Our redemption, our eternal life, lies only in this: an eye for an eye, a plague for a plague.

—*The Truth* by High Reverend Father Ian Clevenger

Nick catches me at the chore board the next morning while I'm debating between cleaning duty or helping Carly fix the rain barrel, which sprung a leak in the night. He takes the chalk out of my hand. "You're with us today. Meet me in ten."

That's how I end up at the back door of the ALC with Nick, Salvador, and the sunburned boy, Cormac. Cormac is tall and sharp with long red hair and a rifle, and he greets me with, "Great. We have to babysit a middle schooler too."

Um?

"Nick," Salvador says, clasping xyr hands together in supplication. "I am literally begging you to let me hit him. Please? Just once. Trevor would want me to."

Nick goes through each of us in turn. "Benji, ignore him. Salvador, not funny. Cormac, one more word, and I *will* look the other way. Am I clear?"

"Clear," Salvador chirps. Cormac scoffs.

My contribution is ignoring Cormac altogether and saying, "So what are we doing, anyway?"

Salvador slings an arm over my shoulder. The sudden touch startles me, but xe is warm and strong, and I don't exactly mind it. "You know how Cormac's been cutting off all those ears? Believe it or not, he doesn't just do that for fun."

Cormac snarls, "Choke on a dick," and Salvador shoots back, "Maybe you can give me some pointers!"

Nick shoves them out the back door and into the courtyard like unruly children, and they squabble for a second before disappearing farther into the grass. A clatter of wood and metal later, they're dragging a wheeled cart toward the gate to the street.

"If you're thinking about joining the Watch," Nick says, "might as well get a taste for what we do." I step out into the sun, squinting up at the early-morning clouds. It's a beautiful day. "Don't want to keep the Vanguard waiting."

The city park—Wagner Commons, according to the sign—has become an infant forest between skyscrapers and dead streetlights. Benches line a gravel path grown through with weeds, and the pond is choked with filth. Squirrels chase one another around a towering maple with a body lashed to its trunk. Flies buzz in a shifting cloud, surrounding the caved-in skull and cross carved into the stomach.

Bodies like this hang in a long, stinking row on both sides of the New Nazareth gate. They're everywhere in this city.

"Shit," Cormac mutters. His trigger finger twitches. "Is that—"

Nick holds out a hand. "It's old."

"Still," Salvador says.

The four of us give the execution a wide berth as we trudge toward the meeting spot at the edge of the pond. It's a pavilion, a roof on stilts above a concrete slab, the kind of thing families used to rent for birthday parties. There's even a sad little grill, blackened with ash. Nick and I pull the sled up beside one of the picnic tables—I switched off with Salvador a few blocks back because I felt bad for not helping—and Cormac glares out over the wavering fields.

He growls, "They said they'd be here."

Along the way, Nick explained the Vanguard: They're a militia group on the other side of the city, made up of a collection of families sitting on top of a *hell* of a lot of supplies. If I ever heard about them in New Nazareth,

I can't remember. We prayed for the destruction of the nonbelievers' strongholds but never any one in particular.

I feel the knife Nick gave me in my pocket. Mom's horror stories about nonbelievers squirm uncomfortably in my skull. Nick wouldn't have given me the knife if this were all a setup, right? If he was just going to hand me back to the Angels? The death squads might make an exception to their no-survivors rule in exchange for getting me back.

"We still have some time." Salvador squints at the sun. "It's not even noon."

"Not even noon," Cormac repeats. "God." I bite the inside of my cheek at the Lord's name being taken in vain, on alert for a grown-up to overhear and scream at us. "I'm going to do a sweep. Come with me or not; I don't care."

Nick sighs. "Salvador, make sure he doesn't get himself killed."

Salvador perks up. "Permission to deck him if he starts saying stupid shit again?"

"Not answering that. Be safe."

They both walk away, and it's just me and Nick. I sit on the edge of the concrete in a patch of sun that shifts as bare tree branches move in the breeze, and I don't let my hand off the knife.

New Nazareth had a lot of green places like this: lawns and wooded areas, creeks and bridges over gullies. I first kissed Theo in one of those little forests. We were fourteen and barefoot in the dirt, obsessed with each other because juvenile crushes meant we could forget about the world choking to death beyond the walls. I could pretend I didn't hate the way my body looked in a dress if it meant Theo would touch me again.

Nick says, so quietly that I know exactly what he's talking about, "When did you join?"

My head snaps up to where Cormac and Salvador are drifting out of earshot. What kind of question is that? I open my mouth to protest, *Are you trying to get me shot?* But . . . I want to talk about it. You can't talk about how much it sucks to be an Angel to other Angels. I tried that once, and look where that got me with Theo.

"Mom took us to New Nazareth when I was eleven. When the High Reverend Father put out the call to the faithful, if you know what that is?"

"The Cloister Order," Nick says.

"Yeah. The Cloister Order. Mom wasn't planning to go, said she had more work to do on the outside, but she was offered a place at the head of the church, and she wasn't about to turn that down." I lean back on the concrete. A flock of birds swirls overhead. "I was eleven. Got pulled out of sixth grade. Never did learn how to do algebra."

But I can recite the Book of Revelation from memory, which I'm sure is an equally useful skill. *The Revelation of Jesus Christ, which God gave unto him, to shew unto his servants things which must shortly come to pass . . .*

"Were you involved with the death squads?" Nick asks.

"Only because my boyfriend was." Calling Theo my boyfriend is easier than explaining that we were engaged, that we still are, even if I don't wear a ring anymore, and I'll die before I go back to him. "I went to his initiation ritual, if that means anything. He got kicked out, though."

I went to Reformation Faith Evangelical Church and watched as Theo kissed the mass of flesh rooted to the altar. I touched his wing tattoos and pretended to love them because he did, and then held him when those wings were ripped off. He just believed *so much.* In the church, in the Angels, in Seraph, in me, because those were all the same thing, really. You could have cracked open his chest and read gospels in his entrails. If I hadn't told him how much I hated Seraph, he probably would have died for me one day.

And no matter what he did to me, I still—

I still love him. The edge of the knife's handle digs into my fingers.

For some reason, I still do.

I keep talking.

"I feel like I'm going to mess this up. Like I'm going to do or say something awful, because I was raised like that." Nick grunts in reply. "I don't know what to do about it. I don't want to hurt anybody. And that's hard when I'm some kind of monster."

Nick finally turns his gaze on me. There's a strange expression drawn between his eyes, one I can't read.

"Are you a monster because you were an Angel," he says, "or because you're Seraph?"

"Shit, either? Does it matter?"

The flock of birds finds a spot in the tree with the body. Across the pond, Salvador throws a rock into the water.

Nick takes something out of his pocket: a toy lizard made of beads, about the size of his palm. The bright yellow beads border on ugly. He rolls them between his fingers a few times.

"I'm autistic," he says.

I splutter, "*Oh—*" not because of anything bad, but because he suddenly makes a lot more sense. Autism was hardly talked about in New Nazareth. When it was, it got the "God never sends trials we can't handle" and "I'm sure it's a blessing in disguise" treatment. Sometimes it was accompanied by glances at the culling fields. I can't make Nick fit that mold, no matter how much I twist him.

"If I can figure out how things work," he says, "so can you."

"Right," is all I reply.

"And take these." He presents me with a set of bobby pins from his jacket. His pockets are never-ending wells of little things. "Your hair is getting in your face."

Then he holds up a hand. Across the algae-choked pond, there are people, and one has a gun raised in greeting.

They're not Angels. I take my hand off the knife.

This is the Vanguard?

This is a group of middle-aged white men (okay, four white men and one white woman, but the Angels have made it painfully clear that's no better) made entirely of wrap-around sunglasses and pilfered army fatigues. They've sewn monochrome American flags and skull patches onto their sleeves, and one even holds his gun with the barrel pointed down between his legs as if to make up for something. I get the feeling I should be grateful they're wearing masks, even if two have their noses peeking out over the top.

Salvador leans over my shoulder to whisper, "Yeah, I know." Cormac shushes us.

"Morning, kids," one says, almost high-pitched, the way you'd talk to elementary schoolers.

"Morning, Joey," Nick drones in return. His head is at an angle that could almost be cocky, eyes cold and tired. Even with his mask, there's an edge to his expression I can't look away from. I am *betrothed*, I remind myself, which has no impact on the fact that I am very gay. I dig my nails into my ring finger instead.

The Vanguard—five people and twelve firearms strong, which is way too many even by Angel standards—claims the opposite table, hoisting their own sled on top. It's covered by a dusty tarp. A guy in the back eyes Cormac like a competitor, as if Cormac isn't half his age. Another stares at Salvador as if he's trying to figure xem out, which has so many racist and transphobic implications that the air goes thick with it.

The one woman crinkles her eyes at me and says, "You're a new one, aren't you, miss?"

The word *miss* hits hard, the way *Sister Woodside* did. A

knife between the ribs and into the lungs that takes all the breath out of me.

For the first time in my life, I defend myself out loud.

"I'm not a girl."

That's it. That's all I have to say. *I'm not a girl.* The world doesn't fall apart. The woman doesn't spit at me and call me a failure of God's vision for my girlhood. She just mutters, "Right. Should've guessed."

As if to cut the tension obviously building in the pavilion, Joey pulls the tarp off the sled. "Let's make this quick!"

It's something out of Isaiah 25—*a feast of wines, of fat things full of marrow.* Cases of water bottles, boxes brimming with canned fruits, vegetables, and tuna, and is that *peanut butter*? Bars of soap, packs of socks and tampons. Batteries, hand sanitizer, and salt. The plastic gleams hard and sharp in the sun, but it might as well be the shimmer of precious metal.

"This is all we could get on such short notice," Joey says. "Water, nonperishables, hygienics. We couldn't spare the antibiotics"—Nick huffs—"but hopefully oxycodone makes up for it. Let's see the goods."

Nick nods to Cormac, who offers a bag to the woman who misgendered me.

"Should be seven," Cormac says.

Brother Hutch. Steven. The rookie. Wedding ring. Three others whose faces I didn't recognize and should have.

The ears come out one by one. Each is held up to the sun, pinched between the woman's gloved fingers, her eyes narrowed as if searching for something. The ears look strange all on their own, discolored and rubbery. Like they came from a costume shop and got fake blood all over them. As she clears each one, it gets placed on the bench beside her. A little parade of body parts, all ears, all *left* ears. Probably so the Watch can't be accused of doubling the numbers.

She pulls out a mangled, fleshy mess. Brother Hutch's left ear. Or what remains of it.

"The hell is this?" she demands.

"An ear," Cormac says. "What does it look like?"

She turns it over, inspecting it one more time. "I'm not calling you a liar, but I am saying—" Without breaking eye contact, she flings it into the grass beyond the pavilion. "Not good enough."

I almost protest, but Nick says nothing so I say nothing too. He just crosses his arms, eyes flickering shut as if begging himself to keep his composure.

Thankfully, the rest of the ears are fine. There are six now, a little two-by-three set resting by the woman's thigh.

That's when she gets to the Grace tooth at the bottom. She hands it over to Joey.

"And this?" he says.

Nick answers, "An abomination tooth." Not a Grace. Abomination. I tuck the vocabulary away for later: *abomination*. Leviticus 20:13—*If a man also lie with mankind, as he lieth with a woman, both of them have committed an* abomination. Deuteronomy 22:5—*The woman shall not wear that which pertaineth unto a man, neither shall a man put on a woman's garment: for all that do so are* abomination *unto the LORD thy*

God. Mom's voice, hissing behind my shoulder the way the Devil spoke through the fangs of a snake in Eden.

"What makes you think this is worth anything to us?" Joey says.

"It's another thing out of the city." How is Nick's voice so calm? "It's what you asked for."

"For all we know, this is from one of those little—" Joey makes a skittering motion with his hand. "Those little bastards. Not anything dangerous."

A lot of Graces aren't actually the massive, terrifying monsters the Angels have adopted into their ranks. Graces like those are a rare blessing, where the mass of mutations creates something useful. Most of the time, your body shatters into something just *shattered*. Dad and I found one a few days ago: a person turned inside out, lungs bulging as they gasped for air again and again.

That's when it dawns.

The Vanguard are too afraid to do this themselves.

With all the skulls and flags, the firepower and muscle, they can't handle what the Watch does. They're too scared to fight back, so they're using kids to do it instead.

Nick says, "It killed our friend."

Silence.

"Right," Joey finally says. The tooth goes next to the ears. "My condolences."

"Is that enough for you?" Nick says. I can hear the grit of his teeth, the tension in his jaw. "We've done what you wanted."

Joey says, "It'll have to do," and turns to the man beside him. "Two cases and all boxes but the big one."

The big one: the one with fresh socks sticking out the top and pill bottles peering from the seam in the cardboard.

Salvador cries, "What the fuck, man!" Cormac lurches forward like he's itching for a fight, and Nick just makes a quiet, broken sound. Even I can't help myself.

"You can't do that!" I protest. I turn to Nick. "Can they do that? They can't just do that, right?"

"Stand down," Nick warns us.

"One of those ears just wasn't up to snuff," Joey says. "Sorry if we're a little cautious these days. We're low on supplies too. Everybody is. And we decide what's worth it. I'm sure you kids understand."

"We made," Nick grits out, "a deal."

"And that deal," Joey says, "is contingent on you doing your jobs. Look, kids. We go through a lot to get this to you. We're taking this away from our own wives and children on the promise that you're making the city safer for us." *I knew it.* "We thought it was a good deal at the time. And if this is all we get on our end, maybe our families will decide this isn't worth it."

A threat.

Nick crumbles.

"Fine," he says. His eyes drop to the floor and his fingers tighten around the bead lizard. This doesn't look right—this doesn't look like him. "Fine. Okay."

"That's what I thought," Joey says. "Let's load you up."

I grab a case of water and carry it over to the sled. It's probably forty pounds, and my hands ache when I set it down. I can feel the woman's eyes on my back, their eyes on all of us. Cormac lingers by one of the pillars holding up the roof, assigned to his spot as a guard, glaring Joey down.

"Bunch of fucking assholes," Salvador whispers to me when our arms brush tying down the boxes. Two cases and all boxes but the big one. Under the mask, xyr face twitches with rage. Xe looks like xe's going to explode as soon as we're out of earshot. "Can't fucking stand them."

This is why the Watch fights Angels. To trade pieces of flesh for supplies that are just stolen right back out from underneath them. Taunted with food and medicine by grown-ups who talk down to them like they're toddlers. Grown-ups who should know better. A bunch of cowards.

Nick shakes Joey's hand, sharp and quick. The bead lizard rattles. He's angry. We all are. They lost their friend to the Angels, and this is all they get in return: some water and disrespect.

That settles it. This is what I want to do. I can help. I can make the Angels suffer for it.

I can do *something*.

When we make it back to the ALC, we're swarmed with eager, curious people. It's the first excitement I've seen from them since I arrived. Someone offers to split half a canned peach with me in thanks, but I feel too guilty to eat it and wave Salvador over instead, because xe'll appreciate it more than I could. Now that I know where this comes from, now that I'm another mouth to feed, food might as well be wet cardboard. I'm sickened at the idea of taking it from a person who might need it more.

I distract myself by tracking down Nick to tell him my decision, but he's nowhere to be found. Erin is so caught up trying to organize the food and the people that it would be a dick move to add one more thing to her plate. So I spend the rest of the day helping Sadaf catalog her dwindling medical supplies, even if, halfway through, I have to duck out into the courtyard, into the weeds in the back corner, to throw up more of my organs. A piece gets stuck in my throat. I have to pull it out with my fingers.

Chapter 7

The LORD's gift is not an easy one to bear. It is painful—but the reverend mother says no blessing worth having comes without pain. You will suffer sickness, agony, and rage beyond your imagining. Bear it with dignity, for salvation is forever yours. (But I would make it easier, God, if only I could.)

—Sister Kipling's notes on the Flood

Trevor's funeral is the next evening. The whole day, the ALC is still as a corpse. Nobody will so much as breathe until the oppressive taste of the air is gone, until the terrible thing seeping into our lungs is looked in the eyes.

The funeral is held in the courtyard at the back of the ALC, boxed in by a bank and the gate. It can barely hold all forty people, let alone the shoebox-size open grave marked by a rock. I've never been to a funeral before. Angels look down on them. Mom's uncle died when I was eight, and her side of the family stopped speaking to her after she refused to attend the service. Funerals are a function of grief and therefore sacrilege. Loss is God's plan. *How dare you grieve what was always His to take?*

It's getting dark, and the sky is orange and indigo. The only person not gathered around the grave is the sniper on the roof, who sits with her legs dangling over the edge.

I'm the last one out. I ease the door shut behind me, where it hits the brick keeping it propped open. People clump together like algae on the pond in Wagner Commons. The Watch clusters by the gate. Erin stands behind the grave, whispering to someone I can't see. And Nick stands away from everybody, alone except for his bead lizard.

Faith tries to wave me over to the Watch. Aisha is leaning against her shoulder, desperately trying to wipe away tears. I wave back, offering a smile I hope comes across behind my mask, but make my way over to Nick. After watching him crumble in front of the Vanguard, I don't like the idea of him standing by himself. Or something. I don't know.

Nick is focused on his lizard. He stares at each bead as he goes over it with his fingers. I like that we don't have to say anything. It's easier this way.

"Thank you all for being here," Erin says, just loud enough to carry across the courtyard and no more. Erin changes when she's in front of a crowd. There's no waver to her voice, no uncertain twitches or nervous tugs at her braids. "The past few days have been difficult, and I am incredibly proud of how we've soldiered through. But keeping a stiff upper lip for too long hurts everybody. It would mean a lot to Trevor that we're letting ourselves come together like this, even for just a little bit."

How dare you grieve what was always His to take? I haven't been able to cry for years. The Angels made sure of it; Mom made sure of it. I watched my father die, and all I did was keep it crammed in my chest where nothing can get out except my own literal guts. I watched his head cave around the bullet, turning his face into a bloody flower of skull and tongue, and I accepted it and kept running because I couldn't do anything else.

"Trevor was our heart," Erin says. A girl sobs into her sleeve. "He fought for us because he loved us. He stormed City Hall when our funding was cut, and he stuck with us through That Day and every day after. He died for us because he loved us."

Dad died for me because he loved me. I'm going to join the Watch, I'm going to be good, I'm going to make the Angels suffer, because I love him.

A boy in the crowd leans on his friend, and I see the person next to Erin: a scraggly white kid in a patchwork coat. In funerals like the ones I've seen in movies, I could picture them as the widow. Instead of a bouquet of lilies, sprawling white funeral flowers, they clutch a charm bracelet.

I wish I had Dad's watch. His wedding ring. A scrap of his shirt, his blood under my fingernails. *Anything.*

"If anyone knew him," Erin murmurs, "it was Alex." She puts a hand on their shoulder, ducking her head ever so softly. I remember Erin asking Salvador to track them down in the hours after Trevor's death, because they'd disappeared and she was worried—and I remember their coat lurking near the ham radio in the lobby, only catching flashes of it as I passed by. They looked so gaunt, so destroyed. They still do. "Is there anything you want to say?"

Alex shakes their head and puts the bracelet in the tiny grave.

They never got to see Trevor's body, did they? Do I pity them for it, or am I jealous? Would I feel better if Dad had been killed behind my back, if Steven had grabbed me by the neck and led me away while Brother Hutch put Dad down? If Dad hadn't died with his hand in my hair and his blood in my mouth?

"You're grinding your teeth," Nick whispers.

I unclench. It takes every muscle in my face to manage it. "Thanks."

Do I believe Dad is in Heaven? What happened when the bullet tore through his brain and turned that delicate organ to sludge? I want to think he's happier now than he was, suffocating under Mom and the church, but I can't stomach it.

"Again," Nick says.

"Shit." I work my jaw and stare at the brick wall beside me because it's better than looking at the grave. "I just . . ."

"I know."

Somebody else is talking now. Alex stands to the side, wrapped up in their coat, head down in silence. They're so small. I wonder if I looked that small beside Dad's body, in the moments between his head shattering and me getting to my feet to *run*.

A prayer for the dead is sacrilege, heresy, blasphemy. I was never taught any, so I have to make one. I dredge up Mom's words, the church's howling screams, and fasten them into something I'm not sure I believe. *O Lord, accept these souls into your arms and ease their suffering.* Do they reach anything? Maybe it doesn't matter if it's true as long as it takes a bit of this weight off my chest. *In Your wisdom, let them be judged and let them rest.* I can't tell if I'm faking it. If I just want it to be true the same way Faith wanted it, so we know there's something more than nothing.

Alex stifles a sob and steps away.

Prayers don't help any of the living besides the one saying them. I can't just stand here. I promised I would help.

I whisper to Nick, "Be right back."

He says nothing, just watches.

Alex is walking away from the grave. They look a lot like me: pale, feminine in the face, bags under the eyes. I catch them by the back door, underneath the sniper's legs dangling off the roof, right before their hand reaches the handle.

"Hey," I whisper. Alex jumps and turns a watery glare on me. "Alex, right?"

They sneer, "Who the hell are you?"

I understand anger, God, I do. "I'm Benji. The new guy. I wanted to say . . ." *I was there when Trevor died. I watched the light go out of his eyes.* "I lost somebody a few days ago too. If you, uh, want to talk about it? I'm here."

Alex punches me in the face.

Pain snaps through my jaw. I hit the wall, my head cracks against it, and I'm frozen long enough to say, "What—" Long enough for Alex to jam their arm under my throat and lean on it so hard, it sends a bolt up the soft part of my esophagus. I fight for air, scrabbling for a hold on their arm.

Their eyes bulge, red and bloodshot, and they growl, "*It was you.*"

"Alex!" someone shouts, shattering the desperate quiet of the courtyard. I dig my nails into their wrist so hard something pops.

"You killed him," Alex keens. They press harder into my throat, and I gag. "You killed him! He would've lived if you hadn't gotten in Nick's fucking *way*!"

"Alex!" It's Faith's voice, louder. "Alex, stop!"

Alex's concentration breaks for just a second, and I wrench an arm around the back of their neck and slam a fist into their ribs and throw my body into theirs. We hit the grass together.

I think I hear Erin, I think I hear Nick, I *think*, because I don't know. I can't hear anything but the rush in my ears now, hot blood roaring through my veins, because I'm on the ground with Alex and I'm making some terrible noise, wet and deep in my throat like a Grace. I'm on top of them. Their knuckles hit my jaw, my tooth clicks, and a piece of enamel hits the back of my tongue right where the rot is boiling over, seeping between my teeth. Every nerve ending is on fire. Red burns into my vision.

I have a knife. What if Alex has a knife too? What if they stick it into my lung?

I lean on them, putting all my weight on them until they choke, their nails cutting into my face. Our shoes dig into the grass, and their knee hits my stomach as they buck and twist. I have to get my knife first, I have to—

A hand grabs me by the hood of my jacket and yanks me back, dragging me down to the dirt. I snarl and lash out with my foot. Alex scrambles back, clutching their neck. Ghost-white marks around their throat fade as blood rushes back into the skin.

Above me, Cormac steps back, heaving with anger. Hair has fallen out of his ponytail and hangs around his face in a mess.

"What the fuck," he spits. *"What the fuck?"*

The stranglehold on my vision eases. The world comes into focus: the entire ALC staring at us. Nick holding Erin by the wrist. Everyone frozen, even the Watch, eyes wide like they caught me reciting an Angel prayer.

"Jesus Christ," Cormac says. He holds out a hand for Alex, who scrabbles farther backward before finally staggering to their feet, ignoring him entirely. Cormac turns to me, face contorted. "What the fuck is wrong with you?"

I don't answer. There are no words. I barely hear him, just the thrum of my heartbeat and the creaking of my bones. Just Flood in my mouth, burning, tasting like corpse flesh. I swallow it down even though I know it will come back up later.

Cormac turns his glare away from me, marches up to Nick, and jabs a finger into his chest. Nick recoils. Erin puts an arm between them.

"If you think I'm going to work with that motherfucker," Cormac hisses.

Nick replies, simply, "Don't touch me again."

Alex flings open the back door and flees into the ALC. Cormac shakes awkwardly for a second, looking from face to face, waiting for someone else to speak up. Nobody does. Aisha, Faith, and Salvador all turn away.

Giving up, Cormac grunts and follows Alex inside.

And all that's left is me.

The burning is stuck under my fingertips, searing hot, my cells breaking and bursting. My thoughts are an angry swirl of words, none of which I can get past my tongue. Everyone saw that they started it, right? I did what I had to. Don't look at me like that. *Don't look at me like that.*

One word gets past the block in my throat: a bloody, rot-splattered, "*What?*"

Nick breaks from the group and hauls me to my feet, not at all gently.

"I think," he says, his face right next to mine, "it would be best if you turned in for the night."

It isn't until I nearly try to pull his arm out of his socket just for touching me that I manage to take a step back from myself and realize.

Something is really, really wrong with my head right now.

I don't do this kind of thing. This isn't *me*.

So what was it?

Chapter 8

As the church is to Christ, a wife is to her husband, and Graces are to our Seraph.

—Reverend Mother Woodside's notes

The Flood works in stages, but they pass so quickly—you're dead by the fortieth hour, tops—that they blur together. It moves more like a parasite than a virus, devouring everything it touches. It starts with the insides, unraveling your organs for spare parts, and it gets into the brain so quickly that you don't notice your spine growing out of your back until you've already tried to put your teeth through the nearest piece of flesh.

Seraph, though, is slow and meticulous. It has a vision in mind, and it's going to do it right. I get to see the stages play out perfectly, all in order, ticking off each box as it goes. I watched it happen to the failed Seraphs before me, and now I get to watch it in the mirror.

This is the second stage. Sister Kipling had a specific word for where it happens: the blood-brain barrier. The virus gets from the blood into the brain and starts twisting it the way it twists the body. The way toxoplasma makes rats love cats, the way cordyceps makes bugs hang from the stem of a leaf. It makes you more likely to pass it on; it makes you angry. First you start puking up your organs, and then you get *pissed.*

I can't say I didn't know what came over me, because I do. And I can't join the Watch if I'm going to hurt the people I'm supposed to be helping.

So I am going to do to Seraph what I can do to any other Grace: Look it in the eye and control it.

If Nick didn't want me to leave the ALC, he shouldn't have shown me how easy it was to get out without the sniper guard noticing. He had to whistle to get the guard's attention when we left for Wagner Commons, and only then did they notice, acknowledging us with a wave: *Fine, I won't shoot you since you asked so nicely.* All I have to do is wait until dark, then pull up on the gate handle so the hinges don't squeal when I open it.

I am alone in Acheson.

The city is beautiful if you can ignore that, for months after Judgment Day, it stunk of dead bodies decomposing in beds, hospital gurneys, carpets, and alleyways. They baked in the sweltering sun, splitting down the stomach when they swelled too large with putrefaction gases. If you can ignore that some of the corpses track you with their eyes when you walk past. If you can hide well enough from the death squads.

But there *is* a beauty to the city. There's no light pollution anymore, so you can look up at the night sky and see the entire universe twinkling between clouds and skyscrapers. Nature creeps back between cracks in the road and up the sides of buildings. I pull down my mask and breathe in fresh, cool, silent air on a street corner.

I understand how the Angels could radicalize somebody. Eternal life and a sky like this could convince a lot of people to join their cause. But that beauty is always dragged down by the desperate hands of the billions of people who were slaughtered to make it. I keep moving.

If I'm going to face Seraph, if I'm going to coax this virus to life and meet it in the middle, I need a Grace.

I'm not sure where I'm supposed to look. I don't know this city nearly as well as anyone from the ALC does, so I count turns on my fingers and memorize street signs to make sure I don't get lost. I open front doors to find bones and don't stay because the dusty picture frames scare me. I startle stray pets and scavenger animals that wander the streets. No Graces.

My path takes me to a bodega between two crumbling storefronts. The windows are plastered with sun-bleached ads and government-distributed signs about water shortages and electricity limits. *Might as well.* I pull open the front door and a bell rings, the first sound I've heard all night that isn't my sneakers on the asphalt. It's immediately followed by the yowl of a cat as an orange blur scatters from the counter, knocking over pens and hissing and spitting the whole way.

I frown. I miss pets. "Sorry, kitty."

The store was ransacked. The shelves are naked and only the most useless items have been left behind—zip-tied clusters of brooms, sludge that had probably once been fresh fruit, stacks of lottery tickets that are all scratched off for some reason. Considering how close this is to the ALC, I wouldn't be surprised if someone I know stripped these shelves of everything they had. If Erin, Aisha, Faith, and Nick lived off Doritos and beef jerky for a time.

I'm about to leave—there's nothing here but brooms and a cat—when I find a stack of Acheson maps in a plastic case. *Perfect.* I grab one and spread it out in a back corner cordoned off by shelves, where a spill of moonlight comes in through the window. The floor is disgusting, but I sit anyway. According to the map, there's an emergency room a few blocks away. Hospitals would have been hotbeds for the Flood. I picture morgues filled to bursting by doctors who are starting to spit up blood, a Grace rising between gurneys as its flesh melts and builds itself anew.

That's my best shot, then. I hunker down, fingers tracing paths through the streets, trying to orient myself. Which direction did I come from? Which direction should I go?

The doorbell jingles.

The cat yowls.

I freeze.

The door eases shut. A black form eases between the shelves, a hand lingering on the front counter. I put a hand over my mouth to muffle my breathing. No white, no robes, so not an Angel. A nonbeliever? Someone who would get scared off if I banged on the shelves or someone who would slit my throat?

I grab the knife from my pocket and ease it open. As soon as the blade peeks from the handle, the silver edge catches the moonlight. Its point is terrifyingly sharp, the way Angels always keep them.

The blade clicks when it settles into place. Loudly.

I mouth *Goddamn it* and don't have time to feel guilty for taking the Lord's name in vain. The footsteps stop for just a second, the hard scuff of a rubber sole against tile, before they pick up again. Faster. Toward me.

That red anger burns up my throat again, the fury that pushed me to crush Alex's throat in my hand. More of Seraph past the barrier, nestling into gray matter and the folds of my brain.

The dark form takes one step past the last shelf.

I lunge forward.

A hand catches me by the wrist, twists me around and smashes me into the shelves. My back pops, and mop pads and magic erasers clatter to the floor. My knife hand is pinned above me. The dull shine of another blade glints between my stomach and a bruised hand.

A raspy voice warns, “Careful.”

You’re kidding.

I struggle for air. *“Nick?”*

Nick lets go, pulling the knife away from my belly. I stumble a few steps and cough into my hands, trying to get breath back into my lungs.

“Your form is messy,” Nick says as I struggle to regain my composure. I lean over to spit Flood rot in the corner but thankfully nothing else comes up. “And close the knife. You’re going to put your eye out.”

Grudgingly, I do what he says. “I thought you were going to kill me!”

“Then don’t be so easy to kill.” I groan. “And put your mask back up. If it was anyone other than me following you, you’d have a lot of explaining to do.” He’s right, I guess—no mask means either *I’m infected and there’s no point* or *I don’t care if I get sick and bring it back to everyone else.* I shove the mask over my nose and crouch to gather the map. He steps on the corner so I can’t. “More explaining to do than now, anyway. What are you doing?”

“Why were you following me?” I snap.

“Because you made yourself easy to follow. What are you doing?”

“I was trying something.”

“Too vague.”

“I’m not a double agent, if that’s what you’re thinking. Give me the map.”

He doesn’t let up. “You can never be too careful.”

I sneer. "You really think the Angels would use Seraph to spy on a bunch of queers that'll starve out by summer? Yeah, right. The *map*."

Nick moves his foot off the map. I fold it up and shove it in my pocket.

I want to join the Watch. I need to prove I'm not a danger. I force my voice to steady and scrub all the anger from it, making sure it comes out quiet and calm.

I say, "I was trying to find a Grace. So I could practice."

"Practice," Nick repeats.

It sounds sad when I say it out loud. "I scared myself at the funeral. This is what I was talking about at the park. Being a monster and everything." But even if it's pitiful, I have to say it. "I want to help you. I want to join the Watch"—Nick blinks—"but I don't want to hurt my friends."

Nick says, "You're not friends with Alex. Nobody is friends with Alex."

"That's not the point."

"It's not," he concedes. "You want to join the Watch?"

"I do." *Make them suffer for it. Be good.* "God, I do."

Nick holds out his hand. "The map."

I give it to him. He points to an unlabeled spot nearby. "There's a homeless shelter here. Let's go."

"So what was that at the funeral?" Nick asks. We're walking down the middle of the road; feral Graces can be heard from a block away, and death squads don't usually roam at night. No need to stick to the sidewalks. "If you know."

I stick my hands in my pockets. "The Flood messes with your head."

He glances at me. The starlight really brings out his eyes. People never talk about how pretty dark eyes are, especially the so-dark-they're-almost-black of Nick's.

"How much?" he says.

"Not a lot," I say. "Not yet, at least."

"We'll deal with it."

We find the homeless shelter a few blocks away, squat and nondescript. I've never seen one in real life before. When I was younger, Mom would have hurried past it, giving me a lecture about the dangers of overpopulation and laziness, how some people refuse to take responsibility for their lives. *They must have done something wrong for them to be punished this way. God is kind; God is just.* That wouldn't fly at the ALC. It's been just a few days, and I know how they would react: "God sure as hell isn't. People were poor because the rich wanted them to be, just like we're fucked now because the Angels want us to be."

The inside of the Acheson Rescue Mission is a massacre. The windows let in just enough light to see by, illuminating rows of stained beds and plastic chairs. It may as well have been a military barrack or maybe a low-security prison. No privacy, no human comfort, just four walls and a cot.

And the bodies. Always the bodies. The Flood is in their bones—splinters break off from femurs and jaws, strange structures grow through chest cavities. I mouth my cobbled-together prayer for the dead as we walk between the beds, because Mom isn't here to stop me.

This is what Seraph was made for. To turn every human being into this. To destroy what's left of the world.

"Maybe there's a back room," I offer. My voice is too loud in the silence. "There's just bones."

Nick goes back to the front desk and sticks his hand in a trash can.

I say, "Um."

He pulls out a glass bottle, weighs it for a second, and smashes it on the floor.

"Christ!" And it feels good to shout it, to *mean* it. It burns through me like blood rushing back into my fingertips, and I do it again because I can. "Christ, what the *hell*!"

A low, long wail keens from the far side of the hall. It rattles in my ribs and puts every hair on edge, the way a child's scream gets under your skin.

A Grace.

I'm across the room before I can stop myself, holding on to the edges of cots to keep myself together. My fingers snag moth-eaten sheets. A Grace. A *Grace.*

I'm at the edge of its bed, wavering on my feet.

This is me.

This is what I'll become.

Its mass of white, whirling eyes lock on me, and it begins to scream. High, shrieking, choked with phlegm. Nick stops a few steps away, but I don't. I move forward because I have to.

It's more human than not, more human than some but less human than the inside-out man Dad and I saw on the apartment floor days ago. A head, a torso, close enough. But its ribs open into a second set of teeth, gray organs pulsing underneath like fat, heavy tonsils. Its lower jaw has melted into its chest, and molars stick out of its collarbones. One desiccated arm is wrenched above its head, lashed to the bedframe by a pair of old handcuffs.

It. I can't keep saying *it*. That's not right. I want to press my hands to its, *their*, *their* skin, reach into their organs the way Theo brought the flesh to his lips, whisper to them, *We're the same thing, we're the same, can you tell?*

Nick says, "Are you all right?"

I'm so much more than all right. "Yeah. Yeah, I'm fine."

The Grace makes a pitiful sound, scared and small. I press my hand to the broken expanse of their chest.

"Hey," I whisper, and I make sure to *whisper* it too. Softly. Gently. "It's okay. I'm not going to hurt you."

They're in so much pain. They've spent two years like this, kept alive by the Flood and nothing else, alone for so long. Their skin is mottled all kinds of colors, green and black and yellow, looking like it might come off in my hand when I take it away. It won't, though. Grace skin is tough and hard, impervious, intensely painful. It's why people like Nick have to get them in the soft parts—the mouth and eyes, into the brain.

Just thinking about that makes my skin crawl. No. I'm not going to let that happen. They're scared. I am too, but I'm here now, and I'm not going to let anything happen.

We're the same, can you tell, can you tell?

Nick comes up beside me. He's been keeping his distance, hands clasped behind his back. I don't blame him. I'll have to scrub my hands raw as soon as we get back to the ALC, or Sadaf will probably have Cormac haul me out back and set me right. The Flood creeps in through the same soft parts of bodies that are so vulnerable in Graces, the mouths and eyes and mucous membranes, and it gets you any way it can. Clinging to skin and clothes, lingering in dead meat, sometimes traveling through the air on an infected person's breath. At least the virus has the decency to show itself quickly.

"It's calm," Nick says, eyes fixated on the Grace's cracked-open chest.

I say, "They're safe now. They know that."

His eyes narrow at the use of *they*, but he doesn't point it out. "How?"

"I told them." But whispering is more than just telling. It's a live wire. Seraph to the Flood, the Grace to me, like the virus is some kind of current thrumming between us. I open my mouth to explain, but none of the metaphors sound right. A language, a connection deeper than that. Even Sister Kipling couldn't put it into words. How am I supposed to?

Any attempt to explain is choked when I take off my mask and spit black sludge onto the floor. The Grace turns in bed as best they can, whimpering, free hand reaching for me. I grab their fingers as I straighten up, murmuring, "I'm okay, it's okay."

Screw practice. I need to make sure this Grace is okay.

"Does it follow orders?" Nick asks.

"They're not a dog," I retort. I don't like the way he says it, and I can't tell if it's just the flat way he talks or if he truly doesn't give a shit about the person in front of us. My skin burns warm, then hot, the way it did when Alex pinned me to the wall.

This is it. I said I would control it. I'm going to control it. I've spent years swallowing down anger the way girls are told to do, so I can learn to do this too. *Breathe. Ask the question calmly.* "Do you see a handcuff key anywhere? A little metal thing?"

Nick frowns. "What?"

Calmly. "Do you see one?"

"I heard you the first time. Why do you want one? You're not thinking about . . ."

I bristle. *No, no, get it together.* "I am."

Nick says, "Absolutely not."

"They're not going to hurt anybody." They've been trapped here for *years*, this *isn't right.* If I can help them, I have to. That's what it means to be good. "Just help me look."

"It's dangerous," Nick says. His calm voice isn't matched by the look in his eyes, nervously flicking from the Grace to me. "I understand that this is important to you"—*Don't take that tone with me*—"but this is taking it a step too far."

"It's not. They're just stuck. They won't hurt us, I swear."

"No." Nick pulls me back. "This is too much." I wrench out of his grasp and shove him away. It burns where we touch. "If you're going to act like this, we're leaving."

I bare my teeth. Even though it's behind the mask, even if he can't see it, it feels right. Showing my teeth like a Grace, like Seraph. "No." I've never said no to anyone before. Not in any way that mattered. "We're not."

We watch each other. I'm skimming him for weapons the way I did in the office that first day. He has a knife in his pocket. He could have it at my neck in a second and slit my throat in another, and I know it.

I have a knife too.

And an idea.

I snap it open and dive for the Grace.

I jam the blade into the crook of their thumb and shove it between the bones and wrench it until something snaps. The Grace shrieks, and Nick's body slams into mine, taking us both down to the floor. He bashes my knife hand into the concrete and the blade clatters away.

"Get *off*!" I howl. His knee digs into my hip. I try to twist him off but, God, why are cis boys so much stronger, it isn't fair, I remember when Theo held me down almost just like this and I hate it, *I hate it*. "Mother*fucker*!"

Nick's weight disappears from my chest. A mass of flesh hits the cot beside us, sending it across the floor with a screech and taking Nick with it.

I sit up. The Grace has Nick trapped against the floor, strings of saliva trailing from their gaping mouth. The thumb

I broke hangs limply by the rest of their clawed fingers, just enough to help them slip their cuffs.

Nick has gone completely still, dark eyes wide and jittering.

It's beautiful, and I come back to my senses immediately.

I clap my hands as if scolding a puppy. "Hey!" The Grace's head snaps up. "Don't hurt him!"

The Grace snuffles and backs away, taking their hand off Nick's shoulder. Nick scrambles to his feet, wheezing. The fire of Seraph chews through my stomach, and it hurts, but it hurts like *growing*. Like setting a bone, or popping a joint back into place.

This is control. This is what I wanted.

This is what I was made for.

"All right," Nick rasps. His hand hovers by his shoulder where the Grace held him down. "All right. You want to join the Watch?"

"I do." More than anything. I do.

He looks to the Grace.

"Good. You start tomorrow."

NICHOLAS

Chapter 9

The Acheson LGBTQ+ Center, Youth Services, is a crucial resource for gay, lesbian, bisexual, transgender, and other queer and questioning youth. From providing free meals for those in need to readying students for a career through job counseling and volunteer work, we do everything we can to offer opportunities to those who need them.

—Acheson LGBTQ+ Center official website

It took Nick a long time to learn to lie.

If he was going to be honest, it took him a long time to learn most of the things that seemed to come naturally to everyone else. Like realizing someone meant "Fuck off" when they pretended he wasn't there, or how to speak without rehearsing the wording of a sentence a dozen times, or figuring out that sometimes it was better to make up something that wasn't true and pretend it was. He'd gotten good at compensating for it over the years. He'd had to. Being autistic was just another thing his parents could hold over his head, could carve into his skin as they reminded him what a failure he was.

But lying was different. Because once Nick learned to lie, he became disturbingly good at it.

He'd spent so long memorizing the rules of interacting with people that he could twist them to his advantage. There are scripts people don't even realize they follow, and if you fit that script, or tweak it just enough to throw them off, they drop their guard. There are certain *ways* to say things, and if you get them right, you can say whatever you want. People hear what they want to and fill in the gaps themselves. There are patterns. There are tells. It is embarrassingly easy.

That's why lying is his job and not Erin's. Erin's job is to make the truth palatable, and if she can't do that, then it's Nick's job to hide it.

Speaking of Erin, Nick has just woken up and is looking for her when something happens in the kitchen. Nick sticks his head in to see if Erin is there, which she is not, just in time for Calvin to shove Aisha against the sink and scream, "*Fucking liar!*"

Sadaf and Carly jump up from their breakfast so quickly, it sends their chairs screeching back on the tile. The sound feels like worms crawling up Nick's spine, but there's no time to do anything about it because Calvin has his hands on Aisha and no, *no*, absolutely not. Nick bolts across the room and grabs Calvin in a headlock, one arm under the jaw and one on the back of the head.

Calvin twists in his grasp as Nick drags him away. He spits, curses, and claws at Nick's sleeves. "Liar! Goddamn fucking liar—let me go!"

Aisha braces herself on the counter, gulping down air. Sadaf tucks against her side while Carly stands in front, one hand on Aisha's shoulder to keep her steady.

"Stop," Nick snarls. Calvin's back is flush against his chest, and the heat and pressure is suffocating. "Stop."

Calvin jams an elbow into Nick's ribs. Nick grabs the elbow and wrenches it back until Calvin howls.

Nick says, "Cut the shit."

He drops Calvin to the floor, where the boy coughs and chokes, pounding his fist on the tile. The first thing Nick wants to do is shake himself out, get the awful feeling off his skin, but Aisha is trembling, which means Nick has to keep it together. Okay. He can do that for her.

Calvin whines from the floor, "You almost broke my arm."

"You're right." Nick does not say that the move would have simply dislocated it. "I almost did. If you have a problem, you come to me. Not my people. *Me.* Am I clear?"

"Your people," Calvin spits. He flings a hand at the skeletal pantry. Aisha flinches. "Fuck you. Where the hell is our food?"

Nick's throat slams shut. Of course it's about food. When one person finally snaps, it means everyone is thinking it, at least a little bit. Seraph was right; they're going to starve out by summer if they don't do something drastic, and soon. The mental image of losing people to a lack of water when the rains stop coming, to heatstroke when summer breaks, to starvation when the animals begin hiding from the heat and the Vanguard turns their back—it hits like an iron pipe to the back of his skull, every time.

But nobody gets to put a hand on his people.

"There is enough," Nick says. "And we will be getting more." Every word is careful. Every word is perfect. He doesn't know if he's lying, so he has to pretend that he is. Lying keeps Aisha safe—it keeps them all safe. "If you touch her again, we're going to have a lot more problems than a broken arm."

Calvin says nothing to that, so Nick turns to Aisha. "Are you okay?"

"I guess," Aisha manages, which is also a lie, but Nick doesn't press. He just nods.

"If he does this again, you come tell me immediately."

Aisha's voice hitches when she speaks. "Can I go back to my room?"

"Of course. Sadaf, Carly, go with her."

Then it's just him and Calvin. Calvin's face is wrinkled in anger and pain.

"That was a bad decision you just made," Nick notes. "You won't make it again."

That's when Erin comes running in, still in the silk scarf

she sleeps in, her mask lopsided on her face. "I just saw Aisha crying," she says. "What happened?"

Nick spends a lot of time being grateful to Erin, and this is why. She sits on the office floor with him, silent and unpitying, while he pulls himself together.

His lizard isn't enough, so he digs his palms into the rough carpet until his skin stops trying to crawl off his body. The Vanguard, the Grace, then Calvin. He has to keep it together. His job is to keep it together. He scrapes his palms red on the carpet, shakes them out, and presses them against his temples, right where he can feel the heartbeat pounding in his skull.

"Can you talk?" Erin asks.

Nick shakes his head. He can, technically, but the idea of it, God, the idea of it. He wants to hide his whole face behind a mask, not just everything below the eyes. Cover the eyes too. Cover everything.

Erin says, "Okay."

It takes a while for the vice to loosen its stranglehold on him. It happens slowly, the threat of a shutdown fading like shadows come noon: still there, technically, but not nearly as noticeable. His breathing slows. He doesn't feel like he's drowning anymore. His leg is still bouncing, but it always does that.

Nick says, "All right."

Erin says, "Aisha's okay. Faith offered to buddy up for a few days, keep an eye on her. Sadaf offered too, but we've been keeping her busy lately."

That makes sense. Faith has been glued to Aisha's side since Trevor died. She wouldn't even leave her long enough to go out to the Vanguard—she had been his first pick, but she refused to budge. A sudden knot presents itself: Are they dating? Not that he particularly cares about the details, but he needs to know for strategic reasons. As soon as he tries to inspect the tangle, though, it fizzles out. It'll be easier to ask Salvador. Xe knows a lot about these things.

"Good," Nick finally says. He puts his work voice on, the low one that never wavers or cracks. If he can't cover his whole face with a mask, this is the next best thing. "I'll keep an eye on Calvin."

Erin leans against the desk, studying him. She's picking at the ends of her braids, which is never good. Nick knows how delicate her hair is. She must be really stressed. "You have better things to keep an eye on. Like Benji."

Seraph. That's why Nick was looking for Erin in the first place. The whole reason he crawled out of bed this early in the morning, even after he spent half the night out in the city.

"Seraph will be joining the Watch today," he says. "And it'll be going to the church." Erin cringes at the word *it*, but they'd had this argument already and agreed to hate the other's opinion on the topic in silence. "Just wanted to keep you updated."

"I was wondering when you . . . ," she mumbles, then stops. "Wait, where?"

"The church. Next week."

"I know that," Erin says. "What I mean is, why?"

The way she's looking at him, like he's a child missing something obvious, makes him hate himself a little more, so he pulls the lizard from his pocket to play with. It's the least rude of his stimming options in the middle of a conversation, and even with Erin, he finds himself trying not to be *too* autistic.

And the thing is, there are a lot of ways to answer her question. Because Seraph is desperate to prove itself loyal. Because it wants to be helpful and offering it the opportunity would twist it around their finger. Because there's no reason not to use Seraph while they have it.

Because they might not have Seraph forever.

He decides on, "I've seen what it can do." The memory of the abomination pressing its face to his bubbles up, all the teeth and skin and stench. "It'll make the church survivable."

Erin doesn't respond. Nick looks up from the lizard—which has fourteen blue beads and thirty-six yellow beads, which he knows because he's counted them a thousand times—to find her staring at nothing.

"We shouldn't have done this," she finally says. "This was a bad idea."

A heavy weight settles in Nick's stomach. "Explain."

"Him," Erin says, and the pronoun feels pointed. "Benji. Seraph. This whole mess." She shakes her hands helplessly;

not the way Nick shakes his hands, but the way non-autistic people do, like she's trying to conjure something out of thin air. "I don't know if I can do this."

"You don't have to lie to it," Nick says. That must be what she's upset about. All he has to do is reassure her. "That's my job."

She breaks out the patient tone of voice that means he's missing something. "And I'm grateful, but that's not what I mean."

It hits. Again. The iron pipe to the back of the head.

He says, "You feel bad for it."

It's an awful thing to say. Saying it out loud means the words are going to stick. The words are going to stay there, in his head, and he's going to keep thinking about them, and he can't let himself do that.

"I feel like shit," Erin says. "It's cruel!" Nick doesn't flinch, only because he's been called cruel before. "Asking Benji to risk his life when he's practically dying? When we're wondering if his dead body will convince the Vanguard not to abandon us? There has to be some other way. Something else we can do."

Nick told her it would be difficult. He said that Seraph would play at being human, and they couldn't let themselves be weak. They've spent the past year killing Angels. This one should be no different.

It can't be different.

"This is our best chance." Nick jams his finger into the carpet. "Do you want to let everybody starve?"

"No, I don't!" Her chest heaves. "Nick, look. Logically, I understand. I do. Don't pretend like I don't understand exactly where you're coming from because I *do*. But I don't want to be the kind of person who is fine with sacrificing a kid."

Nick's face is doing that thing where he can't figure out how to move it, and he is so grateful for his mask because she can't see the way he's sucking on his teeth and chewing on his lips as if that will help, which it doesn't.

"You get me," she says. "Right?"

Deep breaths. "I do. But this is different. Seraph isn't a person."

The words snag on the way out. He tamps down how Seraph looked at him under the pavilion, the way it sagged in relief when Nick offered a little bit of himself in return—*I'm autistic*—to ease the tension in its shoulders. It looks like a teenager, it sounds like a teenager, it acts like a boy exactly his age, reflecting his worst nightmare back at him, desperately grasping for a friend, and Nick *cannot* be that.

Nick can be anything else. He can be cruel. He can build an entire personality out of violence and disconnection, convince everyone that he is unfeeling and uncaring, but he will not betray a friend. He has never gone that low, and he never will. The moment he does, he will be no better than the sons of bitches that burned this world to the ground.

Therefore, Seraph cannot be human.

Erin sniffles. Nick never knows what to do when people cry. It scares him.

She says, "He reminds me of you."

No.

"You see it," she says. "Right?"

Absolutely not. He refuses to listen to this from himself, and he absolutely will not hear it from her. He wants to beg her not to say things like this, because it will only make it harder for everyone, it will only make it harder for *him*, and he'll be the one pulling the trigger if it comes to it, because he always is.

Nick says, "I have no idea what you're talking about."

"You have to see it. It's right there."

He *has* seen it. How could he not? Under the pavilion, Nick almost kept talking. He wanted to tell Seraph everything. He wanted to say that it would be okay, that he'd been through it too. He understood the wild look in its eyes when it saw something it could protect, because he feels the same way every time someone comes to him for help. He understands, and if he so much as acknowledges it he will never forgive himself.

Why did he give it those bobby pins? Why did he reach out like that? What was he *thinking*?

"No," he says.

"Nick—"

She reaches out to take him by the shoulder, but he jerks away and slams into the office door. She knows to ask before touching him. She *knows* that.

"Please," she whispers.

Nick is silent. His jaw is locked, and there are no words in his head, just a storm of anger and gritting teeth and bones grinding in his knuckles. He tries to speak three times and fails, each time the thought burning away into ash before it can form the right shape. He counts the beads on the lizard without looking. Eventually, he pieces a sentence together word by word, bit by bit. The feathers tattooed on his back sear like a cattle brand. Like hellfire.

"Seraph will go to the church," Nick manages, "and if it comes to it, it will be given to the Vanguard."

That is his job. He will do his job.

BENJAMIN

Chapter 10

I've heard of the Angelic Movement. Yes, I agree that the world's situation is dire. Yes, I believe drastic action is required. But the day I ally myself with those who use God as a cover for genocide is the day you'll see me dead . . . America! Come deal with the monsters you've made.

—Head Speaker Ngozi Adamu,
2038 International Climate Conference

I have no idea what's going on when I walk into the media room for my first Watch meeting.

The media room is crammed with mismatched seats, board games, and a cracked flat-screen TV. One wall is stenciled with a vapid inspirational quote from the Before Times that just feels hollow now, like a smile drawn on a dead body. The Watch itself is sprawled in a haphazard pile across torn couches and ripped seats. There are two empty spots. One has to be Trevor's. I try to picture him in the room with us, but his face is a void and bones stick out of his chest.

I'm saved from the thought by Aisha raising her voice to cut off Cormac's sentence, which I'd tuned out as soon as I opened the door.

"It was capitalism," she says, pointing hard at the ground. Salvador props xyr chin on xyr hand, watching lazily. Nick isn't here. "It was always capitalism and colonialism, it—what, no, don't look at me like that, Cormac."

"Rich bastards need to hush," Faith interjects when Cormac tries to retort. "Normal people are talking."

"We weren't rich!" Cormac snaps. I ease the door shut behind me. "We were comfortable."

"Your parents owned the Acresfield Country Club," Salvador groans. "Shut the *fuck* up. Hey, Ben!"

Everyone turns. Cormac glares.

"Benji, actually," is the only thing I can think of to say. "What's, uh, what's going on?"

"Nothing," Faith says. "C'mon, sit."

I take the spot next to Salvador because it's as far away from Cormac as I can get. I can't handle him right now. I barely slept last night, even after Nick and I got back from the rescue mission. I kept having to go out back to throw up, and I saw the Grace every time I closed my eyes, and the prayer for the dead always came back, sacrilege poised on my lips, *O Lord . . .*

I'm getting sicker.

"Are we just waiting on Nick?" I ask.

Salvador blows out a breath. "Yep. Some shit went down this morning, so we're not pressed. He'll get here when he gets here."

I frown. "Some shit?"

"Yeah," Aisha mutters. "Some shit." Faith skims a hand down her arm the way you'd comfort a little sister. Cormac kicks his feet up on the table and keeps staring at me.

"I'm sorry I wasn't there at breakfast," Faith whispers to Aisha.

Aisha ducks her eyes. "It's fine."

It looks like everyone has let the funeral incident go—Erin made it clear Alex and I had both lost someone and weren't doing our best—but Cormac. With Seraph getting into my head, making everything burn, it might be best if I just stay away. Even though it would be *really* satisfying to punch Cormac in the face. Did his parents actually own a country club? Figures.

It doesn't come to that. Nick walks into the room like he just crawled out of bed. His hair is falling out of its pins, and his knuckles are white around the bead lizard. This is the Nick I saw lowering his head to the Vanguard, whispering, *Okay*, *okay*, the one pinned under the Grace—not the Nick that slammed me into the bodega shelves and knocked me to the floor.

We don't say anything. We just look at him.

He stops in front of us and in a second, he's back. "Too quiet in here," he says, rolling beads between his fingers. "What's wrong."

Cormac points to me. "I told you, I'm not working with him."

My face burns, blood rushing to the surface, a *Seraph* burn. It's glorious, getting angry so quickly. Maybe the Flood has given me something in return for my body: the anger I never let myself have as a little girl, the rage I swallowed down every day of my life. It feels like it's slotting into place where it was meant to be all along. Under my mask, I bite down hard on my cheek.

Nick blinks slowly at Cormac, unimpressed. "Yes, I heard you the first time."

"Then what the fuck." As Cormac talks, I suck on my teeth, fingers digging into the armrest. "You saw what he did to Alex."

Salvador hums, "I think you're just jealous they're paying more attention to him than you."

"Oh my God, their boyfriend just died," Aisha says. "Leave them out of it."

"Guys," Faith cuts in. "Come on."

I can't help myself. "I'm *right here*, asshole."

Cormac gets up from his chair, vibrating with anger. "You tried to kill them!"

"They tried to crack my head open!"

Nick hooks his foot under the edge of the coffee table and hoists it up. It flips with a terrible crash, sending books, papers, and pens scattering across the floor. I yelp. Faith swears, cords of muscle standing out in her neck.

"That's *enough*," Nick snarls. My skin prickles with excitement. The noise, the shouting—I could get used to this. I could leave the old Benji behind, the one who cowered behind Mom's robes and fell to my knees on the bridge. "*All* of you."

Cormac sinks back into the chair. Aisha looks away. I take a long, deep breath, expanding my chest until my lungs ache and then letting it out slowly through my nose. The heat settles into a comfortable place in my chest, right below my ribs, under the sternum. Among flesh, bone, and organs. Where everything should be.

"Thank you," Nick says. He primly readjusts the nose of his mask. I wish I could read underneath it, see what's going on there, figure out what he's hiding from us. "We have something important to talk about."

We nod, suddenly one group again, pulled together for what we're here to do. Nick has that effect on us. I allow myself to admit that it is beautiful, the same way he is, even if I still want to dig my nail into my ring finger.

Nick leans against an overstuffed armchair, lording over us.

"In four days," he says, "a pilgrimage of Angels will be heading to Reformation Faith Evangelical Church for an initiation ceremony." *Wait, he's not actually considering—* "After intercepting papers concerning the details last week, and considering the trouble we've had with the Vanguard, it's in our best interest to intervene. If anyone has any objections, speak now."

I open my mouth, but nothing comes out.

"It's decided," Nick says.

In less than a week, we are going to Reformation—where the death squad was taking me, the heart of the Angelic Movement in Acheson, and one of the worst places I have ever been—to kill as many Angels as we can.

The next four days slog by but pass far too quickly. I wake up every day sluggish and crash every night exhausted.

I imagine this is what Theo felt as a new death-squad soldier, reeling from a taste of the Flood and desperately trying to keep up. Cormac avoids me, but I still hear him bragging about his rich parents, as if that matters anymore. I ask Aisha about her doomsday-prepper family, and she talks about underground bunkers in West Virginia until she gets distracted by Sadaf. I learn Faith used to be in the coast guard when she goes on a soft-spoken but firm tirade about the inherent cruelty of the armed forces and what a mistake it was to join. We quiz each other on maps of Acheson to make sure we can get back to the ALC if we're separated. Nick teaches me how to load and unjam a pistol, and I pretend I'm not staring at him more than I'm looking at the gun.

Nobody notices I'm only taking half my allotted water rations and barely any food. The pantry empties quickly. Even when a boy named Micah butchers rabbits and squirrels in the courtyard, it barely makes a dent in how much food we go through a day. Taking even a granola bar makes me feel guilty.

The first respite I get is lunch with Salvador on the second day. We've got a back table in the kitchen, and I'm picking at half a can of tuna. The two of us are supposed to be studying Reformation's floor plans—Aisha found a copy of the blueprints in City Hall months ago, and they're currently laid out on the table—but I already know the layout, and Salvador insists on a meal break.

I don't know much about Salvador, and xe seems quite fine with that. My one question about xyr scars is met with a wink and, "Care to tell me why you were kidnapped by Angels?"

I glare.

"Exactly." Xe leans back in the flimsy plastic chair, gesturing at me with xyr fork. "But I'm curious, so humor me. What convinced you to join? Because the Watch ain't fun. I'm sure it'd be easier to scrub the floors and let us do the hard shit."

There's not much to say. "Nick recommended it."

"That can't be all."

When I frown, xe can actually see it, since eating is one of the few times we take down our masks. I've tried waiting around for Nick to eat, but he always takes his food upstairs. Salvador taps at the scar on xyr lip, which has bent xyr mouth into something uneven.

I say, "If I tell you the reason why I'm here, will you tell me about Nick?"

"That's not fair. Nobody knows jackfuck about him."

There goes that. I drag my fork through the remains of my tuna. I don't even like fish, but I haven't eaten all day, and hunger is starting to make me sluggish. I'm sure there's some Bible quote that's woven itself into my skin about sacrifice, or maybe something from High Reverend Father Ian Clevenger's rambling manifesto, but all I remember is the feeling. Another mouth, more food, I'm sick and shouldn't bother.

"Really?" I manage. I shouldn't even be asking about Nick. He's my commander and nothing else. "That sucks."

"Well, Erin knows everything about him, but good luck getting her to talk. She's a steel trap." Salvador looks over at Aisha, who is sitting on the other side of the room with a book, Faith beside her. "You'd have an easier time getting Aisha to date a white girl."

Aisha pipes up, "Piss off." Faith snorts into her cup of water.

I tuck my head in closer. "Wait, she and Faith aren't—"

"Nope. Besides, Faith is aromantic, and Aisha wants to ask out Sadaf."

"I can hear you!" Aisha protests.

"So what?" Salvador calls back. "We're not talking shit."

I say, "So you know everybody's business?"

"I do my best. Tomi used half our supply of antibiotics last month when they got a UTI banging Luce, which, ew, why would you. Cormac is a bottom. Erin actually used to have a crush on Nick before she found out he's gay, and I'm surprised I even got that out of her. Look, give me something, and I'll give you something. How's that sound?"

Nick is gay? I rein in my expression before xe notices. I mean, I'd figured he was something if he was *here,* but . . .

It doesn't matter. I'm betrothed. I'm an Angel, I am Seraph, I am the avatar of the Flood. Crushes are a waste of time when I'm just weeks away from being God's wrath incarnate. Besides, cis gays are the worst. I've only been part of the ALC for a few days, and I'm already picking up on strange divides in the queer community. I can almost hear one of the other trans guys mocking cis gays to his friend, wrinkling his nose and whining, *"Ew, pussy! I could never!"* Like they think not having a dick makes us lower-tier men, like there's something wrong with us.

It's just that I don't get along with the other trans guys here. One turned up his nose at me, and I've been too awkward to approach the others.

"All right," I say. "I'll give you something, but you have to answer my next question the best you can."

Salvador perks up, eyes flashing. "Go for it."

"I said I'm in it just because Nick thought I should be, but—" There are so many things I could say. I could make myself seem selfless, taking on the hardest jobs just because I feel like I should. Or I could hint that someone who forgives me for being Seraph deserves every ounce of myself I can give them. So I say it all, as simply as possible. "They took my dad. I want to make them regret it."

Salvador says, "So you're in it for revenge."

Yes? Maybe. Distilled down to its most basic parts, yes, but the word feels too heavy. Revenge has lost its weight.

Everyone wants someone to suffer for something. "Yeah, kind of."

"So much anger packed into such a little body." Salvador laughs. "How very *trans boy* of you. All right, intriguing, I like it. What do you want to know?"

"There's this one guy," I say. "Also trans, a little taller than me, shitty stick-and-poke tattoos. What's his name—Carl? Clay? You know him, right?"

"With the bad haircut? That's Calvin." Xe eyes me. "Please tell me you don't have a crush on him."

"God, no. He'll barely give me the time of day. What's his problem?"

"If he's just not talking to you, you're getting off easy." Xe watches the door as if Calvin could walk in any second, which he technically could. "He nearly beat the shit out of Aisha earlier, calling her a liar and bunch of other nasty stuff. He's the worst. Like being a dick will make up for his lack of one." I barely suppress a laugh. "Let me guess what he was throwing a fit about. You're white, so . . . oh, was it because you don't bind?"

It's not obvious I don't. It's not like I have much to work with, but once you know what to look for, it's impossible not to see it. I cross my arms over my chest anyway.

That must be all the answer Salvador needs. "Look, he's awful. He bought into a bunch of gatekeeping rhetoric before That Day, and all he does is lick boots. Said I was making a mockery of the trans movement for using 'fake pronouns,' and I nearly strangled him. Pink-washed colonialism and all that." A long, angry breath. "Feel free to deck him if you want. I'm sure Aisha would appreciate it."

I don't need any ideas.

The night before we head to Reformation, Micah catches a deer. It's small and withered, tongue hanging out of its mouth. He says we're lucky it's small. We're running low on sugar and salt for curing, so we'll have to eat as much as we can tonight to keep it from going to waste.

When the sun goes down, we light a fire in the courtyard with plywood pulled off windows across the street. The deer is laid out on a tarp, and pieces are put over the flames, sizzling and spitting. The sniper guard breathes in the smell of cooking meat and turns back to the streets, just in case the smoke attracts attention. Someone runs up the stairs to give them the first pieces.

There's not enough room for everyone to gather in the courtyard with the fire and Trevor's fresh grave, so most people stay in the ALC lobby. But Calvin is by the radio, getting too close to it for Alex's liking and causing a snarling match, so I wander out to the yard and sit by the fence.

It's a quiet night. The heat of day still lingers, cut by the breeze. Flames crackle, and the sharp tang of smoke tastes warm on my tongue, even through the mask. The firelight itself bathes faces in shades of gold, lighting up eyes that shine with laughter they keep choked up so they aren't heard. People move in packs, leaning on friends, faces tucked into shoulders and against thighs. It reminds me of the movies I saw before Mom took us to New Nazareth: groups of friends cuddling up, close enough to inhale one another's air. Erin lingers by Micah, disgusted by the raw meat but taking great interest in the way his hands work the knife. Sadaf wanders out into the grass and Aisha follows, reaching for her arm.

I stay by the fence, alone. I've been pressed up against the Watch all day, and I don't feel like explaining my growling stomach to anyone, and more than anything, I need some time to myself. I kick off my shoes and spread my hands in the cool grass. The fence smells of wet wood. Weeds creep up the slats and tangle in my fingers. The Milky Way shines in a silver streak above the buildings and clouds.

Revelation 21:1—*And I saw a new heaven and a new earth: for the first heaven and the first earth were passed away.*

No, the first heaven and the first earth were murdered.

I don't notice Nick beside me until the rattle of plastic beads makes it past my thoughts. He's leaning against the fence, toy lizard in hand, staring into the fire.

"You eat yet?" he says when I look up at him, even though he doesn't look at me.

"I'm fine."

"Not what I asked."

"I'm not hungry."

Of course, my stomach picks that moment to growl. Nick kicks away from the fence and walks into the crowd. A minute later, he returns with two handfuls of sizzling meat, using folded-up printer paper as plates. He tosses one down to me.

"Eat."

Grudgingly, I do. It's still fire hot, the same way my hands, stomach, and throat feel, and I balance it on my thighs to keep it from burning my fingers. This is more food than I've eaten at once in days, but it's so warm and smells so good I can't stop myself. It falls apart in my mouth, taste bursting across my tongue. There's so much flavor, it makes my jaw ache. It's barely salted, barely seasoned because we have so little to spare, but it's the best thing I've tasted in forever.

Nick says, "Are you going to be all right tomorrow?"

I shrug, peeling off another piece. When I accidentally touch a part that burns, I stick my finger into my mouth. "I'll have to be."

He snorts and pulls down his mask to take a bite.

I stare without an ounce of shame. He has the squishy face of a teenager, like cookie dough that isn't finished baking, baby fat that puberty hasn't wiped away just yet. But there's strength to his jaw, in the hard way his lips are set. Something that says, sure, he's handsome now, but just you wait, just wait and see what he grows into, it'll be worth it.

He doesn't have stubble. For some reason, that surprises me. Maybe I'd just gotten used to it. Theo was starting to get patchy, awkward facial hair when I left, and he used to rub it on me to piss me off, leaving red burns on my neck and cheeks. I dig my nail into where my engagement ring used to be and shove more venison into my mouth. The flavors aren't as strong this time.

Nick says, "All you have to do is give the signal and make sure the abominations don't kill us."

"I know." We've decided I'll be on lookout since it needs to be done anyway, and it's the way to hide what I can do. As far as the rest of the Watch knows, my job is to find a vantage point, wait until the Angels are distracted, and fire the first shot. Easy enough for the new guy, and still more than most others are willing to do.

"See Aisha for your uniform before we leave."

"Yeah."

We're silent for a moment together. Just eating, catching juice that rolls over our chins. Someone barks with laughter and claps a hand over their mouth in apology. The food settles in my stomach, and I feel warm. Not burning, but warm, like I'm somehow sitting next to the fire even though I'm all the way across the courtyard. Gentle. Cozy.

There's so much bustle over there and inside the ALC. So many bodies, so much silent noise. It's quiet over here. Just us, the food, the grass, and the sky.

Nick says, "It's okay to be scared."

I look up. "What?"

"Your hair is getting in your face again." He digs out another set of bobby pins and hands them over. "Don't lose these. I don't have that many."

It's okay to be scared.

It hadn't hit me until now that my teeth were grinding again.

CHAPTER 11

At the core of every believer is a warrior ready for battle. Every day, you engage in spiritual warfare against evil through prayer. But the LORD tells us: Warfare in our hearts is not enough. Angels, wash the streets red with blood.

—*The Truth* by High Reverend Father Ian Clevenger

In a place like the ALC, after Judgment Day, it's easy to forget you're trans. Or maybe a better way to word it would be, it gets easier for me to forget the *pain* of being trans. Being transgender is who you are, and the pain is what the outside does to you. The pain is what happens when you and the world go for each other's throats. In the ALC, I almost forget that being trans can hurt.

But in front of a full-length mirror, it's impossible to think about anything else. I never liked looking at myself, and that was before the Flood started showing up on my body. Aisha doesn't see it, but I do. The way the skin on my nails has shrunken back, making them just a little too long; the dull dryness to my eyes; the fact that, when I bare my teeth while she isn't looking, my gums have pulled away, giving me a mouthful of half fangs.

I settle my mask back over my nose when Aisha returns with a handful of black clothes. "These should be your size," she says, pressing close to me in the cramped laundry closet. She's in a better mood today, like she's managed to pack away Trevor's death and Calvin's shit, but she's coming unraveled around the edges. There are bags under her eyes and a tremor to her hands. "It's all super masc, promise. Give it a shot. I'll be right outside."

I don't have physical dysphoria the way the workbooks in the ALC office describe it, narrowing in on obvious sex characteristics like that's all being trans is. I don't care about my chest, and I've never once, in my life, wanted to have a dick. My period sucks, but it never made me feel like less of a guy. Still, as I'm taking off my shirt in front of the mirror, I have to turn away. My dysphoria comes from the way other people see me, and I can't help but look at myself from the outside. Why do my wrists have to be so small? Why does every shirt have to sit on my ass like that? Why do *hips* and *chest* and *thighs* have to read *female*?

I won't have to deal with it for much longer. My skin is only a temporary thing. I wonder if I would feel the same way if I ever had the chance to start testosterone, knowing everything about my body would change but being unable to grasp exactly how. I've caught glimpses of the previous Seraph martyrs, bodies of children shattered under the weight of the Flood, but only glimpses. A twist of rotten flesh here, a fang or feather there. I thread a belt through the loops on the black jeans and zip the hoodie up to my throat. This self won't last me long.

I knock on the door to tell Aisha I'm done. She comes in and rocks back on her heels to inspect me.

"Roll up the sleeves," she says, and I do. "Try these gloves," she says, and I do. "There."

Combined with the mask, I must look like the people in the ALC office photographs, like I'm about to throw Molotov cocktails through Wall Street windows. She turns me around to the mirror.

"What do you think?" she says over my shoulder. "Fit all right? Not too warm?"

I blink at myself in surprise. I *like* the black bloc anarchist look. It's soothing to smother everything that could clock me as a girl under black cloth. I'm formless, able to blend in with the rest of the Watch like we're all shades of the same person.

"No," I say. "It's good." I adjust the gloves and try pulling up the hood. "Do you do this for everyone?"

"I insist on it," she says. "I need a little bit of control over *something*."

After Aisha can't justify fussing over my outfit anymore, we go downstairs. Everybody is waiting for us, and like the white cheeks and too-long teeth, that makes it real. Erin twists the ends of her hair while Salvador opens and closes the blade of xyr knife over and over: *click, tp, click, tp.* Nick hands a rifle to Cormac, reciting the plan as he goes. It's the closest thing I've heard to a prayer in days. Beside them, Faith checks her own gun, movements fluid and perfect the way the coast guard would have taught her.

"Morning," Aisha says, taking a firearm for herself. Nick nods. There are notches on the grip, etched with a knife. I don't count them. The city has been devouring Angels lately. An ear every now and then isn't enough for the Vanguard.

Nick hands me a small pistol, still warm from his body heat. He asks, quietly, "Ready?"

It's okay to be scared, he said.

"Ready."

Behind us, Alex stands by the radio, staring as if they might find Trevor hiding between us. When I make eye contact, they huddle deeper into their patchwork coat and avert their gaze.

Only one person comes up to wish us good luck. It's Sadaf, who plants a gentle through-the-mask kiss on Aisha's cheek before slipping away again. Aisha puts a hand where her lips had been, the cracks in her expression etching deeper.

The rest of us just get curious eyes from the gym. Girls, boys, people who are both or neither, they all stare, wanting the details but knowing not to ask. I picture Cormac indulging an innocent question with a vicious smile, gory details making his victim turn green.

"Let's not waste the morning," Nick says. He looks better than he did yesterday, like everything has finally settled into place, like he's right where he's meant to be while swaddled in black cloth and carrying a gun. "Come on."

"Be careful out there," Erin whispers. "Please."

This is happening.

I'm part of the Watch.

After Sister Kipling took the needle out of my spine, Mom said I would be venerated as a true instrument of God's will, just as holy as the cherubim, thrones, dominions, and virtues. Dad begged me to tamp it down, to be quiet, to be better than what the Angels had done to me. Theo told me my power would be as terrifying as the Devil and twice as righteous.

I will be good. I will make them suffer. And I will take the Angel's greatest weapon and turn it against them.

But I'm still terrified.

It's an hour's walk to Reformation, Salvador tells us, and we'll get there before noon. The heat of the February sun clings to our black clothes. Sweat beads under my arms. Roads stretch out in an endless maze of traffic.

The last time I saw Reformation Faith Evangelical Church was when I walked the pilgrimage with Theo.

He was so excited on the way there, transfixed on the squad escorting us through the city because his father wasn't there and that was the next best thing. On the way back, he was so sick, he could hardly walk. As soon as we were back within the New Nazareth walls, I brought him water as his guts revolted the way mine are now, pieces of his insides dangling from his lips. The only difference is that he got better, because he'd only taken a little bit. He'd taken one step closer to God, but only one. He was strong enough to fight off the infection, so he was strong enough to become a soldier. Proof of God's favor.

Theo's future squadmates laughed when I wiped his face, asking when we planned to put a ring on it. I'd touched his bare shoulders, hadn't I? *Kissed* him, even? And the reverend mother's daughter, no less. What a whore. Theo should've done the right thing and proposed already, before word got out and I made a disgrace of myself.

A few months later, he did. Not that we had a choice. Mom caught us having sex, and it was either get engaged or be cast from the family. Mom never would have actually disowned me—she had *plans* for me—but she said it anyway, spitting it in between scriptures, demanding I have more respect for my body than this. What if I had gotten pregnant? Would I have the strength to drown my newborn the way I should? She dragged me out of bed by the hair, threw Theo's clothes at him, and said we had to make a choice.

The choice was obvious. Theo proposed the next day. We were fifteen. And despite everything, he loved me. He loved me through the Seraph trials, through my sobs that I was a boy, through the realization that I would become a monster and slaughter the world. I loved him through the death squads, through the carving of skin from his back, through him slamming me against the wall and squeezing my wrists so tight, I thought they would break.

I raise a hand to keep my hair out of my face as the wind blows, to block out the sun and its searing glare. When Nick isn't looking, I try to put in the bobby pins, but they slide out and hang limply by my ear.

I'm still in love, aren't I?

Reformation Faith Evangelical Church is a time machine made of stone and stained glass—a towering, Gothic-style monster cradled by brutalist ten-story offices and parking garages. It used to be a Presbyterian church, but the Angels consumed it like they did everything else. They invited all kinds of people into their flock, teaching them the purpose of Evangelicalism and tradition and the way of the Angels, and then the martyr masquerading as a preacher smashed a vial of the Flood on the altar and barred the doors shut. *An eye for an eye, a plague for a plague.*

We don't get within two blocks until Cormac climbs the parking garage and snipes the soldiers standing at the front stairs, Faith going with him to watch his back. There's a pair, one leaning against a broken streetlight and the other smoking by the door. Aisha stares at the road so she doesn't have to see it. I watch them fall and wonder who they are. If I'd recognize them if I lifted up their heads.

Who am I kidding? Of course I would.

Cormac and Faith come back through an alleyway, thumbs up in reassurance. We're in the clear.

As we get closer, the ground itself seems to hum, reverberating through my throat and behind my eyes. The church drips with flesh: arteries the size of arms breaking through stained glass windows, root veins spreading out between the stonework. Fingers grow from cracks in the masonry. Bodies hang from the architecture, the mark of wings painted on every door in the same shade of red as blood, like the blood on the doors of the Israelites to spare their firstborn sons. Scrawled messages cry, *GOD LOVES YOU, GOD LOVES YOU, GOD LOVES YOU.*

PREPARE TO DIE. HIS KINGDOM IS NEAR.

The closer we get, the clearer the hum becomes—cries of the Graces, calling to Heaven, the children's choir singing about washing clothes with the blood of the Lamb. It's the same hum I felt when Theo cut his hands and pressed them to the flesh of the church, when he leaned down to kiss it, his blood becoming Jesus's blood, the same way as wine. It sounds like New Nazareth. It sounds like *home*.

When I step down from the curb and into the street, I almost stop. I don't want to go any closer. This is where Brother Hutch was going to take me. This is where I watched Theo fall apart into something other than the boy

I grew up with. The Angels always had their claws in him, but this is where they hooked into his insides so deep he could not pull them out without bleeding to death.

But Nick looks back at me, and I follow like I've been doing this all my life.

"*Are you washed in the blood of the Lamb?*" the choir asks in a warbling, childish soprano before fading into a holy echo. We walk around to the back, where a delivery entrance pushes up against a graveyard meant for the bodies of the church's elders. The door is unlocked; the Watch contains the only people brave enough or stupid enough to come this close.

Nick wrenches it open. We're greeted by a distant sermon, crying loud to the faithful.

"We have gathered here today," comes the faint voice of Reverend Brother Morrison, "to celebrate the achievements of our children." It's a voice that shakes under the weight of its words, the voice of the man who promised to wed Theo and me by the river when we were ready, when God had made me perfect with the Flood. Nick freezes against the door, eyes squeezed shut. My left hand shakes so badly, I have to shove it into my pocket. "To put the worthy through trial. To help them take their places one step closer to the Lord's side."

Nick lets me through first. The room is dark and musty, piled full of boxes and discarded pews. I didn't need the map of the church we studied; I know this building. Theo and I snuck away while the presiding reverend readied himself for the ceremony, creeping through the halls to find a place all to ourselves. He stopped by a hidden staircase and kissed me, and when we got back my braid was a mess, so everyone knew what we did. I look up to see the same tendrils on the ceiling, a fingernail digging into the beams. We all come in, and Nick closes the door tightly. The room plunges into darkness.

I can do this.

"Brothers, take pleasure in your struggle," Reverend Brother Morrison commands. "Learn to love the pain. It is a cleansing pain. It is a glorious pain. Love it the way Jesus loved the nails through His palms, the thorns upon His brow. It is not a soft love; it is not a gentle love, but it is a perfect one."

Nick catches my arm—his fingers on my sleeve, enough that I feel them but no more—and murmurs, "On your signal."

"On my signal," I repeat and step into the guts of the church.

"Your love must be strong enough that it becomes fearsome! It is fear that brings the unfaithful to the Lord. It will be fear that saves the nonbelievers. It will be fear that teaches heretics the truth of our Almighty God."

The back hallways are claustrophobic. Dust cakes the carpets, and cobwebs hang in the stone ribs holding up the ceiling. A rumble shakes the walls as those trapped here on Judgment Day groan in pain. I almost feel Theo pulling me through the corridor, smothering his laughter, glimmers of happiness shining at the corners of his eyes. The memory is beautiful and terrifying.

Focus. I feel out the doors in the dark. I'm not looking for this one, or the next one either. The offices are back here; one of these doors leads to the sacristy, where the priests prepare for service. A kitchen, the little rooms where Sunday school was held. None are what I need.

"Fear will always be what pushes sinners toward God because we are broken things that do not deserve His love. The first step to wisdom is to fear the Lord, to tremble in the face of His truth. And you! Oh, you, my children, will be His terror made flesh."

I find the right one: the back door to the second-floor pews. There are never any people on the second floor since they are kept empty for the brothers in Heaven. They receive a seat, and that is the most thought Angels will ever give to the dead. I yank open the door.

Sound hits like a solid wall, like the reverend holding you underwater for your baptism until your lungs burn and your vision blurs at the edges. Baptism in drowning, baptism in blood, *Are you washed in the blood of the Lamb?*

Up the stairs, slowly, quietly.

I'm on the balcony.

The sanctuary of Reformation Faith Evangelical Church is the belly of the whale. Stained glass glimmers in every color of the rainbow, muted by dust and cut through with white where pieces have broken from the pane. The rafters are ribs, each wood beam another bone reaching up toward the spine. The pews below are full of boys, pale and hunched in prayer, knives in their laps and their allowed loved one begging God for their child's survival behind them.

I duck below the waist-high wall. It's so much harder to breathe up here. Reverend Brother Morrison has his Bible on the altar, hands spread wide, blood smeared down his face and throat in worship. A nonbeliever lies at his feet, head wrenched back to reveal the festering black hole of their throat. The choir of children flocks at his sides, so little, *too* little, staring at him in awe.

The Graces. Oh God, the Graces.

One stands with their handler, their head a mass of skulls lashed together with Flood and sinew. Mouths open and close in a gurgling gospel. And there is the nest behind the altar—a beast made of every soul trapped here on Judgment Day, dragged into the body of this one creature. Hands reach out, torsos press against thin veils of flesh, eyes peeking between bones, lungs, and scraps of jewelry trapped on the wrists of the not-quite dead. Their muscles spread in a quilt across the carpet, up the carved stone walls, under the pews and between the beams of the ceiling.

Soldiers stand by the front doors, watching the boys waiting for the rite to begin. Among the boys, I see Brother Abels, who had such a soft smile and volunteered to stack the chairs after Sunday school. I see Brother Davis, who cried when he scraped his knee the first day at New Nazareth. And I see Sister Davis, his mother, swaying as Reverend Brother Morrison speaks, desperate to drink in his words and save her son. I know every face. If I don't know their names, I know *them*. I've seen them, I've broken bread with them, I know them, I know them, I know them.

Theo told me the nest's flesh tasted sweet, sweet the way vomit does for just a second after it comes up. It killed someone from his pilgrimage. The boy didn't make it a day. A soldier dragged him to the culling fields before night fell, the Flood devouring him whole as his skull swelled and one of his eyes popped from its socket, dangling by a nerve.

If the Watch weren't here, how many people in this pilgrimage would die? How many would survive the rite? How many would go back to families who hailed me as their savior? Who put their hands on me and prayed?

Stop, stop thinking about home. This is for the Watch—for the ALC, for the Vanguard, the way it should be.

The Grace by the door whines, and the handler tugs on a bone jutting out of their jaw. I whisper, "*Hush.*" They quiet, trembling, all their dozens of eyes searching for me in the darkness. The Flood hisses and burns like fat falling into a fire. I whisper, "*I'm here.*" The nest quiets too.

And when Reverend Brother Morrison pauses for breath, I swear I hear my own lungs echo.

There is a sudden, intense calm. Like something terrible being held back.

I'm here. It's okay.

Reverend Brother Morrison says, "Let us pray." Every hand clasps; every eye closes. Even the handler, even the soldiers.

I brace my back against the railing and aim the pistol at a beautiful window above me. Blue and gold and red and green dances on white robes like sun streaming through the leaves of a forest.

The Flood burns.

I pull the trigger.

CRACK.

The pistol jerks back painfully in my hand. Glass shatters. I whisper, and the nest shrieks. I whisper, and the Grace lunges forward to tear their handler's arm from its socket. The sanctuary shatters into gunshots and hellfire.

And I'm not in Reformation Faith Evangelical Church anymore.

CHAPTER 12

I am Alpha and Omega, the beginning and the end. I will give unto him that is a thirst of the fountain of the water of life freely. . . . But the fearful, and unbelieving, and the abominable, and murderers, and whoremongers, and sorcerers, and idolaters, and all liars, shall have their part in the lake, which burneth with fire and brimstone.

—Revelation 21:6–8

It's quiet on the culling fields. It's always quiet on the culling fields, sure, this little grove at the back of campus where a tiny stream cuts through the woods. But this is the quiet of the dead. The kind of quiet colored by the creaking of rope and the rush of water and wind—all the things that *aren't* the quiet that make the quiet so loud it hurts.

Sunlight sinks its teeth into the back of my neck. Trees rustle their dying leaves. The dry grass hisses at my presence, and the stream runs red.

And the third angel poured out his vial upon the rivers and fountains of water; and they became blood.

A body hangs from the sturdiest tree, a branch laden with rotten fruit. One crow watches me, and another flutters its wings as it pulls on the eye dangling from the optic nerve.

I'd know the body anywhere: a boy with two broken legs and a Flood-swollen skull.

And all the fowls were filled with their flesh.

The death squads dragged him to the culling fields because he was a failure whose body was burned out by God's light. He couldn't survive taking upon the mantle of holy war, so the soldiers gave him mercy by putting him down. Theo stood beside me as we watched; we had to watch him die, Theo wiping the last bits of rot from his mouth, knowing that could have been him if God's plan had fallen just a little bit to the left.

I am in New Nazareth again.

No. No, that can't be right. This boy rotted months ago, and it's empty here, too empty. It's not real. It can't be. I was *just* at Reformation. The dust is still in the back of my throat. The howls of the Graces and soldiers still ring in my ears, and I swear those are dust motes swirling in the light coming through the stained glass windows, but—

Right now, somehow, I am in New Nazareth. A dead New Nazareth, where it's just me, the body, and the birds.

And the four beasts had each of them six wings about him; and they were full of eyes within; and they rest not day and night, saying HOLY, HOLY, HOLY, GOD ALMIGHTY.

Something else is here too. A monster among the trees. Obscured by branches and dead legs, split-wound mouth hanging open with teeth and tongue, its body wreathed in a halo of six broken wings. Rotting, growling. Fangs, feathers, flesh.

I stumble back, and my feet sink into the muck.

A Lamb as it had been slain, having seven horns and seven eyes, which are the seven spirits of God.

And I looked, and beheld a pale horse; and his name that sat on him was Death.

It is beautiful. It is terrifying.

The wrath of God made flesh, the Flood made perfect.

And I stood upon the sand of the sea and saw a beast rise up out of the sea, having seven heads and ten horns, and upon his horns ten crowns, and upon his heads the name of blasphemy.

Hide from the wrath of the Lamb. Hide from the wrath of the Lamb. Hide from the wrath of the Lamb.

The six-winged monster sees me, and it rears back with a shriek, white eyes whirling—and I fall to my hands and knees in Reformation Faith Evangelical Church.

I lurch forward, heave, and tear down my mask. I gag so hard my jaw pops. A trail of black spit falls to the carpet. A crash sends dust raining down and shakes the dead lights hanging from the ceiling.

What the fuck? I want to scream it, but all I can do is choke. I want to scream until my skin burns off. *What the fuck just happened?* Was it a vision like the one given to John of Patmos, the prophet of Revelation, or is the virus eating holes in my brain? I can still hear the red stream, the crows, the *beast*. Can still taste the soft, thick smell of wet leaves on my tongue. I dig my fingers into the carpet and feel old wool and the silt of the creek bed.

The Grace. Shit, the *Grace*. I force myself up and find them surrounded by the bodies of Angels, ramming themself into the barred front doors. The wood buckles under their weight. They bellow, long and low and sad, and all the dead from Judgment Day scream in return, grabbing the ankle of a passing Angel and dragging them shrieking into the mass of so many corpses.

I can't see any of the Watch. I know that's the point, but I still feel sick. I just want to know they're okay.

But behind me, suddenly, somehow—

A voice I thought I'd never hear again.

"Benji?"

It's small. Smaller than it has any right to be after what he did to me.

It takes the wind out of my lungs.

"Is that you?"

The Angel behind me is so close we could touch. He's pulling down his mask to show his face, but he doesn't need to. I'd know him anywhere. I'd know every part of him. That mess of curly blond hair, the baby-blue eyes, the stubble dotting the soft skin of his cheek.

A desperate laugh bubbles up from his lips, and he falls back, mouth open in awe.

My heart stopped beating a few seconds ago. It hasn't started back up again.

Theo says, "You cut your hair."

Colossians 3:18—*Wives, submit to your husbands.*

The last time we spoke, I thought he was going to tear out my throat. He was so rabid that white flecks speckled the corners of his lips. I don't remember all of what he said, or exactly how he said it, because I couldn't hear anything but blood screaming in my ears and my prayers that he wouldn't hurt me more than he already had, that he would stop before he broke me. *Lying, ungrateful BITCH.*

I told him I was afraid of Seraph, and he hurt me for it, and I'm still in love with him, I still love him, I still, I still—

I pull the knife from my pocket and snap out the blade. It flashes in the light streaming through the stained glass windows and comes right to his throat.

Theo throws up his hands. "Benji, wait!"

I snarl, "You have five seconds."

"Five?" His voice wavers. "Shit, five? Okay. Um." Deep breath. "I'm sorry."

He's *what*?

"If you're going to hurt me," he says, "I understand; I kind of deserve it." His words catch, and his throat bobs, and he just looks so pitiful on the other end of my knife. "But I wanted to get that in first. Just so you know. I'm sorry."

My knife hand trembles. *He's sorry. He's sorry, he's sorry.* "You *kind of* deserve it? Dad thought you gave me a concussion. I thought you broke my arm, I thought . . ."

I thought he was going to kill me. If not by breaking my head against the wall of my dorm, then by telling Mom what I had said. The church wouldn't have culled me but, God, what would they have done instead?

"Okay," Theo amends. Every word comes out slowly, like he's picking them carefully, like I'm a wild animal he's trying to keep from snapping. "Okay. Yeah, I deserve it a lot. I shouldn't have laid a hand on you. It wasn't right. And when you left, I realized that. I was *so scared*, babe, I thought someone found out what you'd said, I thought you'd been taken away." He's deteriorating, picking up speed. "This is a sign, isn't it? Finding you here? I've been praying for a second chance, and I have it now, so please. Please, I'm so sorry."

Five seconds have been up for a long time. My stomach burns with Flood and Seraph, and so does my ring finger. It feels naked. The knife falls.

I don't know what's going on below us, and I don't want to know. It's just noise and terror. My world has shrunk down to Theo on the ground in front of me, like it always does.

I say, "What are you doing here?"

"The pilgrimage was the only way to get into the city to find you," Theo says.

"To find me."

"To find you." He moves closer, his eyes catching mine and refusing to let go. "I was wrong. And I know I don't deserve it, but I wanted to say I'm sorry for what I did. Because I love you."

I love him too. God, I still do, I still do.

I bare my teeth. "I'm not going back with you."

"I know," Theo says. "I came here to follow you. I couldn't let the city take you alone. If it wants you, it has to take me too."

The blade of the knife bites into the carpet at my side. "What if I don't believe you?"

Because I don't. Being an Angel was Theo's calling. Being a soldier was everything he ever wanted. His father is the general of New Nazareth, and his mother was martyred on Judgment Day. He comes from a line of missionaries and holy warriors. He wanted to be just like them, even if he choked on it, even if it killed him. When he was forced out of the death squads, it broke him. All I could do was watch as his faith got infected and bring him food when he, praying in a fever as if that would sweat out the horrible mistake he'd made, wouldn't leave the damn chapel for days. What that mistake was, I never learned. Mom said it was not a wife's place to ask, and I should start practicing for that.

And leaving everything to follow me into the city . . .

"You can refuse to believe me all you want," Theo says, "but I'm here now, and that has to stand for something."

I hate that it does.

I lunge for him.

He yelps and tries to scramble back, and I grab him by the front of his Angel whites. His eyes widen in terror as he struggles for air.

Good. Let him fight for it. Let him know what it feels like.

Beneath us, the church falls to pieces. The front door shatters as the Grace rams through and stumbles into the sunlight; the gunfire is so loud my ears ring; everything hurts, and I am coming apart.

I kiss him.

Theo's mouth immediately opens for me. His hands find mine like he's going to drown if he doesn't hold on. It's just like it always was, he feels exactly the same, like nothing has changed at all.

I pull back just enough that our lips brush when I speak. He holds on tighter.

"I'm not contagious," I say. "Promise."

"Shit," Theo whimpers. *"Benji."*

"Do exactly what I say, and I'll come back for you." I am so weak for him. I love him so, so much. "I have some stuff to take care of."

Afterward. After I put my mask back up, and everything is quiet.

Downstairs reminds me of Judgment Day, or what I imagine it was like beyond the New Nazareth walls. The carpet is tacky with blood, and the air tastes of death. Bodies cuddle the pews. The nonbeliever lying at the base of the altar stares at the ceiling, mouth open like God took out their tongue.

The Watch didn't kill every Angel. It was impossible to block every exit without spreading ourselves too thin, leaving ourselves vulnerable.

But still, there are a lot of bodies.

The giant Grace, the nest of corpses, whines pathetically, a low moan that trembles the wood under my feet.

"Does it *have* to do that?" Cormac says as he saws off the last strip of skin holding an ear to an Angel's skull. Blood streaks up his wrists. "Christ."

I whisper, quietly enough that nobody else can hear, that it's okay, that they don't have to worry. Some of the mouths settle, but others continue to call mournfully, and there's not much I can do about that. Cormac grumbles and keeps moving.

Nick counts the dead. Aisha runs outside to throw up. Salvador sits in a pew, knees tucked up to xyr chest. Faith stands near the back wall with her hands clasped in front of her mouth. And I'm on the shallow stairs leading up to the altar, by the nonbeliever's bare feet, between little snakes of meat trailing down to touch the pews and Reverend Brother Morrison's body. I stare at the balcony, trying to keep my heart from tearing out of my ribs.

He left New Nazareth for me.

He still loves me.

"Fuck," Salvador says.

There are two children among the dead. One barely looks old enough to be without his parents, the other just about to age out of the choir. Cormac takes their ears too. I don't want to look at them but I do, trying to place them, to put names to the bodies I know. Eventually I stop seeing faces and start seeing a jumble of eyes, mouths, and noses that my brain won't let me put together into a person. Small mercies.

Silently, I pray for the dead. I don't know if it works, I don't know if it means *anything*, but it stops the sick feeling in my chest, so it must count for something.

Nick sits beside me on the steps. His right index finger and thumb tap together over and over and over, a heartbeat in anxious double time.

His left hand offers the pistol.

My face burns. Between the vision and Theo, I hadn't noticed I'd lost it.

"I found this under the balcony," Nick says. No accusation of carelessness. Just a simple statement of fact.

"Sorry," I say. "I must have dropped it. It won't happen again."

I don't take the pistol. He doesn't move it away.

I say, "I don't want it."

"All right." He puts it in his jacket.

"How many Angels . . . ?"

"Fourteen."

Fourteen. Double what we took to the Vanguard. There's no way they can screw us out of supplies this time.

We gather ourselves the best we can. I shake Salvador out of xyr silence while Nick coaxes Faith out of her catatonic state. We try to bring Aisha inside so we can talk about getting back to the ALC, but she bursts into tears as soon as she turns to face the pews, so we meet in the churchyard instead.

The mass of the not-quite dead cry as we leave, and I whisper over my shoulder: *I'll be back*.

I promised Theo I would.

Halfway to the ALC, Aisha staggers. "They were kids," she whimpers. "They were *kids*."

"It doesn't matter if they were kids," Cormac snaps, and Aisha punches him in the stomach. Nobody helps when he folds and throws up on the sidewalk.

Chapter 13

Stand on any roof, wall, or hill tonight and watch the world slow down. Watch it empty. Watch it return to the paradise our Lord intended. This is a once-in-a-lifetime experience. Isn't it beautiful?

—Diary of Sister Kimberly Jones

Three people welcome us back to the ALC: Alex, Sadaf, and Erin. Nobody else.

Erin nearly collapses with relief, wrapping Salvador in her arms because xe's the first person she can reach. Alex counts us twice, checks the blackboard in the lobby, and counts us again. Satisfied that everyone has come back, they leave. Sadaf leads Aisha away, promising Faith she'll take care of her. Every other person in the ALC, if they have the misfortune to come through the lobby at that exact moment, ducks their head and leaves.

We take turns changing out of our black uniforms in the laundry room, except Nick, who disappears upstairs. Some of us take longer than others. I'm in and out in a minute, jamming the clothes in a bin, while Erin helps Salvador get xyr arm out of the sleeve due to a nasty scrape. Erin says she'll let Sadaf know, because someone should really look at it. Salvador insists xe's fine, xe's fine, it's nothing to worry about, please don't take her away from Aisha.

Then we pull just enough water to clean ourselves and draw straws for order. I get the shortest straw, and Faith tries to protest, but I hide it before she can take it. By the time the water gets to me, it's cold and murky. I dunk my hair and scrub an old washcloth across my arms, and I don't let myself take long because if I do I'll try to scrub off my skin.

For the rest of the day, I struggle to keep down food and catch fragments of sleep. People avoid me in the kitchen and the halls. I check the mirror to make sure Seraph hasn't etched itself deeper into my body, but there's nothing there I hadn't seen before.

I did good. I made them suffer. I did it.

Theo still loves me.

But *what the fuck happened*? Why did I end up in New Nazareth, why did I see the body hanging from the tree, why did I see the monster? I want to crack my head open and search through the brain matter for the rot creeping across my frontal lobe. I want to ask Theo to do it for me. He'd break me open if I asked him to, wouldn't he? He understands I never asked for this. He won't hurt me this time.

I'm scared of the beast in the trees, the barest glimpse Seraph has given me of fangs, feathers, and flesh. Because I think that beast—*six wings, Death on his pale horse, the monster of the sea and blasphemy, the wrath of the Lamb, the wrath of the Lamb*—is me.

I don't sleep more than a handful of hours. The next day, I'm so tired that my eyes burn, and I'm so hungry my stomach has given up on growling. Instead, I ache all over and take too long to respond. My hands tremble. *Low blood sugar*, Dad would always say. Or maybe it's Seraph. Does the Flood cause tremors? I can't remember.

I tuck my hands between my knees as the Watch sits in the media room in a terrible, stretched-out silence. We don't say anything. Just look at one another.

It's Salvador that finally speaks.

"Sorry to be a bummer," xe says, slapping the arm of the loveseat, "but I can't do this. I'm going back to bed. Later."

Sadaf untangles herself from Aisha and Faith to reach for xem. "Sal."

"Let xem go," Erin whispers.

Salvador leaves the media room, wiping xyr face and letting the door slam behind xem. Nick watches the ground. Cormac picks at his nails.

"I didn't sleep well," Faith says, her voice teetering on the edge of a whisper. "I mean, none of us ever sleep well. But worse than usual."

"Me neither," Aisha says. "I was up half the night, I just—" Sadaf squeezes her hand. "Sorry. You don't need to hear this."

"Nightmares?" Erin prompts gently.

Aisha says, "It's worse when I'm awake."

Nick meets my eyes across the room. He knows I don't have anything to say here. That I'm used to this, that this is my normal, and all I can do is watch everyone else crumble.

Cormac says, "I don't know why this is any different. This isn't the first time we've killed people. Nothing's changed."

"There were *children*!" Aisha protests. "There were children. They were just *kids*."

"And so was Trevor," Cormac says. "Stop acting like this is so terrible."

I can't take the broken look on Aisha's face. "Cormac," I say, "shut the fuck up."

Erin says, "Nick? What about you? Do you want to talk?"

"I'm fine," he says.

"You always say that," Faith whispers.

"Then stop asking. My job is to take care of you, not the other way around."

Erin either takes the bait or lets it slide, because she keeps going. "Everyone deserves to know somebody is looking out for them. I know what you go through isn't always understood by everyone else at the ALC." She leans over to put a hand on the back of the couch. "Sadaf, I'm glad you're here. This support means so much to us."

I tune it out. The words aren't meant for me. Staring unblinking into the face of death even as it tears you to shreds is just what Angels do. There's no point in fear when God is so much greater. To fear is to sin; don't you trust Him, don't you believe in Him? Have *faith*, you coward. Psalm 118:6—*The LORD is on my side; I will not fear.* What can man do to me?

Afterward, Sadaf gathers Aisha and Faith to go make sure Salvador is okay. Erin tries to talk to Nick, but he pulls away, staring at his hands, taking the lizard from his pocket, focusing on anything but her. Then he mumbles a flimsy excuse and flees.

"Hey, Benji," Erin sighs once we're the only ones left. "You holding up okay?"

"Better than everyone else, looks like," I say. "Is Nick all right?"

"He's . . . hmm." She searches for a word. The lengths she's going to in order to avoid saying *autistic* is admirable, but I can't help wondering if Nick would be grateful or annoyed. "He doesn't like to talk, I know, but I'm still worried about him." She picks her hair for a second, swaying on her feet, before something clicks. "Do you think you could go talk to him?"

I balk. "Me?"

"If it's not too much of a problem," she says. "Talking to you might be good for him. You have a lot in common, actually."

"We do?"

Her smile—something I can almost see past her mask, creeping into her eyes, the crinkle of her cheeks above the flower-patterned cloth—looks desperate. "Yeah. And maybe he'll see it."

A lot in common. I can't think of anything about us that overlaps besides being white gay guys, and in the ALC, that's not special. What else is there? We're both kind of short? We're both way too comfortable with the dead?

With the way Erin is looking at me, all hope and sadness, I can't say no.

It takes me a few minutes to track down Nick. One of the sniper girls points me in the right direction: the roof. "Said he'd take over for a bit. I ain't complaining." I head upstairs—which is just storage and a few doors, one of which has a key that gets passed around if you want a place to hook up or jack off in peace—and open the roof-access hatch.

The roof is flat and full of gravel, peppered with useless HVAC units and other little metal and plastic things. Nick sits in a lawn chair looking out over the street, a rifle leaning against his knee and binoculars in his lap. It's hot up here, and the sky is perfectly blue.

I let the hatch door drop.

"Did Erin send you?" Nick says, not bothering to turn around.

"That obvious?"

"She worries too much."

"That's kind of her job." I come over and sit on the concrete wall running along the edge of the roof. Nick is tapping his fingers the way he was at Reformation. His leg is bouncing too. "I promised I'd check on you, so if you want me to piss off, give me something good."

"Something good," he repeats.

"Yeah. So I can say, *We had a good chat. He's doing okay.* She deserves that much."

"I'm fine."

I throw his words from the corner store back at him: "Too vague." His nose wrinkles. "Just give me something to work with—"

"Already did."

"—that isn't *I'm fine* because holy shit, dude, none of us are."

Nick kicks his feet up on the wall.

"Or we can just hang out," I say. He snorts, almost as if he finds it funny, which would be a first. "That's cool too."

Theo and I used to do this kind of thing. New Nazareth rose from the ashes of a university in the northern quarter of Acheson, and we imagined the students would be jealous of the free rein we had of restricted areas and old basements. Our favorite place was the roof of the student union, where we would chase carrion birds, hide from our parents, and study the world beyond the gates. At first, we watched endless streams of cars and the flashing lights of the city, telling stories of the lives of nonbelievers far beyond us. Then, after Judgment Day, we stared at utter silence, at lights slowly snuffing out, at the world grinding to a bloody, sin-soaked halt.

I look over my shoulder at the city now; at the skyscrapers that are only just starting to bear the scars of abandonment, the green peeking through cracks in the sidewalk, ponds gathering in dips in the road. February is the end of spring. Soon, the city will become sweltering and nigh uninhabitable. Revelation 8:7—*And the first angel sounded, and there followed hail and fire mingled with blood, and they were cast upon the earth; and the third part of trees was burnt up, and all green grass was burnt up.* Come April, the world will be parched. The river surrounding the city will become a siren song, coaxing animals toward the rapids and smashing them against the rocks. *Dasheth thy little ones against the stones.*

Theo's back.

He still loves me.

If I could cry, I would. It's only been a handful of weeks since I last saw him, but it feels like we've been apart forever. I had to pull a knife to keep from falling into his arms, begging him to forgive the transgression that made him raise a hand against me. He did it to me, he *hurt* me, and I wanted to *apologize*.

He came for me. And I'll go back to him. I have to.

The two of us really have changed, haven't we? In so little time? I skim my hand through my hair, and it flops in front of my eyes. He's turned his back on the Angels, and I'm more a boy—more visibly a boy, I guess—than I ever was in New Nazareth. I blow the hair away, but it falls right back down.

Wait. I still have Nick's bobby pins. I pull them from my pocket and try to slide them into place, get the shaggy hair out of my face, but they don't stay. They come loose and sag.

Figures. I never learned how to do anything with my hair besides comb it and messily braid it. Mom practically had to hold me down to put flowers in my hair for the engagement blessing, like she was trying to wrestle *girl* back into my head.

Nick says, "You have them backward."

"What?"

"Here." He slings the binoculars around his neck. "Give them to me."

I hand over the bobby pins. Nick pulls the sleeves of his jacket over his palms, almost like he's trying to create sweater paws, and he sweeps my hair out of my face. My fingers curl against the concrete wall, and I stare at my feet, trying to keep myself as still as possible as his hands skim my scalp. This sort of touch between the unmarried was barely allowed in New Nazareth.

Theo is back. I am betrothed, and Theo is back.

Nick slides one bobby pin into place, sweeps back my hair again, and nestles the second one at my temple.

He steps away and lets his sleeves go. His right hand shakes for a second, like he's trying to get something off it. "Ridged side goes against the skin," he says and drops back into his chair.

I barely remember to reply, "Right. Thanks."

"You did good at the church," Nick says.

"I don't feel like I did." Dad's meaning of the word or Nick's, it doesn't matter. I know I technically did, but I still ache in my chest. Like I did something wrong instead.

"We lost nobody to abominations. You did your job."

"They didn't want to hurt us."

His throat bobs. His gaze focuses on a squirrel balancing on a phone pole, tail twitching as it surveys the rusting traffic jam.

He says, "How much longer do you have?"

"I don't know. A few weeks at most." The skin underneath my fingernails is a bit too pale, verging on gray. Nothing *too* wrong. But just wrong enough. "I'm throwing up all the time, and it's getting worse." I don't mention the vision, or whatever it was, at Reformation. He might think I'm losing it and shove me over the side of the building. "But I'm all right for now."

"It's okay to be scared," he says.

I say, "I'm scared all the time. I'm tired of it."

"Then do something about it."

Like *what*? What else is there to do but split open my skull, beg Theo to take out the rotten parts, peel Seraph out of me cell by cell? All I can do is run away. I ran from New Nazareth, I ran from the Angels and Theo and Mom, and I'm running from this too, as if closing my eyes against it will stop it from devouring me whole.

Maybe I have to run *toward* something for once.

Toward Theo. Toward the beast in the trees.

I say, "This was supposed to be *me* getting *you* to talk."

Nick says, "Good fucking luck."

I laugh.

Chapter 14

The hospitals are full. We have patients on the floor, in the halls. They're dying there. And the ones that don't die . . . Look. My advice? As soon as you start vomiting black, or feel your organs moving inside you, the only thing I can recommend is euthanasia.

—Anonymous nurse at West Acheson Medical Center

Six wings. Death on his pale horse. The monster of the sea and blasphemy.

The wrath of the Lamb.

I chase Seraph.

At first, I'm not sure how. I spend the rest of the day reciting Revelation from memory, and when I get to Revelation 22:20—*Even so, come, Lord Jesus*—I rewind back to the top. The end times, measuring the Kingdom of Heaven, the woman in labor, the dragon, and the bride of the Lord. I whisper to nothing, trying to find some connection to the disease under my skin. I run my tongue over my teeth, chew on my nails, grind the bones in my hands together until they hurt. I take a wad of rags from under my pillow and cough up rot.

Is it visions of the end, or the Flood eating holes in my brain? Seraph is burning through me, readying my insides for the inevitable shattering of my human form into something *blessed*. It's reached my gray matter, burrowed between my synapses, and gotten into the lobes, the neurons, all the little pieces of me, and maybe that's why, when I squeeze my eyes shut and pray, I am given the gift of sight.

Dead New Nazareth and the blood-pink river. The crows. The trees and the underbrush. The beast of fangs, feathers, and flesh across the stream, dappled in sunlight and shadow, baring its teeth. The angel that gave the vision to John of Patmos, and the angel that gives this to me: a body twisted under God's will into something else, winged and sacred.

Isaiah 6:2—*And above him stood the seraphim*. Among the trees is Seraph.

I wade into the water and climb up onto the other bank, squeezing between trees. Seraph rears back and snarls, but I whisper, "*You don't scare me.*" I can make out more of it now—its blazing white eyes, the gleam of the sun on its teeth—but not much else before it clamors into the branches of old-growth trees, sending down a rain of twigs and brown leaves, a massive winding shadow disappearing farther into New Nazareth.

I follow and come out from the trees into the back of campus. The old university has been scrubbed clean of all things secular, transformed into a liminal space between the old world and our next life in the Kingdom of Heaven. For once, it lies silent. The soldier preaching in the plaza is gone. The bell doesn't ring to call the faithful to worship. There are no women walking to the parking lots made fields, no children running through the grass. But there are still blessings painted across sprawling windows, concrete paths winding through towering buildings, trees wavering in the breeze. This was home for five years. I know New Nazareth better than I know myself.

The shadow of Seraph digs its claws into the side of a building and hauls itself up to the roof. I follow.

I've never chased anything like this, not really. Theo chased me, and I let him, both now and when we first fell in love. Dad chased freedom for both of us in Acresfield County, and I just held on to his sleeve. I barely even chased the idea that I might be a boy. I didn't want to think about *why* I never felt at home in my skin, why my name never felt like mine, why I was so apathetic about everything the Angels said a girl should be. I thought I was tired of an Angel's womanhood, of loyalty and purity, of all the terrible things they tried to cram into our heads. But that was never enough, all the excuses were never *enough*, and dysphoria had to wrap its hands around my neck and hold me down, baptism in drowning, before I faced the fact that living as a girl would kill me long before the Angels did.

My boyhood threatened to destroy me unless I looked it in the eye. I'm not going to let Seraph do that to me too.

I follow Seraph into the heart of campus, where towering buildings encircle the student union. I throw open the glass doors and step through the mess of chairs in the old food court, up the spiral steps to the fourth floor and through a hidden staircase to the roof.

Up here, Seraph sits on the other side of the skylight, a towering shadow backlit by the sun. A massive creature of wings and sharp edges. Diseased flesh and exposed muscle.

How close do I have to get? What do I have to do to *face* it? Whisper across the roof, hold its warped face in my hands, look into its eyes and bare my own teeth?

I pause, watching. A long tail made of sinew and bone wraps around its hunched body. I squint against the sun, and I can't make out any of its features, except the hissing of breath and the flutter of so many wings.

I say, "I'm here, you son of a bitch. What do you want?"

Seraph lunges across the skylight and smashes us both through the glass.

I wake up with a piece of glass in my mouth.

I roll off the mattress and hit the cold, waxed floor, kicking my sheets and trying to spit out blood. Nothing comes out. Nothing? I stare at the ground, but it's night, it's dark, and I can't see anything.

There's glass stuck in my mouth.

I run my tongue over my teeth, and it snags on my top left canine. It wasn't always this big. It's scraped my upper lip raw. I didn't think I had another smaller, normal tooth smashed backward to make room for it, and I didn't think it was as sharp as—

As sharp as shattered glass.

For the word of God—it is sharper than any two-edged sword, piercing to the division of soul and spirit, of joints and marrow.

I bolt from my room. I trip over the sheets spilling out from the little apartments and almost run into the gym doors trying to open them. I grab a box of tools from the supply closet, I'll need tools for this, and the only place to hide is the bathroom at the back of the building. Nobody uses it since there's no water. It'll be safe there.

I paw open the door and slam the lock into place behind me. The only light comes in from a small slit window just above the toilet, the moon trickling in lazily. Good. I sit on the floor and squeeze my eyes shut.

It's Seraph. It's the Flood pushing outward. A tooth, like my nails and gums and the red rims around my eyes. Like the one Nick pried out of the Grace.

Let all the earth fear the Lord. I tear open the tool bag and dump out everything. *Let all the inhabitants of the world stand in awe of Him.*

There. Pliers.

Breathe. Okay. Knee up, elbow propped against it, put the pliers against the jagged Grace-tooth sticking out from my gums, destroying my lips and mouth. People pulled teeth all the time before anesthesia was invented. It can't be that hard, can it? I clamp the pliers around the tooth. Don't be a bitch, get it over with, bury the tooth in the courtyard, and deal with it. Breathe. Just do it.

I yank. The pliers scrape all the way down and punch me in the knee. I stare at the empty metal clamped in my hand, dazed. It didn't work.

Of course it's not going to be that easy. This is just the first of many. What am I going to do, tear out all of my teeth as they grow in? One by one?

I groan hysterically and press the back of my head against the wall. Maybe if I push out instead of pulling down, I can snap it off. There's a small, strange sound deep in my throat, almost like the wheezing Grace noises I made while pinning Alex to the ground.

On three. One, two—

Fear the Lord and depart from evil.

The sound is like bones breaking. Like Trevor being crushed against the road. A bullet of pain shoots up my skull. Blood gushes from my mouth and cascades down my chin. My tooth skitters across the floor.

Holy shit. Holy *shit*. I tear handfuls of ancient toilet paper from the dispenser and jam them into my mouth. Blood pools in my throat. It soaks through the paper as quickly as I put it in my mouth, and I grab another handful, trying not to choke in pain when it snags on exposed nerves.

But something isn't right.

My hands are numb. My mouth still feels too heavy, too full. In the dim light of the bathroom, I pull myself forward, groping across the floor. The tooth clatters away and comes to rest in the grout between two cracked tiles.

Oh.

Fear the wrath of the Lamb. Fear the wrath of the Lamb.

The tooth on the floor is small. And round. And not sharp at all.

In what world has my God ever been a benevolent one?

I tilt my head forward so I don't choke on the blood the way I choked on Mom's words, on the bruises Theo left on my wrists. The Grace-tooth is still in my mouth, taunting.

FEAR THE WRATH OF THE LAMB.

Seraph is here, and it's inside me, and—just like my dysphoria holding my head underwater, demanding to be acknowledged before it drowned me—it's only getting worse.

There's nothing I can do.

Chapter 15

Wives, remember: The way to a lasting marriage is faith and loyalty. You must have faith in your husband the way you have faith in God. When your husband turns from you, it is your duty to pray, Lord, how can I change?

—Sister Kimberly Jones, *A Biblical Love*

This is what I steal for Theo: two bottles of water, a near-empty jar of peanut butter, a can of tuna, a sleeve of stale crackers, and other little things nobody will notice. A pair of socks with a hole in the heel. A face mask hanging up to dry. All in a backpack with a broken strap.

I'm sickened with guilt just looking at the backpack. I've barely eaten anything since I got here, taking just enough to keep myself on my feet. This is just what I *would* have taken if I'd actually eaten. Half that, a quarter. I guess. Plus, we're meeting the Vanguard in Wagner Commons tomorrow. Alex gave the news this morning. With fourteen ears, we'll be getting enough food. Nobody will notice everything I'm shoving into the backpack. It's fine.

I do some quick math: Nick only takes three people with him to the Vanguard—something about their sensitive egos, wanting to keep the numbers in their favor, whatever—which means I have a 33 percent chance of *not* getting picked to go. Those numbers don't look good. I can't hide the Grace-tooth from him, not from someone who knows what to look for. Not from someone I want to tell.

Not from someone I *need* to tell.

I checked the mirror as soon as the sun rose, and it confirmed my suspicions. I took out my actual canine with the pliers. My tooth, not the Grace-fang. I don't know how I did it wrong, how Seraph *made* me do it wrong.

At least I can hide it for now. I tried talking to myself, and the words don't come out too badly. But there's more coming, and it hurts, and—

I'm doing the right thing. I'm being good. I'm just not telling anybody.

When darkness falls, the night before the Watch is called to the Vanguard, I sneak out the back. This time, I make sure Nick isn't following me.

Brother Hutch and Reverend Brother Morrison weren't the only ones who spoke at Theo's and my engagement ceremony. Mom did too. She read a passage from Kimberly Jones's book on marriage, *A Biblical Love*. I remember because I saw her flipping through the book for hours beforehand with a pen, trying to find a passage that would hammer home my place as a wife. Like *that* could somehow beat the boy out of me.

Kimberly Jones was a writer in the early Angelic movement—still alive, I think, in a settlement in California—who got really popular a few years before Judgment Day. She was especially beloved by white women thirty and older and was one of the best propaganda machines a fascist Evangelical terrorist cult could ask for. It's amazing how locking down one key demographic, white people in rich countries, means you can get your claws into the world so tightly, you can tear it all to pieces around you.

This is what's best for you, Mom told me. It was that or be shamed for giving up my body before marriage. As if I hadn't been forced to give up my body to something far, far worse.

I could at least pick Theo. I could pick the when and how.

I'd never gotten that anywhere else.

By the time I reach Reformation Faith Evangelical Church, it's late. The moon is high in the sky, cradled by the Milky Way and all the thousands of stars. Maybe Mom is looking at this same sky right now, thinking it will all be okay when she brings me home.

Me, with a knife to Theo's throat. *I'm not going back with you.*

I step through the back door to find nothing. No ambushes by death squads, no Angels lying in wait. I hate that I was thinking it, but I'm always thinking it.

Anyway, Reformation reeks. It smells like bodies and Flood. The nest howls my arrival, rattling all the dead of Judgment Day. *I'm sorry,* I whisper. *I didn't mean to disturb you.* It quiets, slowly, murmuring and rasping through the rafters.

I take the bobby pins out of my hair like a housewife taking off her wedding ring before meeting up with her boyfriend.

"Theo?" I step into the dark hallways, into the belly of the church. "You still here?"

"In the back."

He's in one of the Sunday school classrooms, sitting on the teacher's desk and reading an illustrated kids' Bible. We didn't have those in New Nazareth. Kids don't need to be able to *understand* the scripture. Nobody's asking them to understand, just obey. He's pilfered clothes from the donation pile, and it's the first time I've seen him in something that isn't Angel whites. Bulky shorts that cut off at an unflattering place near the knees, which, same. A plain T-shirt that's a little too big on him. And his hair has grown out since he was torn from the death squads, finally long enough that a pale, little curl falls over his forehead.

My stomach turns. I want to kiss him. I want to be sick. I want to hold his jaw in my hands and feel his body heat against my skin. I want to pretend he never hurt me, that everything is fine, that this is something we can move forward from. I'm scared; I don't want him to put a single hand on me, I don't want him to *exhale* in my direction; I want to wrap my arms around him and stay there forever.

I want things to be how they used to be. It would be so much easier that way.

Why does this have to be so hard?

"Oh," Theo says, because he's looking at me. Really looking at me. He has the time to take it all in.

He slides off the desk, and I think he's about to rush to me and wrap me up in a hug, the way people used to do in old movies. But he stops halfway. Teetering. Not exactly sure what to do with me. He's got that confused look in his eyes, fumbling between wanting to touch me and wanting to back away. One mistake, and we're back to the beginning of our relationship: kids who were thrown together and just don't know what to do with themselves.

"Um." I hold out the backpack. I want this thing away from me. "I brought some stuff." I *stole* some stuff. "Thought you might be hungry."

He takes it like a starved dog takes meat from an outstretched hand. "Thanks. You look . . ."

"Like hell," I finish for him.

"No. Just different." He gestures at the back of his neck. "You cut your hair."

Instinctively, I touch where my braid used to be. My head felt so light when Dad cut it all away, as if he'd taken off some terrible thing that'd been dragging me down for years. Which was true, in a way.

Theo says, "You actually look like a boy."

My first instinct is to snap, *I was a boy before I cut my hair and stopped wearing dresses, and I'd still be a boy if I hadn't*, but I don't. I can't be mad at him for saying the same thing I thought when I looked in that bathroom mirror. He's just being nice.

"I look awful," I say. I force a smile even though he can't see it, not really. "I guess that's the same thing as looking like a boy, right? I've worn cargo shorts three days in a row. If that's not awful, I don't know what is."

Theo snorts. "How did I manage to land a straight guy?"

"How *dare* you imply I'm heterosexual. I am disgusted and appalled."

And we're quiet again, because we got close to the way things used to be and neither of us knows what to do with that.

Theo clears his throat. "Did you come here alone?"

"Of course I did."

His throat bobs. I get the urge to pick out from under my nails blood that isn't there anymore.

"Benji, I . . . ," Theo says. "I'm so sorry."

I've been doing pretty good at not thinking about Dad.

What would thinking about him do, anyway? It won't change anything. "It's fine."

"Are you sure?"

I wave my hand at him. "I brought you stuff. Make sure it's okay."

"Right." He sets the broken backpack on the teacher's desk and opens it up. "Sorry." I can't watch him take out the food, the socks, the water. Still, as he replaces his old, ragged mask, I get a glimpse at his awkward half stubble. My dysphoria burns. I'll never get to have that. I've come to terms with it, sure, but that doesn't mean it doesn't hurt.

He stands there, hand over the mask as if feeling it. "You came back."

"What, you thought I wasn't going to?" I sit underneath a corkboard filled with coloring pages of the ark and the apostles. "I'm not that much of an asshole."

"I just wouldn't have been surprised if you didn't. I would've been hurt, but I'd have understood. I haven't exactly been . . ."

He doesn't have to finish his sentence. No, he hasn't.

He folds up his gangly limbs and sits beside me. He never did fill out as much as he thought he would, not the way his father did. Instead, he's wiry like a wound-up spring, maybe one of those garage-door springs that can take off your face if you mess with them.

He's so close. His thigh presses up against mine. I have to stop myself from leaning against him the way I always have.

"I lost it," he says, "and I ruined the best thing that ever happened to me." God, I hate apologies. He knows that. Why can't we just admit that it's all fucked up and move forward without talking about it? "I hurt you because I wasn't mature enough to deal with you making a decision."

What is he, a therapist? "You shouldn't have had to be mature. We're kids."

"Don't change the subject," he says. I wince because he's right. "I'm serious. I messed up. I'm glad you're back, and I'm sorry."

There it is. The *I'm sorry*. I never know what to say back. If he knows what he did wrong, he doesn't have to say so. He just has to stop doing it and tell me he learned that way.

But I should be demanding that he apologize, over and over, until it's the only thing he can say.

I can't help myself. I want him to know.

"I thought you were going to break my wrist," I say. "Or my arm. Or something."

He looks away.

I say, "I was scared of you."

"I know. I'm sorry."

"*Please* stop apologizing." I want to hear him say it over and over. I want to sew his lips shut. "Please."

"If it makes it even"—which is a terrible way to start a sentence—"I'm scared of you now."

"That's not difficult. A lot of people are scared of me."

"Well." He stares up at the ceiling. When I follow his gaze, I find little paper angels hanging from the tiles with string. They're angels the way I haven't seen them since I was so much younger: chubby cheeks, halos, holding crayon-pink hearts. Still, though, their heaven-white robes and feathered wings put me on edge. "I guess *scared* isn't the right word. Fear is probably better. Fear God and keep His commandments"—I blink in surprise to hear Ecclesiastes coming from Theo of all people, he was always bad at recitation—"for this is the whole duty of man."

Theo's eyes fall to me. His smile shines in the crinkle of skin at his cheeks, in the light in his gaze.

"The duty I accepted when I agreed to marry you," he says, "is to fear you and keep you. I should have remembered that. I won't forget again. So if the Angels hurt you, then I'll fulfill my promise here."

Our faces are so close, his body is so warm, and I missed him so much. I missed him. I missed him. No matter what he did. I am disgusted with myself.

I believe him.

"I'm not contagious," I say and take down my mask.

I pull down his too, and I kiss him.

Kissing him is water after a drought, deer meat in my belly after days of refusing to eat. He freezes under my lips for just a second, the way he had before, then he gives in, his hands greedily reaching for me and tangling in my hair. I wonder if I still feel the same to him without the braid there, the braid he learned to tie back up so no one knew we had been together.

He stops. He pulls back. His gaze zeros in on my parted lips.

Without asking, I open my mouth all the way so he can see the fang. The pale, receding gums. The cruel curl to my lip that comes so easily these days.

"You're turning," he whispers. Of course he's disgusted by this. Why wouldn't he be? I'm coughing up rot, my skin is turning ashen, my nails are one forgotten trim from turning into claws. I've told him about the martyrs. He knows what Seraph will do.

Instead of telling me how gross I am, he says, "I kept the ring."

As quickly as I was against him, I'm pulling away. Night air rushes in between us, freezing the parts of my arms and chest that were warm so close to him. His face falls.

"Theo," I warn, "I don't think now's a good time."

"No, no, I get it." He swallows hard. "I shouldn't have brought it up."

"I don't want to talk about it." It's too soon. I dig my nail into where the ring used to be. I took it off before Dad and I left. I put it in a little box and left it by his dorm. Which means I wore the ring in the hours between him throwing me against the wall and Dad finally telling me it was time to go. I can't believe that was the same day. I can't believe it's only been a few weeks. It feels like months. It feels like forever. "Please, I don't want to talk about it."

"No, I understand. I understand." He catches my face and makes me look at him. "Hey. We don't have to talk about it if you don't want to."

That's exactly what he said when I broke down crying when we were so much younger, when we had just fallen so hard for each other, when I was terrified of being a boy. He wouldn't pull that phrase out if he didn't mean it.

He says, "I just want to be with you again."

I hate myself for how much I've wanted to hear those words.

I tell him that if we want to make this work, then we need to go over some stuff. It's the only thing that keeps me from feeling like a girl in a classic movie, falling for the man who kidnaps her or holds her down. I look him in the eyes and say there can't be any apologies, because I don't want to hear them, but we need to talk about the things the Angels would never let us.

The nest whines as we step into the atrium. Pieces of the front door lie scattered at the mouth of the sanctuary, spread out across the carpet and front porch. The smell of rot isn't as bad as it had been. The bodies have all been moved. I look to Theo with a frown.

"The Grace wanted them," Theo says in explanation. In the pale moonlight coming through the stained glass windows, I try to find body parts that weren't part of the Grace before, but nothing sticks out as particularly old or new. It's just all the same flesh.

"Didn't know you got along with Graces now," I say.

"I don't," he says.

Even with the front door broken, I don't feel particularly exposed here. Living things know not to come too close, and things that aren't 100 percent *alive* are what I'm best with. So we find a seat in the pews and sit, because we're too used to the smell of rot, and messed up like that.

Grace-meat has grown into the carpet under our feet. I whisper, "*To me*," and hold out my hand. A tendril of flesh peels itself from the ground and finds its way to my fingers, weaving through them like a child holding tight to a parent's hand. Theo's throat bobs. I hold out my palm.

"You want to try?" I ask. "It's not going to hurt you."

"I'm fine," he says. "Really."

"It's not going to make you sick this time."

"Still."

It's a strange closeness, this flesh curling between my fingers. Something primal, almost paternal.

We came here to talk, so we're going to talk.

I say, "You never told me why you left the death squads."

Left is the safest word. No connotations. I pick it because I know better; I saw what happened when people asked at all, let alone used words like *kicked out*, *failed*, *exiled*. I was the one pulling him away when he got upset. Even now, I still expect a darkness to wash over Theo's expression.

It never comes.

"No, I didn't tell you."

"This is me asking."

"Tell me how you left, and I'll tell you why I left."

"Fine." I let the Grace crawl farther up my hand, to my arm, where it gets caught in the hair and rears back in confusion like a startled inchworm. "We'd been planning it ever since we realized Mom was serious about putting me in the Seraph program. We wanted to get out before Sister Kipling actually injected me, but . . ." My back twinges with the memory of the needle slipping into my spine. "That didn't work out." Theo makes a sad sound. He knows damn well it didn't work. "We eventually smuggled ourselves onto a caravan headed to the D.C. compound. Ended up having to ditch halfway into the city when they caught us."

I don't mention how I whispered to the Grace escorting us and slaughtered every Angel who laid eyes on me that day. That the Watch and I are the reasons New Nazareth has lost so many people in just the past few days.

"We got stuck in the city after that," I say. Another tendril of meat comes up to wind between my fingers. "We were about to make it across the bridge when a death squad found us. So."

"They killed him," he says.

"They did."

"And that group you were with a few days ago?"

"Saved me."

His jaw works under his mask. I know what he's going to say. "No. You know it won't work." He looks away. "They don't know who I am. If they did, they'd kill me." But Nick knows who I am, Erin knows, and for some reason I don't say that. "They kill Angels. It's what they do. You can't come back with me, if they see your scars you're dead, and—" I say this instead. "I can't lose you again."

He takes my hand, the one not twined with the Grace-meat.

"Thank you," he says. *To fear and to keep.* Mark 10:9—*What therefore God has joined together, let no one separate.* Not even ourselves. "Not going to lie; I'm impressed you got so far. How did you get past the gate?"

I snort. "Carefully and with our heads down."

We give that time to settle. For everything in our chests and stomachs to calm.

This time, Theo starts.

"Did word ever make it back about Squad Calvary?"

It takes me a while. I don't know the squads by name. But it does sound familiar, and when it clicks, my stomach sinks. "That was your squad, wasn't it?"

"Yeah. Was." To my surprise, he reaches out for the meat curled around my hand. Behind the altar, hundreds of eyes watch carefully as it grasps for him. "One of the members went rogue. Killed everyone but me and asked if I wanted to leave with him." A breath. "And the thing is? I thought about it."

I swallow, hard. "You didn't."

"I did. I thought he'd kill me if I refused, you know? Figured he'd put a bullet in my head if I said no, just like he did the others." I touch my cheekbone, right where Dad's face caved in on itself. "But he didn't. Just walked off. And when I came back alone, they called me a failure and tore the wings off my back."

There's nothing to say, not really.

"I could have stopped him, was the thing. He'd gotten injured in the firefight, and I could have stopped him if I'd just—" He scrapes his hair away from his face. It's sticking to his forehead; even at night, it's just a bit too warm. "He's probably dead. The wounds probably got infected, and the son of a bitch died."

"Yeah," I say. "Probably."

"That's why I was so mad when you said you didn't want Seraph," Theo whispers. "You were just handed the thing they took from me."

I finish for him so he doesn't have to say it. "And I rejected it."

"Yeah," he says. "Yeah."

I practically spat in his face; I dug my nails into the wounds in his back.

I guess . . . I can't blame him for being angry. We all get angry these days.

"I'm glad you're here," I say.

He puts an arm around my shoulder and pulls me close, my face nestling in the crook of his neck like it always has. He smells exactly the same.

He says, "Me too."

When I get sick a few seconds later, Theo rubs my back as I spit rot onto the floor. He kisses my temple and brushes hair from my face because the bobby pins aren't there to keep it back. My stomach cramps, and it doesn't feel like it's in the same place it's always been. If you cut me open, my torso would be a mass of sludge and flesh. Sister Kipling described it as the way a caterpillar dissolves before reforming into a butterfly. I gag and cough, and Theo holds me close.

To keep and to fear.

CHAPTER 16

If you feel the Flood within you, do not fret.
God is calling you home.

—Reverend Brother Morrison's Judgment Day sermon

Cormac kicks me awake the next morning. His designer boot-clad foot hits the edge of my mattress and waves around like a worm sticking out of a hole.

Shit, did he notice the missing supplies? Did he catch me sneaking back in last night?

"What the hell do you want?" I snap.

"You're late." His foot disappears just before he knocks aside the bedsheet curtain. I pull my blanket up to my nose. "We're heading out, and Nick wants you with us. Get cracking."

Great. I got back from Reformation late, and now the sun is barely up. "I can't change if you're watching me. Piss off."

"Well, hurry up." Cormac drops the sheet and leaves.

I press the heels of my hands into my face and give myself three seconds to rest before shoving myself out of bed.

This time, it's me, Nick, Cormac, and Faith, which makes sense because Aisha has been a mess recently and Salvador skipped the last meeting, which is never a good sign. Plus, with the way Salvador was being stared at last time? I wouldn't blame xem for not wanting to come.

I help Faith pull the cart, and I think she smiles, but it doesn't get to her eyes.

"How's Aisha holding up?" I ask her on the way, while we're cutting across a street littered with potholes.

"The best she can," Faith sighs. "Sadaf is with her now. I know she doesn't need a babysitter, but I'm still worried about her."

"She can hold her own," Cormac cuts in. Nick's eyes flick to him preemptively. "She's a grown-up."

"She's eighteen. She's younger than us both."

"And yet we're carting around the elementary schooler."

I snort. "I'm sixteen."

"Jesus! You're sixteen?" Cormac looks to Faith and Nick in turn, like one might also see the *obvious* absurdity of having a slightly younger teenager in a militia made of teenagers. "No wonder you didn't do shit at the church."

"Easy," Nick warns.

"Why are we even bringing him if all he does is stand there or *hide*?"

I bare my teeth under my mask. It would solve everything if I just lay it out for him—I'm the reason the Grace didn't tear his head off at the church the moment they realized he was there. I'm the reason he's not just as dead as those Angels. I am turning into a monster, and I am using this monster to *help him survive.*

Nick slams the flat of his arm into Cormac's chest and pushes him back. "Aisha already did a number on you," he says, "so I'm not going to repeat it. But do everyone a favor and shut up."

"And you're still defending him." Cormac sneers in Nick's face. "God."

Nobody likes the way that sounds. We all get a little too quiet. Or maybe we're just as quiet as we should be, walking through a city like this.

We meet the Vanguard at the same pavilion in Wagner Commons. The body at the tree shows the days of rot, sagging against the ropes, skin mottled and eaten away by scavengers. The sad trees and skyscrapers feel more oppressive than they had before. Everything has eyes—everything is watching, trying to catch a glimpse of Seraph, the Flood creeping out from my veins. If we really do *walk by faith and not by sight*, 2 Corinthians 5:7, then I have faith that every damn thing in this city knows what's wrong with me, and it's worming its way into my head with everything else.

"Morning, kids!" Joey chirps, helping his buddies haul their cart up on the table. The others, with their patches and stocky body armor, make a semicircle around us like we'll lunge for the supplies if we aren't held back. "What have you been up to? You called us awful quick."

He isn't happy to be back, no matter what his tone says. It's in the way his squad holds their shoulders, the way they study us.

Of course the Vanguard isn't happy. They don't want to be this deep in the city. They don't want to be this close to us. They don't want to give their supplies to a bunch of kids, but they made a deal, and now they have to live with it.

Nick says, "Let's see it."

"Skipping the pleasantries." Joey and a second man—the one who holds his gun weirdly at his crotch—tear the tarp off their cart.

There it is. Water and food and socks. Masks and bandages and painkillers. Replacements for what I stole for Theo.

"All right," Joey says. "Pay up."

Cormac hands over the bag to the woman, who holds it with one hand and a rifle against her chest with the other. They're mirrors of each other, and for the moment when they're both holding the ears, they look like they're going to lunge and wrestle each other down to the concrete.

They don't. She takes the ears, plastic-looking dead things, and counts them. She holds every one up to the sun between the skyscrapers, checks that each is from the left. Faith stares at the cracks in the floor, at the grass coming up between her boots. Cormac watches Joey, and Nick watches the rafters. I watch the city.

That's why I see the girl.

At first, I'm not sure what I'm looking at. Maybe another corpse across the pond, one I hadn't noticed my first time at the Commons, clothes fluttering in the breeze coming in low over the grass. Maybe a deer on its hind legs to reach a tree's softer branches.

But there's hair held back with a clip, torn jeans, and a shirt stained all the way down the front with rot.

"Nick." I move my lips but I'm not sure any sounds come out. "Nick."

The time it takes for Nick to look at me, figure out something's wrong, and track my gaze across the pond is probably less than two seconds, but it feels like forever. And when Nick sucks in a sharp breath, that's the death blow—that's when everyone notices it at once. Something is very, very wrong.

There's a girl across the pond.

She's eleven, maybe twelve, the same age as one of the boys who died on the floor of Reformation Faith Evangelical Church, whose ear sits in that bag. The age of the tiny skeletons Dad and I found while crossing Acheson, curled in bed when their parents realized the world was burning and it would be better for the little ones to die quickly.

She moves slowly. Too slowly. Dragging one foot behind her.

"Ah, shit," Joey mutters, pulling his rifle to his front. "We got a sick one."

No. No, no, he's going to shoot her. Cormac takes the safety off his gun, pushing through the crowd to the edge of the pavilion. Seraph burns in my throat, right where the Flood comes up.

They can't do this. She's a kid. She's harmless.

Just like the choirboys were harmless.

They had weapons. We did what we had to do.

"Cormac," Faith says, voice trembling. "What are you doing?"

Cormac doesn't look at her. "Don't play stupid."

He's going to shoot her. Her foot catches on a rock, she stumbles, and sludge falls from her mouth to the grass. She makes an awful keening noise, barely human. Nick winces. The fingers on his right hand stretch so much, he's going to shatter something.

I whisper, so quietly I'm barely speaking, "Please go."

Go. They're going to hurt you.

I remember when the Grace stood over me and a pile of Angel bodies. When the Grace at the café stared into my eyes, recognizing me for what I am. When the Grace in the rescue mission threw Nick to the ground to protect me. When the Grace broke down a door to flee the Angels, when the nest of the not-quite dead in Reformation cried for me. *I'll be good, I'll be good, I promise.*

I don't want them to hurt you too. Please, *go.*

Nothing happens. The girl hits the gravel path. The cracks in her skin are visible now, breaking open like a bloated corpse.

"God," the woman in the Vanguard whispers. "What the hell?"

"I'm gonna need you to back up," Cormac calls out, sharp and commanding, everything that Joey is trying and failing to be. The members of the Vanguard look at one another warily. Cormac's gaze does not falter. "We *will* fire."

GET AWAY.

Nothing's happening. It's not working. Her eyes are too bright, she's still too alive, the Flood is devouring her, but it hasn't devoured *enough*. My words mean nothing. She's not a Grace; she's just a scared little girl. The same kind of little girl I was when Mom took me to New Nazareth, when she became more of a monster than the heathens, the people lost to the Devil, who would be sacrificed to the Lord to save our souls and theirs in turn. Or maybe she'd always been that way. I can't remember these days.

"I said *back up*!" Cormac snaps.

"No." I say it before I can stop myself, grabbing his sleeve. "Put that down."

"What?"

"Just trust me."

Cormac coughs out a sick-sounding noise. *"Trust you?"*

Joey says, "What the hell are you talking about?"

"She's not a monster," I say. "She's a kid." I could have said the same for the choirboys. I could always say the same for something else. "If you won't talk to her, I will."

Joey says, "*Talk* to her?"

Faith says, "Benji, don't."

Cormac says, "Don't you dare."

Nick says nothing.

Nick is the only person whose opinion I give a shit about.

I step off the concrete foundation and into the grass. The sun soaks into my black clothes, turns what should be winter into near summer, burning the earth like God's wrath setting fire to the grasses and trees.

We meet between the pavilion and the pond, on the edge of the path. Her head lolls, and her eyes whirl like a scared animal. Her breathing is wet and labored, her lungs full of fluid. Dissolving from the inside, turning into something else, the same thing that's happening to me.

Oh God, this is me. This is me.

"Hey," I murmur. Soft nonsense, anything to calm her, to keep her from screaming. *This is me, this is me.* "Hey, there."

She says, sick burbling up with each word, "It hurts."

This is me. If Nick hadn't found me, I would've become a half-dead kid wandering the city, stumbling up to the first person I saw, begging for help they couldn't give. My skin cracking, black shit coming up my throat as my organs are eaten away.

I am still going to be this, no matter what. Just with four walls and some people who might not kill me, might, *might*.

"I know it hurts," I whisper, "but you need to leave. It's going to hurt more if you keep walking toward us." She stares, but her eyes aren't focused on me. She doesn't have long. "You need to get away."

Get away.

Almost like this can make up for the dead boys in Reformation, for the ears in that bag, for what the Watch has to do to keep our people safe, alive, and *okay*.

Instead of Seraph's warmth, there is a deep, rough sound. The sound of grinding teeth.

Of breaking bones.

Her face shatters into a spray of pieces, coming apart in chunks barely held together with stretches of sinew and Flood—eyes, teeth, tongue. Rot splatters my mask and hair. Her fingers curl back, and bones tear out into claws. She shrieks loud enough she could bring the world down around us, and she yanks me closer by the lapels of my jacket until her massive, dripping teeth are inches from my face.

I say, "*Stop*."

She stops. Trembling. As her body crumbles and breaks apart around her, she stops.

And there's a *crack* like thunder and her body jerks once, *crack*, again. Black-red blood seeps out of her shirt as she stumbles and tries to hold on to me, but it isn't enough, and she hits the grass, dead.

Her body doesn't make nearly enough noise for how loud it feels.

Exodus 21:23–25—*But if there is harm, then you shall pay life for life, eye for eye, tooth for tooth, hand for hand, foot for foot, burn for burn, wound for wound, stripe for stripe*. Those boys died in Reformation, and she will die in turn because that is how the world works. In what world was my God ever a benevolent one? I didn't even try to save them, so what gives me the right to save her just to make myself feel better? How *dare* I call myself good? How dare I even try?

She convulses once. Her insides leak into the dirt just like Dad's insides did, her face broken like Dad's face. Bile rises in the back of my throat, and I swallow it because I can't throw up here, not in front of the Vanguard and everyone else. My eyes water with the strain of it, and it's the closest I've come to crying in a long time. I hate it.

A stick snaps behind me. I turn, trying to breathe and failing. Nick is stepping down from the pavilion. Every member of the Vanguard has their guns trained on me.

He holds out a new mask, taken from the Vanguard's cart, still wrapped in plastic.

"Catch," he says.

He tosses it to me. I fumble, it hits the grass, and he backs away to let me pick it up. We do the same dance with a rag taken from the Vanguard's stash, wet with water from Faith's bottle. I clean myself and show off the gore-stained rag, fingers splayed. It goes on the ground too.

Everybody waits. We wait a long time, long enough that a flock of birds comes to the trees and sweat trickles down my spine, pooling in the excess material of my sports bra. Long enough that my feet start to hurt from standing so still. The body smells, but I'm used to it. I stand in the sun with a dead girl until I finally say, "None of it got in my mouth."

"Or your eyes?" Joey says.

"Or my eyes." I think some of it did but it doesn't matter. "I'm fine."

"She didn't bite you? Or claw you?"

"I'm *fine*."

"Unzip your jacket."

I do what Joey asks even though they can make out the curve of my chest. I even pull down the collar of my shirt so they can see the skin her claws grazed. There's no mark.

Finally, Joey relents. He nods, and I walk back up to the pavilion, trying not to notice the way the other members of the Vanguard keep too close an eye on me, too hard a grip on their weapons.

The lady in the Vanguard doesn't bother counting the rest of the ears. She dumps them out, gives them one good look, and says, "Take the supplies and leave."

We get every box and every crate, but it feels just as hollow as failure.

Halfway back to the ALC, Faith calls an apologetic stop for a leg cramp, and Cormac takes the opportunity to drag me behind a tractor trailer. I've been thinking about the girl the entire walk, and I barely recognize that Cormac is in my face until he's shoving me. I hit the side of the truck and my guts burn, but slowly. A dying fire, exhausted and smothered.

I snap, "*What*."

It takes Cormac a second of seething to put words together—his face flushed almost as red as his hair, pieces of it sticking to his forehead—and when he does, he says, "Do you have any idea how badly you just fucked us over?"

The girl's broken face swallows me whole when I blink. I want to stick a finger down my throat and get it all out. "I messed up. Leave me alone."

"Who knows if the Vanguard is gonna answer us next time we call?" He jabs a finger into my chest, right into the empty space of my sports bra. As much as I would love to grab Cormac's hand and bend it back so hard it snaps at the wrist, I don't. "And it's on you. Even if Nick won't say it, I will. When we run out of food, I'll make sure everybody knows it's your fault."

"Nick won't let you," I say.

"I don't give a shit. He'll come to his senses. He'll admit it. Because you want to know something? You want to hear something, Ben?"

He comes up close. Too close, close enough that his hair gets in my face, close enough that I can feel how warm he is. If it weren't for the mask, I could have tasted him.

Cormac says, "Nick's been calling you an *it*."

Chapter 17

Violence that begets evil will always be worse than the violence that ends it. The LORD will guide our hands. We will drive a wedge between the faithless through blood, and they will understand the evil they come from. They will understand the truth of salvation and come to us in repentance.

—*The Truth* by High Reverend Father Ian Clevenger

Don't say shit like that.

You don't believe me? Ask him. See what happens.

And I said, *Fine. I will.*

The ALC erupts when we bring in the supplies. I clean up and change clothes at Sadaf's urging, then help with inventory because it keeps me in the same room as Nick. People flow around me, peeling open boxes, handing off packages of socks, cradling painkillers like Fabergé eggs.

"You good?" Aisha says as she piles cans in the pantry.

"What?" She's staring at me. I'm glad to see her out and about, even if she looks like she hasn't slept in days. "Oh. Yeah, I'm good. Just waiting for Nick to finish up. Sorry, I'll get out of your way."

She picks up a few tins of Spam. "Rough trip?"

"Something like that."

When Cormac said Nick was calling me *it*, my first thought was awful: What if Nick is just super transphobic? But that doesn't make any sense. Nick and Erin are so close, they might as well be siblings. He hovers around her like some kind of guard dog, making sure nobody steps out of line. He wouldn't dare do something like that, not when he adores her.

And there's no way he thinks I'm just a Grace. An *abomination*. No, he can't. That's just not an option.

The only explanation is that Cormac is lying. He's sneered at me in the media room, talked down to me, wants me *gone*. And now he wants me to turn on Nick. Make a scene. Get myself kicked off the Watch and even out of the ALC.

I'm going to call his bluff.

As soon as we're done restocking and everyone has taken a small treat from the pantry—a can of pears and juice split among so many people, a handful of stale chips for the rest—I see Nick's jacket slipping through a crack in the kitchen door, and I give chase. Erin squeaks as I blow past her.

"Nick!" I call. "Nick, can we talk for a second?"

I catch him at the bottom of the stairs to the second floor, leaning against the door with a sign reading: *FIRE DOOR—KEEP CLOSED, DO NOT BLOCK*. He turns with a start.

"About what?"

I don't know how to explain without just spilling everything right here. "Can we go somewhere private first?"

He nods for me to follow him up the stairs. I do.

I just have to talk this through, and everything will be fine, it'll be *fine*, but my jaw is still chattering with nerves.

Nick takes me to a room on the second floor with a label beside the door: *Volunteer Coordinator*. Another office. It's been converted to a small bedroom, complete with a mattress in the corner and shoes shoved by the door. He's collected piles of books on warfare, white supremacy, religion, and the history of environmentalism, and stacks of old newspapers gone soft around the edges. Containers of plastic pony beads and half a dozen incomplete bead lizards sit on a desk in the corner. And, of course, the windows are boarded shut from the inside.

I hadn't realized Nick gets his own room, but it makes sense. This must be where he goes when he disappears. I imagine him locking the door and dropping his head into his hands, sucking in deep breaths, preparing to hold his chin high the next time we need him. Nick ushers me inside.

"So," he says, wandering over to the desk and picking up a pink bead. "Talk."

I start with, "I want to say upfront that I'm not accusing you of anything." Since being raised a good Christian girl will do things to you, will make you hedge topics and soften blows, no matter how much Seraph you have in you. Though maybe that makes it worse, because Nick's eyes narrow. "Frankly, I don't believe it. I just wanted to get it out there and—"

"Spit it out."

Right. No beating around the bush. "Cormac said you were calling me an *it*."

The bead stops rolling between his fingers. A lump appears in my throat, but I keep going.

"That's what I want to talk about. He's been like this ever since I showed up and, look. I can put up with a lot, believe me, but he's actively trying to turn me against you, and that is *not* okay. I wanted to bring it up to you before it gets worse. Does that make sense?"

Nick says nothing. The silence makes me itch.

"That makes sense," I say, "right?"

"I," Nick says, then he stops like the word got caught on something. It takes him a second to start back up. "I can't discuss this right now."

Um. "I don't . . ." My eye twitches. "I don't get it."

He repeats, slower, as if I didn't hear him the first time, "I can't discuss this right now."

"Right. Okay." I gesture to the door. "If you need me to piss off and give you space after this morning, I totally get it. I'll give you all the space in the world. I just need you to,

I don't know, clear the air. Tell me Cormac is a liar. Then I'll go. Okay? Just tell me he's lying."

He doesn't. He doesn't say anything. My heart throbs in my throat like it's trying to come up.

"You can write it down if you can't talk," I say. "Or, or you can tell me that he's telling the truth. I don't think he's telling me the truth, but if he is, you can tell me that too. Because if he is, I feel like we should talk about that instead? Just, whatever it is, give me a yes or no, I don't care how, and I'll leave you alone. I swear."

What if Cormac is right? If Cormac is right—

"Benji?" Nick says. His jaw barely moves. He's trying really, really hard to get the words out. "I won't talk about this."

Nick read the letter. He knows what I am. He knows what I *was.* He knew the girl I used to be, the twentieth host of the virus, the Angels' monster. He knew that long before he ever met me.

Oh God, what if that's all he sees?

Now I'm fighting to get words out too. "Fine. Then I'll stand right here until you will."

A long, heavy breath shakes in his chest. He puts down the bead, and that's what gives his fingers free rein to curl into something painful, knuckles turning white.

I almost feel bad. Almost.

Finally, he manages, "I know what you're thinking." This isn't him standing in front of the Watch. This is him crumbling in front of the Vanguard. This is him *weak*. "I know what you're thinking, and it's not like that—"

"Like hell it isn't." I step forward, and a flicker of fear passes behind his eyes, the first time I've seen it since the Grace forced him down at the shelter. I relish it. *Good.* I tear down my mask and bare my teeth so he can see the jagged tooth sticking out of my gums. "So you did? And you're too much of a coward to admit it?"

It's like flipping a switch. Nick roars, "Get the *fuck* out of my room!"

I stumble. For half a second, that's it, but it's long enough. Enough to remember how Theo screamed at me before he hurt me, the way I cowered, the way I begged him to stop. I was so weak then. Helpless.

But I'm not helpless now. The virus burns so hot it turns the edge of my vision white. Angel robes, the white horse, one of the most dangerous parts of the flame.

Nick was supposed to get it. Out of everyone, he's supposed to be the one who understands I'm not what the Angels made me. He's supposed to be the one that *gets it.* And here he is, using a pronoun like it. *It.* Like I'm not even an animal, just an object, a hunk of flesh, a vessel for something else. The same things the Angels thought I was.

I hate that I can't cry. I want to sob, I want to do something, anything, to get this pressure out of my head, this awful thing building behind my eyes, I hate it so *much*, and if I can't tear Nick to pieces, I need to get it out.

"No, you listen to me." My voice comes out in a terrible, pained rasp. "*Listen to me.* My name is Benjamin Woodside.

I'm gay and trans as hell, I am a boy, my pronouns are he/him, and I am a goddamn *person*." That is everything the Angels never let me have. Everything I am. "I joined the Watch because I thought you understood that. If I knew you were going to be like my fucking mom, I never would have stayed. I thought you were *better* than them!"

It feels like I've pulled out a thorn, yanked a spear out of my ribs, and now there's an open wound I don't know what to do with, just the relief that it's *out*.

Nick's eyes widen. His pupils are so dark, they've devoured every part of his eyes. The whites gleam in terror. Good. I hope he's scared. I hope it hurts him as much as I hurt right now, as much as it hurts for Seraph to burn across my cheeks and sink its fangs into my jaw. I hope—

I hope . . .

Pap.

There's a soft noise at my feet. So quiet I almost don't hear it.

Pap.

I look down.

A black-red drop sits on the tile floor. Splattered from the impact.

Another falls from my chin and hits the ground. *Pap.* Soft but sharp on the tile.

Something hot and wet trickles down my cheek and gathers at the point of my jaw, where it soaks into my pulled-down mask before finally falling. Again. *Pap.*

I open my mouth—probably to say, *What's happening?*—

and half my face goes loose. There's air on parts of me that shouldn't feel air. Nick won't stop staring.

Slowly, I touch my face.

My right cheek has torn all the way back to the muscle of my jaw. An open wound streaks from the corner of my mouth halfway to my ear, exposing the Grace-fang and all the teeth, tongue, and receding gums. A flap of loose skin dangles.

Pap. Pap-pap-pap—then the whole piece sloughs off and hits the ground with a wet splat. It's festering at the edges. Pocked with decay. Yellow and black and gray and red.

I watched this happen to the martyrs.

I stare until Nick pushes a ragged shirt against my face. The white in my vision swallows almost everything, and I slump to the floor. I tilt my head forward to keep the rot from taking up my entire throat and choking me. I let it all fall into the shirt until it soaks through and trickles between my fingers, warm and slick.

"Just tell me if he was lying." When I speak, all this shit splatters my hands. It trails off my chin, and I can't catch it all. There's so much. "And I swear I'll clean this up and leave."

I will. I'll bundle up the piece of my face and bury it out back with my tooth so nobody will find it. I'll make sure my mask covers the wound and pack it with tissue so it doesn't bleed through. I'll clean it up and go.

Instead of answering, Nick picks a notebook off the table. My hair falls into my face, and I remember the bobby pins he gave me. Why did I ever take them out? I reach into my pocket with my free hand—I need to keep my hair out of the blood, it's just one more thing to clean—and find my knife instead.

The click of a pen is almost deafening. Nick writes for a second and, very carefully, hands me a little note.

It reads, *I'm sorry.*

He did.

Cormac wasn't lying.

I take a deep breath because it's all I can do right now. In, out. Blood and sludge comes out with the air.

Maybe I need to start getting used to this. It's only going to get worse.

"All right," I say, and it sounds like something final.

I hand him both the note and the knife. When I free the knife from my pocket, bobby pins fall out and scatter on the tile. Nick doesn't move to take it, any of it, so I put it all on the floor between us instead. I don't know what the hell this means, so I'll leave that up to him.

I just don't want that knife in my pocket when he's the one who gave it to me.

Chapter 18

Do you want to know why we do this?
Love. It's always love.

—Reverend Father Duncan of Washington, D.C.

I don't want to think about what I said to Nick. I don't want to think about what he said to me.

We clean the floor of his room in silence, refusing to look at each other. Then I hide in my own room to peel off the rest of the rotten parts. It doesn't hurt, the same way peeling a sunburn doesn't hurt. It's all dead tissue anyway. No nerve endings. Nothing capable of feeling pain. I spend a minute or so staring at the collected shreds, all the little pieces of me.

After I sneak out to bury the mess, I stop in the laundry room to look at myself in the mirror. My left cheek, or what remains of it, is a riot of tattered flesh and open wounds. You can see my Grace-fang and pale, receding gums. Even with my mouth shut, my tongue pulses in the gaps between my teeth. Saliva glitters in the dim light. I test my vowels, my consonants, my syllables to make sure I still sound all right. A bit garbled, but nothing I can't keep hiding.

When I can't stand looking anymore, I put my mask back on, a thick fabric one that hides everything from the eyes down. With this, I just look tired. Hungry. Distant. Not like I'm falling apart.

I fall asleep early and wake up while the moon is high in the sky, so I can go back to Reformation Faith Evangelical Church. I sneak out the courtyard gate and into the city, where the stars still shine, the clouds still move across the sky, and nothing cares that I might as well be dying. It's a beautiful night. I could watch it forever.

I can't, though. I need Theo, the way I've always needed him.

Halfway through the walk, I pull off my mask. There's nobody to hide from anymore. It's like changing out of the dress I ran in, like watching snips of dark auburn hair gather around my feet. Not quite sure what to do with myself, desperately trying to understand this new body. Trying to figure it out: What does it mean? What does this flesh want? What does the world want from it?

What kind of monster do I want to be?

At least a face like this will make people think twice before making snap judgments about what I am. It's harder for someone to pin you down as a girl when they need a moment to pin you down as human.

Theo is in the sanctuary, praying. In the front pew, hands clasped, head hung and eyes closed. He's so perfectly still, he could be a statue or a corpse.

The sight doesn't sit well with me. All I can think of is him whimpering for forgiveness at the foot of the altar in New Nazareth, the wounds on his back weeping blood, so lost he wouldn't answer even when I laid my hands on him and said his name.

Here, now, I stop in the threshold and gently call, "Theo?"

He doesn't open his eyes, but he says, "Back already? My supplies will last me another few days at least."

I shuffle my feet. No, they won't. I hate that he thinks I'd only come back to keep him from going hungry.

"Bad day," I explain. "I just wanted to see you."

He pats the spot next to him. Still not looking. Every eye of the nest turns to me instead, mouths opening and closing as if beckoning. I do as they ask, sitting beside Theo on the pew, and Theo settles a hand on my leg and goes right back to praying.

I managed to find solace in prayer. I found respite in it, even if I had to force it. It's a chance to step away from everything for a little bit, in a way I couldn't get even when

I was with Theo. I could follow along with the reverend's chant, my own silent words, or the prayers I memorized down to their bones, and forget everything else. It was just me, the words, and the air in my lungs.

The problem is, I always felt like I was talking to myself.

All the other Angels talked about their personal relationship with God and Jesus. How prayer was a conversation with their savior. How they took the spirit inside themselves and knew the Lord was listening. Even when I was little, before New Nazareth and the Angels, Mom would take me to church and say, *Can you feel it, baby girl? Isn't it glorious?*

I tried to feel it. I did, I swear. I reached for it, squeezed my eyes shut as tight as I could and begged for it. I pretended I was stretching my hands out into the darkness behind my eyelids, fingers splayed wide, trying to find even the barest touch of something out there in the abyss. To feel the warmth Mom always assured me was waiting once I accepted God into my heart.

There was nothing. Always nothing.

Maybe that's how it's supposed to be. Maybe you're not supposed to feel that touch—maybe it's always been a metaphor. God is an absent parent who demands loyalty despite never coming around, and I just have to keep throwing my prayers into nothing and trust He gets them. Or maybe I am just too broken to feel Him in the first place.

So instead of prayer being a conversation, it became something else. A time to myself. A time to relax, to center, to set things right.

Do I think He exists? Heaven, Hell, all of it?

I don't know, I don't know, I don't know.

So I sit beside Theo and pray too. I pray for everything I can think of. For this world to hold together for as long as it can. For the Angels to stay away. For all the survivors to make it another day. For everything to turn out okay this time. *O Lord, we need You today and every day. Please lend us Your strength, lead and guide us—*

"Amen," Theo says out loud, startling me.

"Amen," I say in turn, even though I wasn't done.

His eyes flutter open, and he looks at me, jerks back, and says, "What the *hell*."

There it is. I offer a smile, but Lord knows how it looks on my face. "Told you, I had a bad day."

"I—" Theo stammers, mouth uselessly flapping as he scrambles for words.

"To fear and to keep," I remind him.

"I know. God, I know." Finally, he collects himself. He blinks, slowly. Wrangles his breathing into something even. "Does it hurt?"

"Not really. Not anymore." I run my tongue over my exposed teeth. "But my pain scale is screwed, considering everything."

He pulls me closer, hands lingering on my hips, shoulders, arms, cheeks, the way they always have.

"Look at you," he says. It's so soft it almost scares me. "It's still you."

"You don't have to say that."

"I mean it," he insists. "It's still you. I'll prove it."

He takes off his mask and kisses me.

He *what*?

I push him away. "Theo. Theo, what are you doing?"

"Kissing you?"

There's a smear on his cheek. Flood rot. Infected blood.

Seraph isn't contagious. Sister Kipling made sure it couldn't be transferred through any of the usual paths—spit, blood, nothing. The way Mom put it, Seraph was always meant to bear the weight of salvation alone. It wouldn't do to have the gift of God's strength be diluted through the unworthy. It wouldn't do, she said, for an army to be half generals. Just like there is one God, one king, one leader, there shall be one Seraph.

The point of Seraph has always been control.

"That's not—you can't seriously—"

His face falls. "Do you not want me to kiss you?"

I don't know if the idea disgusts me or intrigues me. Both, probably. I don't want to find out. "You don't have to."

"But I want to. And I want to do other things too." The way his voice dips, his hands tighten, oh God, he's talking about sex. I want to hide my festering face in my hands. "This is you, this is still you, and I missed you." He cradles my jaw and despite myself, despite everything, I lean into him. "I don't care about this. It's still you."

He's not lying. He is completely, utterly honest. I want to tell him how awful of an idea it is, how he'll regret it, how much I missed him, and I'll take anything he gives me.

He says, cautiously, “I can kiss something else.”

My embarrassed laughter comes out as a squeal. “*Theo!* Do *not* phrase it like that!”

“I phrased it that way for a reason?”

“I swear to God!”

“Don’t bring Him into this!”

But we’re both giggling, and his hands push under my shirt and find the edge of my sports bra and get under that too. He kisses my not-torn cheek, the crook of my jaw, all the way down my neck. He gets to the dip of my collarbone, I unzip my jacket for him. The quiet noise he makes when he gets to the soft skin of my shoulder makes me brace myself on the pew.

It’s just like it used to be.

“Your . . . ,” Theo mumbles against me, fingers winding through my belt loops.

“Cargo shorts.” I bite down a laugh as I fumble with the button. “How sexy of me.”

He snorts. “I put up with a lot for the sake of being into men.”

Men. I’m a man. Theo has seen me as a man from the moment I told him. I’ve always been his boyfriend, his fiancé, his future husband. Always Benjamin. Always me.

All that gets reduced to an elegant, “Gayyy.”

“That’s kind of the point,” Theo says.

He kneels on the dirty carpet between my knees, and I missed this, I needed this, Jesus, I needed *him*.

"Let me do something for you," I insist afterward, even though I couldn't move if I tried.

Theo pulls a pack of ancient tissues out of his pocket, which means he planned this, and I don't have the energy to be annoyed. I just wrestle my ass back into my pants and stare up at the ceiling of the church, where the ribs arch up toward the spine.

"Nope," he says. "Don't even think about it." He climbs up off the floor to sit beside me. "Been a while?"

"I can't believe you—"

He brandishes the used tissue like a weapon. I yelp and throw my hands up.

"Still you, remember?" he says.

Still me. "Yeah, whatever."

The church is beautiful at night. The Grace rustles gently, all their eyes half closed as if trying to catch the smallest snippet of rest; night wind blows in through the destroyed front doors; the barest streams of moonlight shine through the stained glass windows.

I can't stay long. There's no telling what will happen tomorrow, considering what Nick and I said to each other. At the very least, I need a few hours of sleep to tackle the inevitable shit show.

"Help me up," I plead.

Theo pulls me so that as soon as I'm on my feet, I'm against his chest. He doesn't waste a second in wrapping his arms around my waist and pressing his face to my shoulder.

"I almost feel bad the Grace had to watch," he says. "Almost." I laugh into his neck, right where I come up to on him. "Call it payback for making me puke my guts out."

Theo has no idea what it's like to *puke your guts out*. Not like I do.

"It's late," I murmur against him. "I should head out."

Theo snorts. "C'mon, you're gonna leave after that?"

I nudge him, almost knocking the two of us off-balance, but it does make him let me go. "You want me to stay and cuddle? Look, as much as I'd love it, I have to get back before somebody notices I'm gone."

"Do they have nightly check-ins? Like a hospital?"

"Well, no, but—"

He squeezes my arms. "I miss you."

I don't like the way he's holding me. I remember him wrenching my wrist so hard I screamed for him to let go, he was hurting me, he was going to break something; his spit dripping down my cheek and drying on the neck of my dress.

"I miss you too," I say, "but I can't look suspicious. They don't take risks." And I'm making the ALC sound worse than they are, just because I want him to let me go. He *needs* to let me go. "They'll kill me if they find me sneaking out."

Theo's grasp tightens once, just enough that it sucks the air out of my chest, and then releases. He takes a half step back, but it's not far enough.

"Benji," he whispers.

"I'm sorry." *I'm* the one apologizing. Why is it always me? "It's late, I'm tired, and—"

"Please stay."

He sounds so, so small. The way he did in the balcony when he first found me. The way he did on the chapel floor, at his father's feet, bleeding out.

He says, "Please."

I say, "Okay. Okay. Can I just—is there a decent place to go to the bathroom around here?"

"I can show you."

"You are *not* walking me out to take a piss. Just tell me."

He points me to where, and as soon as I'm out of his sight, I yank open the back door of Reformation Faith Evangelical Church and leave.

I do not look back, not once.

And when I reach the Acheson LGBTQ+ Center, it's burning.

Chapter 19

Those who obey God and His commands shall be blessed, the way faithful men have always been blessed. But to those who turn from Him, He is wrath. He is fire. He tells us where to burn.

—Reverend Mother Woodside's sermon

Genesis 19:28—And he looked toward Sodom and Gomorrah, *and toward all the land of the plain, and beheld, and, lo, the smoke of the country went up as the smoke of a furnace.*

Hebrews 12:29—*For our God is a consuming fire.*

Luke 3:16—*He will baptize you with the Holy Spirit and fire. O Lord our God*, what the fuck happened?

The planks that used to seal the front doors of the Acheson LGBTQ+ Center lie in shards across the steps. Flames billow out of the gaping hole left behind and reach through every broken window, up to the sky, with a low, demonic rumble cut by the high-pitch cracking of embers. Just like the bridges burning on Judgment Day, columns of smoke rising high over Acheson as they all crashed into the water.

A gunshot, and another, and a scream, and a shriek. Long, high, and furious.

I would recognize the cry of a Grace anywhere.

I put on my mask and sprint toward the flames.

The heat hits half a block away. It's a dry heat that sucks the moisture from my eyes and makes me choke. Bright white flame shines in shards of glass on the road, on abandoned cars, doubled in storefront windows, hemming me in like the Lord casting us from Him. *Depart from me, ye cursed, into everlasting fire.*

I've kept running through worse.

The courtyard fence is demolished, broken to pieces just like the front door. I clamber over splinters and nails, and I scrape my palm on a jagged edge.

An Angel. There, flinging open the back entrance of the ALC, raising a hand against the smoke that comes out to greet him. And a Grace. A Grace built like they were gutted doing a backbend bridge, stretched to grotesque proportions, extra arms lashed to limbs, another face peeking from their neck.

They see me.

The Angel sees me too.

He lifts his gun. He can't pull the trigger, he wouldn't dare kill *me*, but can he tell who I am? With the smoke, the fire, and the screaming? Dad's bloody-flower face comes crashing back, teeth and tongue gleaming in his broken head and it's all I can see, it's all I can taste, until the Angel opens fire on the Grace.

The Grace wails, heartbroken and pitiful, staggering back and hitting the courtyard wall. Too-long arms wrap around their head to protect their brain. The flash of gunfire and the orange glow of the blaze lights up the Angel's robes like twilight, looking more like one of Lucifer's angels than God's.

I plunge into the smoke and throw my body into his.

My shoulder hits his ribs. We both fall to the weeds. The gun keeps chattering until it drops, shooting bullets into the sky. The Angel roars and rolls on top of me, blood streaming from his temple where he hit a rock, grabbing me like he's going to rip me apart.

Then he doesn't have a head anymore. His spine snaps cleanly as his skull comes off in the Grace's mouth. The body collapses onto my chest. The Grace toys with the severed head, turning it over and testing each angle with their tongue before finally biting down. Bone gives instantly under their teeth.

I stay in the grass, gasping for air under the weight of the Angel, watching the Grace and the wounds on their body. The Angel *did* recognize me. Why else would he have turned on the Grace? They're God's holy warriors, blessed and perfect, and a soldier only has orders to put them down if they become too dangerous.

I make them too dangerous.

The Angels know I'm at the ALC.

The ALC is burning because of *me*. This is my fault, oh God, it's my fault. My fingers dig into the Angel's rancid robes as the Grace whines and the neck stump spits blood. It's my fault.

I have to stop this.

I shove the Angel's body off mine and reach for the Grace. Part of their jaw was torn off by a bullet, the wound trickling black sludge between their eyes. They have so many limbs, some touching the ground and some not, grasping and reaching with so many hands. I let them touch me. I lean forward so they can grab my hair and pull me close. They smell like rot and Dad's corpse.

I whisper, "*Help us.*"

The answer I get is soft and perfect. Their eyes flutter closed. A hum shakes deep in their broken-open chest. It's all I need to hear.

They press their shoulder against me to steady me, nudging their face against my stomach. I leave a red handprint on their neck.

We enter the burning building together.

Fire lights the narrow halls an otherworldly pink and orange, smoke muffling it all under an ugly gray. Roiling flames lick across the ceiling and devour pride flags and old posters. I raise my hand against the haze. But there's so little oxygen, my lungs scream. It's so hot, the soles of my shoes are going to melt to the floor. There's so much noise it's all a roar, so loud it hurts, all the fire and my own heartbeat and ragged breathing. There's more gunshots, *more Angels*, and I pray: *O God, Your shade is what protects me, our struggle against flesh and blood, against wickedness in heavenly places.*

The Grace charges ahead, barreling through furniture and barricaded fire doors. We weave through back halls and erupt into the lobby, where flames have engulfed everything, even the bodies on the floor. The Angels broke through a defensive line here. Spent bullet casings shimmer; two Angels burn in the doorway, between the bodies of people I know. Don, who helped me do my laundry a few days ago; Lindsey, who laughed when my jacket sleeves fell over my hands.

They're dead. For the first time in a while, I have to stop at the sight of a dead body because God, oh God, *O God, Your shade is what protects us.*

Something moves over my shoulder. I turn to find Carly staring at me, at the Grace, tears streaming down her cheeks. She's supporting someone whose left arm is charred beyond recognition.

I point to the back door. *"That way!"* Carly nods and takes a step back, and the smoke swallows her.

A scream from the gym. Shit, the gym. I fling open the doors.

It's an inferno. Apartments crackle and collapse, and there goes everything. Our beds, our belongings, the trinkets and pages of books held up like wards against evil. All gone.

Through the smoke, I see them: two Angels sweeping the aisles, checking apartments one by one and setting them alight. Glimmering like demons, ash smearing the hems of their robes.

Brother Faring. Brother Heard. Of course I recognize them. I always do.

I jam my shoulder into the Grace's side. They spring forward, clattering across the waxed gym floor, and grab Brother Heard by the torso to fling him into the fire. His robes catch immediately. Brother Faring lifts his rifle but—

CRACK. He falls. An ashen hand bats aside a sheet door from an apartment just feet away, and Aisha crawls out, smeared with soot and cradling her gun like a baby.

"Benji," she gasps, "Benji, you're okay."

I grab her arms to steady her as the Grace digs into the second Angel to make sure he's really, really dead, pulling out ropes of dripping insides. Aisha is shaking and wheezing.

"I'm okay," I manage. "Where is everybody?"

"I don't know, I don't know. We got split up." She's clinging to me, barely able to pull herself out of the apartment. My head feels like it's going to explode under the heat and the pressure. I tell myself there's more than one way to the back door, and just because I didn't see anybody on the way in doesn't mean all my friends are burning alive. "Some people are still upstairs, I think? We need to go."

She looks over my shoulder and freezes.

"What the fuck," she whispers, "what the fuck, what the fuck."

I look too. The Grace is staring at us, head tilted and wreathed in smoke. Part of their skin bubbles where they're too close to the fire.

Look away, I whisper, and when they do, I shove Aisha toward the door. She tries to drag me with her, but I peel her fingers off my sleeve, and she sobs, turns, and runs.

It's too hot in here. The high ceilings aren't doing anything for the smoke anymore, and my chest feels too tight, like my ribs are squeezing in. I'm slick with sweat, but my eyes are so dry, they hurt when I blink. The Grace wanders up, rumbling, and nudges me.

I need to get out of here. Get away from the fire and into fresh air where the smoke won't suffocate me.

But I'm the reason the ALC is burning. I can't just *leave.*

I promised I would be good.

The Grace comes back to my side, and together we run. Out of the gym, through the lobby, down another hall. The Grace rounds a corner ahead of me, and I follow to find them bashing an Angel against a wall, over and over, until there's nothing left of him but sludge.

We reach the media room.

It's white with fire, so bright I have to squint. Breathing feels like swallowing rot. I shield my eyes, tears of strain gathering in my lashes. It's hard to see, but I make out the only shapes that matter: an Angel behind Nick's shitty armchair and Cormac behind the couch. He's stuck. No weapon and no way to the door. And people never hold positions alone.

I don't care that he tried to turn me against Nick. I whisper to the Grace, "*Go.*"

They screech through the doorway, descending on the Angel like something from Heaven, dragging the soldier toward their gaping maw. The Angel screams and is cut off with a crunch.

I stumble through the flames and grab Cormac by the jacket. "Come on!"

"What the fuck is wrong with you?" Cormac shrieks. The whites of his eyes burn. Soot smears his face. "That *thing*—"

I whisper, "*Find someone to help*," and the Grace tosses their head and disappears into the blazing halls. Cormac stares at me, and I hiss, "Get your ass up," and he's with me.

"Why didn't it kill us?" he rasps.

"I don't know," I lie and pull him toward the door.

There's something awful building in my stomach, a pounding in my head like Seraph is clawing through, but I get Cormac into the hall. The flames are as tall as a person, and it's impossible to breathe without hacking. Cormac wrenches himself out of his jacket and presses it against my mouth. I shove it back at him, he needs it more than I do, but he takes one half to block the smoke and shoves the other against me again, and I let him.

We stumble through the back door.

Dozens of people are out here. It's chaos. Salvador smashes a window on the other side of the courtyard and boosts someone through, into the safety of a strange building.

Sadaf shouts at Sarmat to hold someone down while she cuts clothing away from a festering burn.

People are alive. This is my fault, but people are alive, God, they're alive.

I get two steps into the courtyard before the Grace dies.

I feel it in the Flood, in my skull. My knees give out from under me. Cormac stumbles, trying to catch me under the arms, but he's too late. Vomit wells up in my throat. I can't take down my mask to throw up, it'll show my face, I can't—

"Benji?" Cormac whimpers.

I snatch his jacket.

"Shit," Cormac says, "Nick! *Nick!*" I hold the jacket like a shield and barely pull down my mask before I vomit. My jaw opens so far it hurts, and the tear across my cheek strains. Something big comes up, and I have to get it out with my tongue, and it falls into the grass, wet and heavy and way too big. *"Nick, where are you?"*

Two sets of hands bring me to my feet, around my waist and under my arms. I cling to the jacket, vision blurring. Acid burns the back of my tongue.

"You're fine," Cormac says while I work my mask back up. "You're okay."

I slam the jacket against Cormac's chest to get it out of my face, and the first thing I see is Nick—to my left, our sides pressed together, holding me tight. Then he lets go. He's in front of me, climbing through the window, holding out his hands for me. Salvador boosts me through and says, "Glad you made it, kid."

"Sit," Nick says, a hand hovering over the back of my neck. Like he knows I thought, for a second, of running back in. "Now."

I collapse against the wall and slide down. This building—a bank, I think?—is full of wide-eyed, fire-red kids, checking on their friends or lying on the floor, eyes closed. Some cry and some are too shocked for tears. Some have marks from bullets, blood soaking their clothes and hands. Lila, a girl with a cane, has found a first aid kit in the back room and is going around with what little supplies she has, picking up the work Sadaf can't manage.

Nick says, "Are you okay?"

For the first time, I look down at myself. My skin is red from the heat and shimmers with sweat. Ash cakes my clothes. Blisters are starting to form on the backs of my hands. Parts of the soles of my shoes really *have* melted, and it looks like the hems of my jeans were singed. I toe off one of my sneakers to find the bottoms have stuck to my socks through a hole in the padding.

Nothing too bad, considering. I didn't even notice, but I can't tell if that's a good thing or a bad thing.

I decide on, "I'm fine."

Nick's hair has come out of the bobby pins. Strands fall across his sweat-slicked forehead. He's just as much of a mess as me, singed and overheated and exhausted.

He's not moving. God, does he even want to see me right now?

Do *I* want to see him?

"Are you sure?" he asks.

"Um. Can I get some water?"

Nick disappears and comes back with a bottle. I shove it under my mask and drink as much as I can, head tilted to keep it from falling between my teeth. He waits until I finish, standing at my side to block the torn side of my face from view.

"Stay here," he says when I'm done and shoves a piece of paper into my hands.

"Wait—"

But Nick is already gone, climbing back out through the window. "Cormac," he says, "get in the bank."

"I'm fine," comes Cormac's voice from the courtyard. "Benji got me just in time."

"You've been inhaling smoke for too long. Absolutely not."

"I'm fine."

Alex sweeps up beside me and leans out the window. They look awful. Bloody hands, a scrape on their chin, mask stained gray. What happened to the radio? I don't remember if I saw it in the lobby. There are so many things to worry about that I just add it to the list.

"Get in here," Alex snarls through the window, "or I'm going to make you regret it."

"All right," Cormac snaps. "All right."

Salvador gets him through the window, and he collapses next to me, head held between his knees.

We both do nothing else for a little bit. Eventually, Alex

takes up the spot beside him, the three of us in a line next to artificial plants, a writing desk, and chairs.

"The abomination just *killed* those Angels," Cormac says. "Did you see that?"

"Yeah." I sure did.

"What the hell?"

"It helped you."

He groans. "I know."

I hold out the bottle. "Water?"

He yanks down his mask and tips half the water into his mouth. He pours some into his hand and splashes it onto his face. Then he passes it to Alex, who takes a gulp before dumping the rest over their head.

I unfold the note in my hand.

I'm sorry.

The same *I'm sorry* Nick wrote in his room, the same *I'm sorry* I left on the floor with my knife, the same *I'm sorry* he couldn't say but needed me to know anyway.

I press that *I'm sorry* hard against my upper lip and pretend the smoke tears on my cheeks are actual, human tears, the kind I haven't been able to cry in years.

I'm sorry too.

Chapter 20

There's some kind of awful, enduring myth: that after the end of the world, people will turn on one another. That people will become hateful and selfish. That's just not true. It's never been true.

—"The Wasteland Lie," a 2031 essay by Toni Quaye

We work long into the night. Breaking into buildings for fire extinguishers, doing head counts, soothing burns and pulling broken glass out of wounds. I help Lila, Sadaf, and Sarmat, sterilizing needles with a lighter for stitches. The cool night air is the one thing keeping me from vomiting again. My blisters ache, but I have better things to do than nurse them.

"Are you all right?" Sadaf asks me, her pale pink dress splayed out in the ashes while Sarmat helps her last patient stand. Lila measures out a length of bandage. In the moonlight, with her rescued medical kit and bloody hands, Sadaf looks more like an angel than any Angel ever has.

"I'm fine," I say, which I've been lying about all night.

"Do you want a looking over?"

"No." A wave of sick clenches my throat, and I press my tongue to the roof of my mouth to keep from heaving. I choke out, "I'm good."

"If you say so. Also, tell Aisha to take a break, please? If you see her? I'm worried." She nervously picks crusted bodily fluids out from under her nails. "You need some rest too. My professional medical opinion is for you to get some shut-eye."

She's right. I can at least try to sleep this off.

The inside of the bank sprawls with rough carpet, dusty mahogany desks, and gold accents. Micah sleeps behind a fake plant. A girl named Zarah cuddles a blanket as she waits for her girlfriend. I hop the front desk, taking a moment to steady myself once I'm on the other side, and open the door to the hall of offices.

Erin is there, in a little nook under the window.

Finding her alone in the dark just isn't right. She's hunched, hidden in the folds of a charred shawl, braids falling around her face. In middle school, I'd carry hair ties for girls who needed them, and even now I reach for them around my wrist.

"Hey," I whisper, quietly so as not to scare her.

Her head jerks up. "Fuck," she says. I'm not sure what's more shocking—the broken look in her eyes or the fact she just said fuck. "Sorry. Hey, Benji."

A tear slips out from the corner of her eye. I sit on the floor beside her, our knees touching.

"Sorry," she says again. "I should be out there helping, but here I am."

"I'm just glad you're in one piece," I say, tapping my fingers against my thigh to keep the sick down.

"I hate that *one piece* is all we can hope for these days."

"You need anything?"

"I sound like such a child," she says. "A hug? Nick isn't great at them. No offense, but."

I brace myself, and Erin just falls against my chest. She's . . . so small. She has such a big personality and a few inches on me, but God, she's so soft and frail. She's shaking with fear, adrenaline, and exhaustion, like we all are.

"Thank you," she whispers.

No. No, I should be the one saying that. I should be thanking her, Nick, and the ALC. For this, and the bobby pins, and the hands holding me upright, and the people I saved and who saved me. Those are the things I would burn down the Angels for.

It's the least I could do, considering what I've brought down on them.

I wonder where Nick is right now. What I could say to him now. If I could find the words to apologize to him, after all this.

Erin pulls back just enough that our temples knock together. Her hands rest on my arms, where I rolled up my sleeves against the heat, showing the ashes and angry red marks that weren't there earlier. Marks that the fire could have put there, but I know they didn't.

"Does it hurt?" she asks.

I shake my head. She doesn't need to worry about me.

I shut myself in a copy room at the back of the hall. There's still smoke on the air, seeping in through cracks, windows, and doors. I lie on the floor and stare at the ugly tile ceiling. In the silence, there's nothing to focus on but my burned skin and nausea.

Before I fall asleep, I think I see feathers on the edge of my vision; I think I see something strange.

Eventually, the door opens. I don't know when. The sound drags me out from sleep, and I look, just a little bit, thinking maybe it's Erin coming in to check on me or more feathers lurking in the shadows.

Nick stands in the doorway.

He peers in for a moment, awkward and stiff, and leaves.

Those red marks climb up my arms, skin dying in rivers along what used to be veins. They make the heat blisters stand out on my hands, looking like something trying to erupt.

Seraph pushing out, the Flood pushing out, hungry.

Later. The door opens. The door closes.

My eyes open just a crack. Nick stands in the room, unsure, doing that tapping motion again—*tp-tp tp-tp*—over and over, until it's not enough, and he violently shakes out his hands. He tips forward a little bit, back a little bit, forward, back, and soon his expression doesn't look as pained. Still hurting but not unbearable. Another shake of his hands. A breath with eyes squeezed shut.

I say nothing. Not just because I'm pretending to be asleep, but because I know this is something private. He's gone to such lengths to hide this side of himself—the side that flaps his hands and rocks until he's together again—that admitting I'm a witness to it feels wrong.

But I do make sure he's in one piece. That's all we can ask for.

He is, eventually. His breathing evens. He pushes his hair out of his eyes and primly fixes his bobby pins. He stands with his feet firmly on the floor.

He crouches beside me.

I fight to keep myself still. As still as possible. His breath gently huffs behind his mask; his shoe scrapes on the carpet as he keeps his balance. He smells like smoke and sweat.

Nick's fingers hover, for a moment, over my arm. Over my cheek, over my hair.

"Shit," he whispers. "Shit." He gets up and goes to the door but stops, reaching for the doorknob but unable to grab it, and he turns away like he can't consider the idea any longer.

He takes off his jacket.

And his shirt.

The pale expanse of his chest is cut through with awful scars. He's not as muscular as I thought he would be, but there's power in the way his arms move. He turns his shirt over, inspects it. There's a scar on his shoulder and a few on his collarbone. One on his soft stomach, shiny and white. He pats his pockets, then digs in them.

What—what *are* we? Am I still mad at him? He apologized, and I guess I accept it. I need to apologize to him too. I want to get past this, I don't want to worry about this anymore; I want to sit down, talk about it, and move on. I'm sick of worrying about where I stand with the boys in my life.

I have the apology in my pocket. And right now, Nick is with me.

Nick, seeming to accept that whatever he's looking for isn't in his pocket, turns to shake it out of his jacket. With the faint moonlight coming in through the narrow window, I can make out the mass of scars on his back. There are so many, it makes my stomach turn. They're dark, all the way from his shoulders to his waist, a pattern—

A pattern I know.

Those aren't scars at all.

They're tattooed wings.

What the FUCK.

That doesn't make sense. That can't be right. No, I'm seeing it wrong, that has to be it. The shadows are playing tricks on me. I'm seeing feathers where they aren't supposed to be. I saw them before I fell asleep, it's Seraph messing with me. That must be it.

But he shifts in the light, and they're still there. They're carved into his back, scoring all the way down like acid poured across his skin, like a monster tore him apart with its claws.

Nick was a death-squad soldier. Nick was an Angel.

A knife falls out of his jacket and hits the carpeted floor with a muffled thump. His shoulders go with it, sagging like he's suddenly carrying an unbearable weight. He sinks to the floor, absolutely unreadable behind his mask, and he starts to cut his shirt into strips. His arm strains when he yanks at the fabric. I stare at the muscles there, at the edges of feathers creeping onto his sides. There are so many little scars in lines down his sides, right where they would be if he'd tried to claw them off with his fingernails.

Breathe.

He told me to keep *Judgment Day* out of my mouth before I'd even said it. He'd had to figure out his own rules too. Breathe. He didn't cry when Trevor died, he didn't cry at the funeral. Breathe. He moves and leads like a trained soldier, and he tried to tear the tattoos out of his skin with his bare hands.

Oh God, and I told him he was just as bad as Mom.

Nick rips the last strip off his shirt and works my arm out from under my head. I let myself go limp and close my eyes all the way so I don't have to pretend.

He ran from the Angels. He *made* it. He got away from the Angels, found a home, and *survived*.

He wraps the bandages tight around one arm, then the other, to cover the rotting pieces, blisters, and burns, and he slips in bobby pins to keep it all in place.

Nick did it. He did exactly what I've always dreamed of; the thing Dad died trying to do for me.

I keep my eyes shut as he moves to the other side of the room. I tell myself I'll look when he leaves, but he never does. When it's been quiet for long enough, I peek and find him asleep against the door.

I lie awake, measuring the air in my lungs. The bandages are warm against my already hot skin. They smell like him, like smoke.

He knows what I've been through. He understands.

I press my face into my arm, right where the bandages wind into the crook of my elbow. He called me a monster, and I called him one back. He suffered as an Angel, and I led them to his home to burn everything to the ground.

Lord, we can't keep going like this.

Chapter 21

Suffering is the price of flesh. Be grateful for the gift of it.

—Sister Mackenzie's Sunday school lesson

The Watch and a few others—Sadaf, Alex, Erin—stand in the courtyard too early in the morning. None of us could sleep. Birds chirp, the sun barely breaks the horizon, and everything still reeks of smoke.

Nick stands by the broken fence, having found a replacement shirt that shows off the hard lines of his forearms. I keep thinking about his wings, long and beautiful and torn to shreds on his sides. As soon as I open my mouth, everything will come spilling out, so I chew on my bottom lip and pick at the makeshift bandages. At least I don't feel the urge to puke every time I turn my head.

Did Nick think I'd wake up and *not* notice the bandages? It's kind of endearing.

"You know," Salvador says, rubbing xyr scars, "I was gonna ask Chris how he made that cool ace patch. I wanted one."

Aisha says, "God, that's not important."

"I know. It's just . . . sinking in."

"Chris died?" Alex says. Erin squeezes her eyes shut like she can will it not to be true if she just tries hard enough. "I thought I saw him—"

Cormac says, "You didn't."

Alex sighs. They spent most of the night trying to find a good place for the ham radio, like putting down a baby for a nap. At least it's still in good condition. Not great, but it turns on, and that's what matters. They're probably the most put together of us all right now, although that might be because adding one more thing to mourn doesn't change much.

"Do you think we can fix the fence?" Sadaf asks, holding Aisha's arm. I can't tell which is supporting the other.

"I don't think the fence really matters, does it?" Faith says. "What if they come back?"

Cormac's eyes flicker to me.

"We'll discuss that later," Nick says. "Right now, we need to focus on what's in front of us." He shakes his hands, almost like he's brushing dust off his jacket. I recognize the motion, and I'm sure everyone else does too, but he starts giving orders like always. Sadaf and Alex still have work to do in the bank. Erin heads back in to grab extra people for sniper duty, since we might have become a target in the night, with all the fire and smoke. Salvador is put in charge of recovering what's left of the kitchen; Faith, the storage rooms. Aisha and Cormac each get a gun, directions to scope out the surrounding blocks, and a map from Micah detailing any traps, just in case they can bring back extra food for the night. We're going to get hungry, and quick.

I get to deal with the bodies. With Nick.

Downstairs is a charred mess. Dust from the fire extinguishers coats the floor, and we leave footprints in it as we walk. Some of it has settled on the bodies, like a gentle flurry of snow resting in hair and the creases of agonized faces staring up at the ceiling. A pair of open eyes even has dust on top, like cataracts. It makes my face itch.

We count fifteen dead. Six Angels, eight of ours, and the Grace. I know everybody whose bodies are recognizable, and about half aren't. My first thought—we won't have ears for some of the Angel kills; they either melted in the flames or were eaten by the Grace. The second—what the *fuck is wrong with me.*

I stand by the twisted, burned mess of bodies lying in the lobby, right in the midst of the broken front door, and I press my lips to my knuckles. I pray until Nick comes over, brushes my shoulder, and nods for me to follow.

Revelation 21:4—*And God shall wipe away all tears from their eyes; and there shall be no more death, neither sorrow, nor crying, neither shall there be any more pain: for the former things are passed away.*

You will return to the earth for out of it you were taken; for from dust you were made and to dust you will return.

We find the Grace in the gym. It's curled atop a melted body, the Grace's back-bent form desperately huddled around them.

I trace the timeline in their corpses. The Grace's head is crumpled on the side, the same way Dad's was. Between the media room and the gym, we found an Angel whom I don't remember. The pieces click together.

"The Grace was trying to protect them," I tell Nick. I lead him through my train of thought. I don't know what happened to the person—maybe they were shot, maybe they died of smoke inhalation, maybe they were immolated, Lord knows, God knows, *O Lord our God*—but the Grace was gravely wounded before killing the Angel in the hall and coming back to the gym. Maybe the person was dead when they arrived. Maybe they weren't. But the Grace curled around them, or what was left of them, and died.

"At least, that's what I think," I say. "I don't know."

"No," Nick says, crouching beside me. "That sounds right."

You will return to the earth for out of it you were taken; for from dust you were made and to dust you will return.

"Are you okay?" he asks.

"Okay enough." I have to say it. I have to get it out of my head. I twist my hands together and steady my voice. "Which squad were you in?"

Nick coughs. "What?"

"Which squad?" I whisper. "Nick? Which death squad were you in?"

His Adam's apple bobs in his throat. "It doesn't matter which one," he rasps, "does it?"

After a second, I say, "No. I guess not."

"How did you know?"

"I saw your tattoos." What I can see of his face is even paler than usual. He's staring at the mangled bodies, jaw working under his mask. "Last night, when you were in the room with me."

"You were pretending to be asleep," he accuses.

"You thought I wouldn't wake up while you were putting bandages on me?" I hold up my arm. He won't look. "You thought I wouldn't be a little on edge after *everything*?" Deep breath—no, no anger, no Seraph, not now. I can't believe it's only been a day since Cormac told me Nick was calling me an *it*. And what right do I have to be angry, after everything I've done?

I say, softer, "After yesterday?"

"I'm—" Whatever he's trying to say gets caught in his throat. "I'm sorry. I shouldn't have—I didn't mean to—"

He scrapes at his cheek. His hands are shaking a little. I want to grab them to hold them still, but I shouldn't.

Instead, I reach into my pocket and pull out the *I'm sorry.* I hold it out to him, keeping it open with my fingers so he can see exactly what's written there.

I've never been good at saying it, either. I don't like hearing it, and I don't like saying it, but this little token already means so much.

He takes the paper.

"I shouldn't have lost it with you," I say. *I shouldn't have brought the Angels here. I should never have come here. This is my fault.*

"I deserve it," Nick mumbles.

"I really shouldn't have compared you to my mother. That was a dick move." He was raised an Angel, he read the announcement to the faithful—he knows *exactly* who my mother is. "So. Yeah."

We look at the bodies instead of each other. The Angels have hurt so many people. So many it's almost unfathomable. It's a number so big, you can't even start to wrap your head around it—a number in the billions, whittling humanity down to a bottleneck, down to scraps and stragglers. They find any way to hurt you they can. It's their duty.

"You could have told me," I say. "How you were feeling, I mean. I would've understood. I feel the same way sometimes."

"I didn't want to think about it," Nick says. "I was scared."

"Why?"

He takes the bead lizard from his pocket and pulls down his mask so he can chew on the beads of its tail. "Why what?"

"Why you were scared. Why you were calling me *it*. Why anything."

"I was scared of you. And what you meant. I thought it'd be easier if you weren't you."

If I weren't me?

"I wanted to pretend you weren't a person," he says. He sounds like such a little kid, barely the teenager he's supposed to be, let alone the adult he's convinced us all he is. "So I wouldn't think about how much of the *same* person we are."

The same person. Just like Erin said.

Are we really that similar? The only thing we have in common is being gay boys who ran away from home.

. . . Who ran away from the Angels. Who suffered under them and survived.

"You didn't want to think about us being the same because I'm a monster," I say.

"No."

"It's fine. You can say it."

Nick makes a hiccupping sound. I can't place it, and I don't want to.

"I've seen the monster," I say. "I keep seeing it."

"Is it scary?"

"God, yes." I peel back part of the bandage. My arms are so much worse than they were. They look like the skin would slough off if I started peeling, like a sunburn that goes all the way down to the fat and tendons. The blisters on the back of my hands are pitiful in comparison. "I don't have long. Maybe a week or two."

"I was wrong," Nick says. "I won't call you that again."

"And I was wrong too." *More than you know, but I just can't bring myself to say it.*

Silence, then: "I was stationed at New Nazareth," he says.

My brain short-circuits. I knew everyone at New Nazareth. This doesn't add up. "You were?"

"We never crossed paths. My parents weren't all that important, just some Baptist pastor and his wife." He's right; that could be describing a lot of people. "I was a year ahead of you in Sunday school."

Plus, with the way Nick spends most of his time alone, and his being in the death squads . . . Okay, maybe it does make sense we never met. I never really focused on cute boys when I had Theo to occupy myself with.

"Did you ever have Sister Mackenzie?" I ask. "She was the worst."

"She was awful."

"Do you remember when she brought in that crucifix? The one with the naked Jesus that had his dick out and everything?" Nick makes a spluttering noise, which I realize is his laughter, and I laugh too. "I can't believe she did that. Just. The *entire* dick was out. I swear it's the only reason I don't want one now." I make a flaccid motion with my finger. "It looked like a sad worm."

He splutters again. My cheeks hurt from smiling. A small moment of calm in this burned-out building, surrounded by bodies, both of us aching, nervous, and so, so tired.

I should apologize for burning this place down, but I don't. I want to keep this moment safe. I wish I could stay here forever, surrounded by ash and death and his laughter.

Cormac counts the ears we manage to retrieve as if there will be more the next time he does: three. Three isn't nearly enough for what the Angels did to us. What they *took* from us. Our food, our water, our home, our safety.

Alex brings up the idea of taking the ears of our dead friends. The Vanguard won't be able to tell the difference. We consider it. There is nothing in the traps, our food stores are mostly ash, and we *can't* risk disappointing the Vanguard. Not after what I did.

A lot of things are my fault these days.

Nick says, "I'll leave it up you, Cormac."

"Jesus." Cormac pulls his hair. "Don't make me choose."

"Then we'll vote. No looking."

We vote with our eyes shut. I vote for it. Nick whispers the results to Cormac, who swallows hard. "All right," he says, "all right."

Afterward, as I slog through the mess, peeling apart sticky Angel corpses to find anything that could help us, I heave so hard, a trail of spit comes up. I take down my mask to wipe it away, but when the cloth touches my throat it happens again, and I end up with my head against the wall, gagging, waiting for the wave to pass.

It doesn't. I take a page out of Nick's book and find a pen and a piece of scrap paper in the bank and write to pass to him: *I feel sick, I'm gonna go lie down*. He walks me to the copy room and gives me a salvaged blanket, and I stay there until he comes to find me again.

"Erin wants to talk to everybody," he says. "Should I tell her not to wait up?"

I push myself upright, a sick taste lingering in my mouth. "No, I'll be—" I clamp my jaw shut to keep stomach acid from creeping up. "I'll be fine. Give me a second."

"You can rest."

"I'm coming," I insist and stagger to my feet.

In the lobby of the bank, Erin is sitting on the help desk, looking slightly better but not much. Everyone gathers around her like a gaggle of baby ducks, staring at her or anywhere but her, depending on how they deal with this kind of thing. Some nervously leaf through old deposit slips, click pens, or scratch the carpet. I sit by the desk, staring out the window to the courtyard. Nick takes his spot next to Erin, arms crossed.

Her gentle, wavering words break the silence.

"We don't need to talk about what happened," she says. "We all know what happened, and we all know what we lost. Moving forward, we'll be staying here. The Acheson LGBTQ+ Center is not safe to inhabit, at least for now."

A few pained cries rise up from the crowd. So much of their lives went up in flames: the books in the office; the photos on the walls; the flyers, apartments, and friends whose bodies were eaten away by the inferno. It's what the Angels have always done to humanity—what society has always tried to do to *us*. Always taking, always sinking in its teeth. My fingers dig into my arm and pieces of skin start to come off. I stop myself by biting the inside of my remaining cheek until I draw blood.

Erin says, "We'll do what we can with what we have. That's what we've always done."

Calvin raises his hand. If I have to listen to him, I might actually be sick. Aisha, where she's sitting with Sadaf, turns away.

"We need to get the hell out of here," Calvin says. "If the Angels know where we are, we're fucked. They're going to come back and finish us off, and, personally, I don't want to be stuck waiting for them when they do."

Another person, Lux, wrinkles eir nose and spits, "I can't *walk*, dude." E picks up eir thigh almost as if to shake the bloody bandages in his face. "You going to carry me across this damn city? Find me a wheelchair, maybe?"

"That's your problem," Calvin replies.

Faith snaps, "*Hey!*"

"I'm right, and you know it!"

Salvador leans over to Nick's ear, whispers something. He nods, and Salvador disappears into the back room.

"Calvin, please," Erin begs. "We can work through this together."

"I don't want to work with a bunch of pussies who think the idea of just *sitting here* is—"

Salvador comes out of the back room with a backpack and slings it across the floor so it hits Calvin in his side.

"If you don't want to just sit here," Salvador growls, "you're free to leave." Calvin goes whiter than he already is. "I mean it. Get off your ass and do your own thing if you think we're *pussies.* If you hate us so much, then *go*!"

Calvin stammers for a moment, then snatches the bag and stands. "Fine."

"Fine," Salvador repeats, and Calvin looks over his shoulder once before slamming out the front door of the bank.

Half the mouths in the room hang open. I can't see it past the masks, but I can feel it, the collective stunned silence. Aisha, the first person to make a single sound, starts to laugh. Tears stream down her face as she presses her hands to her head and wheezes until she can't get any air, and Sadaf has to talk her down. Faith crouches beside her.

"He'll come crawling back," Cormac mutters. "I give it a day."

"Not even," Salvador says.

Erin says, "Nick, please talk to them. I can't do this."

Nick bangs his foot against the desk to get everyone's attention. "If anyone else wants to follow him, now's your chance."

Aisha breathes into her hands. I fold my arms over my knees and lean my forehead against the bandages.

"That's what I thought," Nick says. "We are safer staying here than we are wandering out to find a new place. The local Angel encampment doesn't have many soldiers, according to their documents. They're a research facility, not a military base. After a defeat like this, they'll be keeping their distance for a while."

No wonder Nick knows all this. How much did he have to fake to avoid suspicion?

"So what are we going to do?" Micah asks.

That's when Alex, from the other side of the bank, says, "Everyone shut up!" They tear out the cord of their headphones from the radio, and the air suddenly fills with the sound of static and an eerie list of deadpan numbers—*five*, *one*, *eight*, *five*, *six*—over and over. "It's the Vanguard."

Erin slides down from the desk and sprints over. Nick follows close on her heels. Everyone else glances at one another and slowly stands to follow. I prop myself up on the desk.

"You okay?" Salvador asks, stopping beside me. I wave xem ahead with the rest.

Alex picks up the radio and a piece of paper with what looks to be a script. It's Nick's handwriting—looks like there's some kind of radio communication etiquette. "Victor Romeo Delta, Victor Romeo Delta, this is Alpha Lima Charlie, come in, over." Alex pulls away from the mic. "I still say that sounds stupid. It's just us, why do we need these call signs? Is it *lima* as in lima beans?"

"Shh," Nick says.

A rough voice from the other side of the line: "Alpha Lima Charlie, this is Victor Romeo Delta"—VRD, Vanguard—"we read you." I'm in awe of this *thing* Alex has built. It looks like it's running off a modified car battery, turned into a beast of wires. This is Alex's domain; we all know better than to mess with it. "You previously contacted us about a meeting. Is this request still in effect? Over."

Alex hands the mic over to Nick, who straightens up like the Vanguard can see him somehow. "Affirmative. As soon as possible, over."

"We hear you." The disembodied voice rattles the lobby. I press closer, leaning against the teller desk, digging my nails into the wood. "Loud and clear. However, due to recent developments, we will not be returning to the Commons until a month passes or you can provide us with proof of twenty kills. Over."

Twenty. The word hits like a cinderblock, the way a bullet hits the chest, the way Calvin's words jammed into our skulls. *Twenty.*

"Did he just say—" Faith whimpers.

"Motherfucker," Cormac growls. "Mother*fucker.*" He looks at me, and for a moment I think he's going to take the steps between us and slam me into the desk until my skull splits open. But his head drops into his hands, and he sits on the floor and says nothing.

Erin stares at the radio as if that will change what she just heard.

Nick grabs the mic. "Repeat, was that twenty? Over."

"Affirmative. Do you have twenty? Over."

Nick looks at me too.

Erin says, "Jesus Christ, Nick. No. We can't. Please, no."

I whisper, "What?"

Nick swallows hard.

"Nick, *what*?"

"We're not," Nick says. He grabs the mic again. His other hand taps against his leg like he's trying to puncture it. "We do not have twenty. Over."

"Then we will not meet. Contact us only when you do, or when a month has passed. Victor Romeo Delta, over and out."

They're not going to help us.

That's what it takes for the bank to shatter. It's too much. Everything we had burned to the ground. We've lost so many people. We don't have enough food or water to last us a week, let alone a *month*. Someone starts to cry. Erin makes a noise like a wounded animal; Faith, Aisha, and Sadaf are as silent as corpses; and my stomach turns, and bile floods hot and sour up my throat. I stumble out of the lobby, through the window into the courtyard, and drop to my knees before vomiting into the grass.

This is the worst it's ever been. It's *so much*. So much is coming up, clumps of wet flesh, red and black and slimy, leaving trails over my chin and across my hands as I peel them out of my throat. What Seraph has rejected of my insides and replaced with the virus, what it's built from my body, what it's doing on the inside, is all pushing *out*, and I have to dig my fingers into the dirt to keep from ripping the skin off my arms. It's taking me apart. We don't have time. I don't have *time*.

We're fucked, and it's my fault. I led the Angels to them. There's no other reason they would come here if not for *me.*

Nick comes up to the window and hops out into the grass, standing as if blocking me from the inscrutable gaze of the road past the broken fence. As if he couldn't spend a single moment longer in that damn building, just like I couldn't; just, Jesus Christ, I'm so tired. *I can't, I'm sorry, I'm so sorry. I brought the Angels here. I did this.*

Nick says nothing, and neither do I. He just crouches and pushes my hair out of my eyes. I groan and cough and throw up again.

It's almost like divine justice. I steal from the ALC to give to Theo, and God sends Angels to ruin it all. I visit Theo, and everything goes to hell, the way it always has, the way it always will. I should have learned when he hurt me. I should have *learned.* I was supposed to be good, and I ruined everything because I was lovesick and *selfish.*

But it was a little perfect, wasn't it? I made it back just as the Angels arrived—why else would the Grace still have been outside? If I hadn't left Theo when I had, I don't think I would have seen the Grace. We would have lost so many more people. What if I had stayed with him the way he asked? How many people would have died? How many more . . .

Wait.

Theo didn't want me to leave that night. He was still praying. How could he have joined the pilgrimage if he was exiled from the death squads, how could he have run away from the Angels when he spent so much of his life prepared to die for them, how could—

How—

He knew.

That motherfucker.

He knew. The Flood burns and Seraph screams, painful and red hot and furious. *He knew, he knew, HE KNEW.*

HE LIED.

HE DID THIS.

Chapter 22

Upon the wicked He will rain fiery coals and burning sulfur; a scorching wind will be their lot.

—Psalm 11:6

***This is what I was made for. Romans 12:19—Dearly beloved,** avenge not yourselves, but rather give place unto wrath: for it is written, Vengeance is mine; I will repay, saith the Lord.* The Angels were made to be the servants of God, but I am the *wrath*, the *flaming sword*, the *six-winged beast*.

Vengeance is mine; I will repay, saith the Lord.

As soon as the sun sets, I slip from the bank and into the streets, wrapped in bandages and every stitch of black clothing I could dig from the ashes. They reek of charred bodies and too much smoke. I want Theo to smell it on me.

My hand twitches as if Seraph is an electric current tightening my muscles, the way mad scientists make dead dogs move. Black sludge trickles down my nose and over my lips, and I throw my mask into the gutter. I wonder for half a second what part of me that used to be, but I can't keep a thought in my head besides what Theo's face will look like when it's smashed to bloody pieces.

I should have seen this coming. I should have known. I tear off my bandages and dig my fingers into the flesh peeling up from my arm. Pieces come off in long, wet strips. The same black-veined raw flesh as my face, the dissolved inside of my throat, the slurry of my stomach cavity. Theo is going to see me, he is going to see the *real* me, and I am going to kill him. I'll bring the Vanguard all the proof they need. I'll bring them Theo's skull and as many heads as I can fucking get.

Leave room for His wrath. *I am His wrath made flesh.*

Seraph and my feet know the path to Reformation Faith Evangelical Church better than I do. A flock of birds sits on the power lines, flapping their wings at one another as they fight for space like crows on the culling grounds. The Angels thought they could take the ALC from me. That without the ALC, I would have nowhere else to run except back to Theo. I'll give them what they want. I will come back to him, and I will make them regret it.

My jaw aches and cramps, the muscles moving on their own. My next breath comes out in a snarl. Inhuman and so deep in my chest, deeper than I've ever felt anything. I pass the bodega and the cat sits in the window, tail flicking anxiously. Something cracks in my gum line, and I pull out an old tooth. There are new teeth there, uneven in my mouth like shattered glass.

I will hunt the Angels who did this. The ALC will be safe.

Everything hurts. I want to take handfuls of my face and pull it off. I'm halfway to Reformation, I think. I only stopped once. When the pain got too bad. When I couldn't keep my eyes open anymore. I pressed my head against a wall to push back whatever was breaking it apart from the inside and screamed. I thought my skull was going to split, and so much more rotten shit came up, and now there's something else sitting heavy in my mouth. A tongue like something alive anchored in my throat, threatening to fill me up, falling out in a rope of flesh. I have so many teeth. My mouth opens all the way to my ears. It *hurts*.

I look like the billions of dead with the Flood tearing them to pieces. I look like the people who didn't survive. I look the way I should, and Seraph isn't even done with me yet. Nick and Erin will have to tell everybody when I get back, but that's fine. That's fine, because after I do this, they'll understand. They'll forgive me. It'll be okay. I can fix this.

On the wind, I hear prayer.

I don't feel the stab of panic in my chest like I should. Like I used to. Instead I stop, lifting my head to the breeze, letting it wash over me.

"Lord, we praise You and thank You this glorious night!"

Death squads usually don't work in the dark. They've been on the hunt; they've been chasing their prey for hours. They're high on the kill and lost in their purpose.

"We cleanse in Your blessed name, we fight in Your blessed name, we bleed and die in *Your blessed name*!" The words slur together. A Heaven-drunk chorus of soldiers howls, frothing at the mouth under their masks. I press myself into the shadows, white-hot fury and pain rising through my bones until I feel like my body is going to come apart at the seams. "O God, accept this pound of flesh as our love!"

A death squad in my path to Reformation, standing around a pair of crumpled, broken bodies. They are beaten and crushed. Their deaths were not quick. It was a game.

"Ashes to ashes," one of the soldiers says, "dust to dust, abyss to abyss."

"Rot in Hell," says another. "Fucking heretics. *Fucking rats*."

Seraph spreads its wings of fire in the hollow expanse of my chest, where my insides used to be.

Walking away from them is a mercy they don't deserve.

Vengeance is mine; I will repay, saith the Lord.

NICHOLAS

Chapter 23

These feathers are a promise. Do you promise to do the works of God and light His fires? Do you promise to be His hands on this earth, no matter the cost? Keep your promise close. Remember that it can be taken away.

—The general of New Nazareth

Nick wakes up, and Benji isn't there.

He and Benji turned in a few hours ago, together. Together. That was the key word. Benji was sick, and Nick was going to keep an eye on him. He wasn't leaving his friend alone. Benji was his friend, and they'd hurt each other, and now they were trying to make it right. Even if he couldn't get words to come out the way they should, even if saying sorry didn't come naturally to either of them, that was something he knew he could do.

But now Benji isn't here. Nick reaches over to the balled-up jacket on the other side of the copy room that Benji had been using as a pillow. It's still warm. He hasn't been gone long.

Maybe he got sick again? Nick grabs a bottle of water and heads to the courtyard, practicing what he's going to say when he finds him. He can't say, *Are you sick?* because that'll be obvious. Maybe, *Are you okay?* But the answer has been "No" for so long, what's the point in that?

Benji. So instead he says the name over and over. Not Seraph. Benji. He, him, his, not *it*. Benji's real name comes so much easier than any other name ever did, and it is a relief to let go of the wrong pronouns. The actual ones are a blessing because they are the truth, and as much time as Nick spends lying, the truth is beautiful.

How could he ever have thought he could turn Benji over to the Vanguard? The moment he looked Benji in the eyes and refused, said they didn't have the ears, said they couldn't afford the Vanguard's help, it was a relief like drinking holy water. He wouldn't have to be a monster. It was proof he still knew the value of a human life, no matter how much the Angels tried to beat that out of him.

Fuck them.

There are some people awake in the lobby when Nick passes through. Sarmat is on guard duty, face smushed into his hand. Probably waiting for Calvin to come back. Nick will offer to let Salvador and Aisha decide if Calvin is allowed to step foot within the group again; it's only fitting.

"Have you seen Benji?" Nick asks Sarmat.

"Benji?" Sarmat holds up a hand to his chest. "Brown hair, yea big?"

"Yes."

"I think so?" Sarmat points in the direction Nick just came from. The window to the courtyard, as suspected. "Didn't look like he was in a good mood, though. Everything okay?"

"It's fine," Nick lies. "Thank you."

But the courtyard is empty. He checks the shadows by the grave, ducks inside the ALC, even stops by the Grace corpse. Benji isn't there.

That's how Nick finds himself on the sidewalk just beyond the broken fence, rolling his beads between his hands. Maybe Benji's just going to the bathroom. It's no big deal. Benji's not a little kid. Well, he's little, but he's not a kid, not really. He's practically grown in the grand scheme of things. Benji is allowed to do what he wants.

God. He deserved it when Benji yelled at him. What kind of person is he anyway, keeping a sick boy tucked away as a possible sacrifice, a living backup plan? Pretending Benji isn't a person when so many people have done the same to him? Erin was right, like she *always* is. Hadn't he spent years begging to be seen as anything but a horrific collection of fuckups? That he wasn't just the mistakes he was made of and his parents' condescending pity and God, *I'm a person, I'm a person too*?

Nick almost laughs. He doesn't laugh much, because it

comes out weird, but he does because there's no one around to listen. What the fuck is wrong with him? *What the fuck is wrong with him*—

In the distance, at the far end of the street, right where his vision ends: movement.

Nick stops. Every nerve narrows to that single pinprick.

A dark form stumbling away.

Nick runs back to the bank for exactly the amount of time it takes to grab a pistol, an extra mask, and some bobby pins.

He doesn't know much about people, but he knows a hell of a lot about anger. He knows what anger will make people do.

God, he knows that much.

The monster Nick finds halfway between the ALC and Reformation Faith Evangelical Church does not look much like Benji at all.

Consciously, Nick—hiding in the shadow of a pickup truck and digging his nails into the corner of his eye to calm down, just *calm down*—knows this thing is Benji. This thing has Benji's hair, Benji's tiny body, Benji's clothes. This thing looks like Sister Kipling took out all of Benji's insides and sewed a wolf under his skin, and it's only now that Nick is seeing it for the first time.

It's not him, but it *is*, and Nick is transfixed.

Benji's eyes are locked on the death squad just yards from him, ghosts with blood on their robes praying to God. Their guns are down. Their eyes are closed in the shining glory of the Lord, the invisible light beaming in their chests in the darkness of night. Nick knows the type. Their job is to flush out survivors like vermin. They're soldiers who can't be trusted with anything else, the ones too bloodthirsty to guard caravans, the gates, or the bridge. The ones New Nazareth can afford to lose, the ones they unleash like rabid dogs to clean up what the Flood, mass shootings, executions, and suicide attacks missed on Judgment Day and every day after.

No matter how expendable these Angels are, Benji can't take six full-grown men on his own, he *can't*—

As soon as the thought crosses Nick's mind, Benji lunges from the shadows and sinks his teeth into a soldier's throat.

Everything else turns off like a switch.

Nick lifts his pistol. At least the Angels taught him something.

CRACK. He drops the Angel closest to him—aiming between the shoulders, right above where the spine emerges from the Kevlar vest under the robe. The bullet casing spits from the gun and hits the ground with a distinctive *clink*.

Nick counts his rounds. One.

The man with teeth in his neck gurgles, and Benji rears back with a mouthful of flesh, a spray of red following in an arc through the space between them.

This is the easy part. This is what Nick is good at.

CRACK. Clink. Two. The bullet hits a thigh and distracts the soldier just enough for Benji to grab him by the face and smash him into the brick storefront. Nick counts the shells and not the bodies because it's what the general taught him, saying the number should be the same anyway.

Nick counts Benji's "shells" too. Three, four. Benji isn't tall enough to reach any important vein in the next neck, so he tears open a forearm instead, right where the brachial artery splits. The amount of blood is impressive. Five. A bullet to the side of the head. Six. A hand shoved into a mouth and the jaw snapped like a tree limb cracking from the trunk. The Angel screams and chokes, and Benji tears it off the rest of the way. The Angel stumbles once, twice, grasping for his face, before finally falling. He coughs and writhes, and Benji just watches.

Then, after the Angel gasps one last time, blessed quiet.

The world creeps back in, past the lockdown clamping Nick's senses, the adrenaline easing its grip. The rustle of debris, the flutter of robes, his own breath.

It's him and Benji now.

Benji isn't what he used to be. He stares at the bodies on the ground like he's trying to figure out where the bullet wounds on the corpses came from through the haze of anger. Thin threads of entrails drip from his mouth. The blood on his face catches the starlight.

What is Nick supposed to say? What kind of words work here? Will Benji even understand?

Benji rolls his shoulders, and his body cracks like the wolf is trying to claw its way out. One of the Angels wheezes as his weight forces air out of his dead lungs. It smells like copper, gunpowder, and shit.

Nick starts forward. Farther into the road. Between the cars. Onto the curb.

He holds out a hand and whispers, "Benji."

When Benji turns to face him, it's almost lazily. Slowly, showing every single jagged tooth in his open-wound mouth. As if he knew Nick was there the whole time and was just waiting for him to get too close. His tongue—the length of a forearm, longer—snakes out of his mouth, testing the air, jaw unhinging and the glint of the moon traveling up the length of his serrated fangs. He looks like he plunged half his face into acid. When a piece of flesh falls, Nick can't tell if it was in his mouth or part of it.

Nick says, "It's me."

Benji replies with an ear-shattering shriek.

Nick is slammed against the sidewalk and into the wet, heavy bodies of the dead Angels, and Benji is on top of him. His gun arm is pinned, and those teeth are *inches* from his face, Benji's tongue dripping with spit, gore stretching between his fangs, fingers digging into Nick's shoulders hard enough to bruise, to break skin.

Nick does nothing. He does not breathe. He does not blink. If he moves a single muscle, Benji is going to tear out his jugular. Those teeth will go in like knives, and he will bleed out onto the sidewalk before he can think to staunch the wound—unrestricted blood loss from a major vein leads to unconsciousness in seconds and death within minutes. Benji's weight presses him into the ribs of a corpse, into a squelching mess of shredded insides and robes that reek of bleach, sweat, and gore.

The next noise Benji makes is not a shriek. It's a whimper. It crawls up from his throat like a dying thing.

Those eyes are still his. Seraph hasn't touched them. They're a little red, strained, but they're his.

Nick is about to do something stupid.

He whispers, "Your hair is in your face."

Benji does not kill him.

All he does is blink.

Nick lifts his arm and presses it flat against Benji's chest, just enough pressure to push him back. Benji shuffles away, eyes wide, and Nick manages to sit. Benji's fingers leave red marks on the concrete. He's so small. He's so light. Black liquid trickles from his nose, and Nick can't imagine Benji has any insides left to lose.

"It's me," Nick says. "I'm here now. It's okay." It's not a lie. He makes a mental list of everything they'll have to do to get Benji into the bank without raising suspicion. Clean the blood off his face. Get him into new clothes and a mask. Soothe the curled-up cramping thing his hands are doing. Cover his arms.

Just make sure he gets home.

One last push, and Benji falls back to the ground. Nick takes the last of the bobby pins from his pocket, selects exactly two, and clips a stubborn clump of Benji's hair away from his forehead. It's like trying to fix the Hoover Dam with duct tape, but Benji's shoulders sag, and another sad little noise crawls up his throat, and his eyes finally focus.

"Nick?" he whispers.

They've lost the Vanguard, but Nick hasn't lost Benji. There is no way in hell Nick could have brought himself to give Benji over. How had he even thought he could? God, what is wrong with him? How could he?

"There you go," Nick says. "Thought we lost you for a second." Even though he wants to cry, *Thank God*, *thank God*, *thank God*, and Nick hasn't thanked God for anything in years.

BENJAMIN

CHAPTER 24

Lesbian, gay, bisexual, transgender, and other queer and questioning youth often face unique challenges in finding community. Whether you are helping build an accepting family at home or searching for one who will support you when others don't, the Acheson LGBTQ+ Center is here for you.

—The Acheson LGBTQ+ Center official website

Nick takes me back to the bank. I remember that much.

He gives me a bottle of water and makes me drink as much as I can. He wipes my face, puts a new mask over my mouth, and gets me a change of clothes. I'm too tired to register the embarrassment of just being in my sports bra and boxers, open wounds creeping across my stomach and thighs. Nick doesn't linger on my body. I am reminded of Jesus and the leper, and Nick helps by not turning away in disgust.

When I'm finally presentable, my crumbling body hidden under bandages and clean clothes, Nick boosts me through the bank window and sits me on the floor of the copy room. I'm so lightheaded, I'm going to pass out. I need to say something, but how do I even start? *I made a bunch of really, really bad decisions and this is all my fault, please don't be mad? I am divine retribution, but I'm also just a scared little kid, and God, why would you call me your friend?* I grind my jaw and try to breathe past my massive tongue. I'm not getting enough air. Or maybe I'm hyperventilating.

Nick crouches beside me and says, "What happened," and it's not a question because it doesn't need to be.

I open my mouth to speak but can't.

Nick watches for a moment, then scratches that little spot under his eye. "It's okay," he says. "I have trouble talking sometimes too." He takes off his jacket and wraps it around my shoulders. "I'll be right back."

I don't want him to go. I reach for him, but he pushes my hand away.

"It won't take long," he says, and leaves.

His coat smells like him. It smells like all of us, like sweat, musty closets, and smoke, but it smells like *him*. Like he's spent too much time with mothballs and old paper. I bury my face in the sleeve.

Nick comes back with a plastic grocery bag that rattles when he moves.

"I know it's immature of me," he says, sitting across from me and unpacking the bag. It's full of beads. Bright plastic pony beads, all the colors of the rainbow and then some. He sets one large container between us and clicks it open. "But when I have a meltdown, I make these. It helps." Out comes a handful of string. "I'm glad it survived the fire."

He takes the bead lizard out of his pocket. The one with the gaudy yellow and blue beads and with bite marks on the toes.

"I can show you," he says. "If you want."

He doesn't have to. He doesn't have to do anything for me, not after what I brought down on us. We lost the Vanguard, we lost so many people, we're *fucked.* But Nick just pulls out a length of string and cuts it with his teeth.

"Pick out some beads."

I half-heartedly pick a few random ones—green, red, whatever—but eventually I find ones that look like the trans flag.

Nick shakes his head. "Other colors," he says.

I narrow my eyes at him. He pulls a half-finished lizard from the bag with the same pastel pinks, blues, and whites.

"Already working on it," he says.

I pick out a rainbow instead. He holds out his work to show me what he's doing.

"You put on one of these," he says, stringing a red bead, "and then double thread it. Like this." He hands me the awkward mess of beads and string. "You do the next two. And don't forget the eyes."

My hands shake, but after a try or two, I get the next row. When I reach the toes, though, I get frustrated trying to make them look right. Nick tells me to stop pulling the string so taut. I can't. There's anger curling up in my hollow chest, but it isn't Seraph's anger; it isn't the white-hot violent thing that made me tear out those throats and slam Nick into the bodies. It's—it's helpless. I never asked for this. I never wanted to be an Angel, and I never wanted to be their martyr. I'm a *kid*, and all I ever do is *ruin things*.

The ALC would be better off if they'd never brought me in.

I yank the string so hard, it snaps. The beads tumble to the floor. Nick sucks in a breath. I can't look at him. I focus on the rough carpet speckled with all kinds of colors, dizzy from the heat, exhaustion, and dehydration, desperate to think of anything but him and what I've done.

After a moment, Nick takes the broken string out of my hand and gives me another.

"Do you want me to start it again?" he asks.

I shake my head and pick the beads up off the floor.

It doesn't matter what I asked for. There's nothing we can do about what's already happened. I was raised by Angels. The world ended. They got into my head and turned me into *this*. That may not be my fault, but it is my responsibility. I'll take the blame for what I've done and do everything I can to fix what I didn't. If I can fix this, I have to. If I can find a way to keep my friends safe, I will.

That's what it means to be good.

This time, when I get to the lizard's toes, I've gotten the hang of it. Nick finishes his trans lizard and ties off the end.

"Here," he says, holding it out to me. "You can have it if you tell me where you were going."

"You drive a hard bargain." My words are wet and raspy but still recognizable as words. Just like I have a particularly bad sore throat or lost my voice screaming.

"Where were you going?"

I can't say it. I should, I *know*, but—"Out."

"Why?"

"Does it matter?"

Nick says, "It does."

I need to tell them. I have to tell them.

I can't do this alone.

"Can we get Erin?" I say. "I really, *really* need to tell you guys something."

The only place I can talk is the roof of the ALC, where nobody but the birds will hear when I inevitably lose it. Ash streaks up the sides of the building. The night-shift sniper has been sent down to get some rest. Our footprints track soot in the gravel. The moon is high in the sky, Erin has her hair up in a silk scarf, and I'm still wearing Nick's jacket.

The city is beautiful. I stare at it instead of Erin and Nick standing close together, watching me.

I've been up here with Nick before, but it's so different at night. The empty, still city. Perfectly quiet, perfectly dead. It'll take decades for this world to start breaking down, centuries for it to fall, and eons for Earth to swallow every bit of it and wipe all trace of us from the world.

"Are you okay?" Erin asks. "I don't mean—" She gestures helplessly at my face. "Because I know that isn't—it can't—"

I say, "I fucked up."

Erin laughs a little. "What?" She looks to Nick, who says nothing, and back to me. "If it's about the Flood, we can figure something out. If you want to tell everybody, we can do that. They'll accept it, I promise. Nothing bad is going to happen."

God, I need to *tell everyone*. "It's not that. I've been lying to you."

It all comes crashing out.

My voice is high and desperate. The words tumble out like prayers, or maybe begging, or maybe they're the same thing. I do not leave out anything. Finding Theo at Reformation and how happy I was to see my fiancé again. The food and masks I stole for him. How I went back to him. How terrified I was when he asked me to stay. When I realized it was him that brought fire down on the ALC, and it's all my fault.

My fault. I did this to them.

I stop, eyes burning. Erin holds her stomach like she might be sick. Nick just stares. Nothing else, just staring. I hate it. The silence hurts like a gaping wound filled with every little thing in this city: the quiet murmurs of the bank; the howling of feral dogs; a gunshot far, far in the distance. The smallest things that let us know we're not the only ones left alive.

They should be doing something, *anything*. Walking away, yelling at me, dragging me to the side of the building to throw me off. They could do anything, and I'd understand. Anything except just stand there.

A terrible whining noise rises up in my throat, small and pathetic like a kicked animal.

"I know I should say sorry," I whimper, "but that's not going to make this right. There's nothing I can do to make it okay, but I want to *do* something to fix it anyway. Which is why I wanted to talk to you. Because I trust you, and if anyone can figure out what I can do, it's you."

Nothing. Oh God, there's nothing. James 5:16—*Confess your faults one to another, and pray for another, that ye may be healed*. I don't feel healed. I don't feel anything, I just feel hollow.

It's Erin who speaks first.

"Oh my God," she says. "Benji."

I whisper, "I know."

"I mean, you're right," she says. "Sorry isn't going to change anything. But I still want to hear it, you know?"

It doesn't want to come up. I dig my feet into the gravel of the roof and force it out the way I pulled flesh from my throat. "I'm sorry."

"Thank you." She doesn't say it's okay because it's not. I want to look away, but I have to face what I've done. "I don't—I don't know what else to say. This is . . ."

"A lot," I finish.

"Yeah."

Nick pulls out his notepad, the same notepad he had in the meeting room, and a pen from his pocket.

He starts to write.

"How sure are you that Theodore knew?" he asks, not looking up.

"I was headed out to confront him about it. I'd bet a lot of things on it, but . . ." Like I wasn't heading out to tear him to pieces. "Why?"

"Because *I'm* sure." Nick crumples up a sheet and throws it on the ground. "That son of a bitch."

"Did you know him?"

"Well enough." Of course he did. There's no way soldiers the same age wouldn't know each other. "I have an idea, but I need you to trust me. Do you?"

"Yes." I don't have to think about it for a second. "Just tell me what to do."

"If New Nazareth wants you so badly," he says, "that they're willing to come all the way out here and risk an entire squad to force you back to them, then we're going to give them everything they asked for." He jabs his pen against the paper. "And we are going to make them regret it."

Erin looks over his shoulder at the notepad. Her eyes flash. "You *brilliant bastard*."

In the middle of the night, bathed only in the moon and stars, we go through the plan.

I am going to walk into the Angels' arms. I am going to repent, twist them around my finger, and then turn the Graces against them like the tide. I will rip salvation from their hands because that is what it means for them to suffer. The *good* the world needs right now is teeth and claws and a taste for blood.

I am going to shatter them, and I *will* be the vengeance of God, I *will.*

And the Watch is going to get me out of it alive. They are the only people I could ever trust to do this.

Acheson, Pennsylvania, will be free. We won't need the Vanguard. There will be nothing to run from. The city will be ours, and we will survive the summer when we don't have to hide like mice under the floorboards.

"They'll hold absolution down by the river," I say, pointing at the western edge of Nick's crude map of New Nazareth, right at the edge of their territory. "It'll probably be the second day because there's no way they're risking not locking me down as quickly as they can." I know how Mom works. I know what she'll do to me—but I have to suffer it for this to work. "Is there anything you can do with that?"

Nick squints. "I think so. That's close enough to the road. We'll position there and get you out as soon as possible."

I'm going to make this right. I'm going to fix it. The ALC will be safe, and the Angels will never hurt us again.

All I have to do is walk right into the mouth of Hell.

CHAPTER 25

Do not be afraid. Have faith. What is right will be done.

—*The Truth* by High Reverend Father Ian Clevenger

"You wasted backpack space for a bottle of . . ." Faith squints. "What is that?"

"It's Brunello," Cormac says, as if offended that Faith can't recognize it on sight. "Classic vintage, 2019."

"Just say *old-ass wine*, nerd," Aisha says. "Let me see it."

"Absolutely not. This cost four hundred dollars."

Salvador puts up a hand from where xe's sprawled on the carpet. "I think we're in a situation where eating the rich is not only allowed but acceptable, encouraged, and part of a well-rounded diet. Essential vitamins and minerals, you know."

"We hardly counted as rich," Cormac says.

"You have a four-hundred-dollar bottle of grape juice. I'm literally going to kill you."

Cormac wrinkles his nose. "I hate you all. Do you want any or not?"

The lot of us—the Watch, minus Nick—sit in a back corner of the bank in the late afternoon. Sunlight comes in through the high, dusty windows, dappling the carpet in gold and making everything just a little too warm. Our exhaustion seeps into the walls, deadens our eyes as we try to laugh and pretend we aren't terrified of Angels, starvation, and the summer. Of everything now.

I want to tell them that there's a plan. That they're going to be okay, that we all are. I want to wipe the pained looks off their faces, the ones creeping behind their masks even as they act like they're smiling. The looks of people who are realizing that in a month, we will probably be dead, and there's not much they can do.

But I need a little more time with them before everything changes.

"I thought you were saving it for a special occasion," Aisha says.

Cormac stares at the bottle, its beautiful black glass wrapped in gold lettering. "I was. But it almost burned with the rest of my stuff, and wine is shit after it gets too hot." He pulls out his knife and pops the cork with it. "And, you know, we're fucked! Might as well get drunk. You guys better thank me."

He drinks straight from the bottle before grudgingly

handing it to Faith, who takes a large swallow to the hooting of Aisha and Salvador. Cormac grumbles that you're supposed to savor the taste of something like this, even if it isn't as good as it should be. Aisha makes a show of taking a dainty sip with her pinkie finger up, and Salvador somehow manages to drink without picking xyr head off the floor.

Xe taps the bottle against my leg. "Hey, short stuff. Want some?"

I shake my head. It'd mean taking my mask down, and besides, I've never actually had alcohol before. This doesn't seem like a great time to start. "I'm good."

Cormac wrinkles his nose. "You sound awful."

"Seriously," Aisha says. "Everything okay?"

I try to force a smile, but as soon as it reaches my eyes, I find I'm not faking it at all. They're my friends. I don't have to fake it for them.

"I'm fine," I say. "Just trying not to think about, you know, everything."

"Don't I know it," Aisha says. She takes my hand and turns it over. Thankfully, the blisters from the fire overshadow the growing discoloration of my fingers, and my arms are *very* hidden. "If you want something to take your mind off it, I've been wanting to do someone's nails for a while. It won't be too feminine if you don't want it to be. I just need a test subject."

"I want my nails done," Salvador whines.

"The offer's only open for Benji. *He* didn't steal my favorite skirt last summer." I lean my head against Aisha's shoulder and shoot Salvador a petty look. Xe pouts. "And he doesn't like coffee, so he needs something good in his life."

"Yeah, like a guy is going to want his nails done," Cormac says, saving me from having to turn down Aisha. I won't have fingernails soon. "Learn how to give stick-and-poke tattoos, that's way cooler."

Salvador gets an empty water bottle from xyr bag and pours some of the wine into it. Cormac scoffs. "Here," xe says, pushing the water bottle into my hand. "For later. If you'll actually drink it, you picky fuck."

I take it carefully. When it sloshes, it leaves purple marks against the thin plastic.

Friends.

"Thanks," I manage.

"No problem. And get some sleep or something."

"I think I have some cough drops?" Faith says. "If they're not expired."

I would cry if I could, so my body kicks up the closest thing it can get, where my eyes burn and my chest hitches. I laugh like I might be able to hide it. "I'm good. Really. Wait, you've got some wine on your lip—no, over there, just—here, let me get it."

I sit with the bottle between my knees while the rest of them bicker, the lighthearted jabbing and snickering that comes with being so close in a place like this. Alex wanders over and steals the wine from Cormac, only to hack in disgust when it hits their tongue. When Sadaf comes to kiss the top of Aisha's head, Salvador offers her a drink too, leading to a bout of awkward spluttering when Sadaf reminds xem she's Muslim.

"Besides," she says, resting her cheek against Aisha's temple. "It's nasty."

There's a knock on the wall beside us. We look up, almost guiltily, like we've been caught slacking off on the job. But it's just Nick, as calm and quiet as always. I have no idea how he does it, how he stays so still when the world falls apart around him.

"Hey," Salvador says, holding up the bottle to him. "Want some?"

"No," Nick says. "Benji, can we talk?"

Right. It's happening. Maybe I can convince Nick to wait—to let me stay here a little longer—but that would be selfish. Everyone turns to me, confused frowns pulling at their masks.

"Sorry, guys," I say. "Gotta go."

"Wait." Cormac catches my bottle and takes the wine back from Salvador. He adds a little more and tosses it to me, with what I think is a mumbled *yeet* under his breath. "If you're not going to drink it, at least give it to someone who will."

When—if—I survive this, if they're still here, I am never leaving them again.

We meet in the copy room. I set the plastic bottle of wine on the fax machine because my hands are trembling, and I don't want to make a mess.

Nick says, "Erin will be here soon. She got tied up with Micah."

"Yeah. Okay." I take off my mask and shove it into my back pocket. My tongue writhes in my throat, and I wipe rot off my chin. "They're cute together."

Nick takes the wine from the fax machine, sniffs it, and takes a cautious sip. His own mask rests under his chin, showing off his squishy teenage cheeks and sharp nose, his tired eyes and hard jaw. The things that made me tell myself I was betrothed and always would be.

It doesn't matter now, does it? After what Theo did?

Funny how I'll go back to him after he hurts me, but as soon as he hurts the people I care about, he's dead to me. If only I had seen it from the start.

"Did you try this?" Nick asks, holding up the wine to the light.

"No," I admit. "You can have it if you want."

"Fine. Trade."

In exchange, he gives me the trans bead lizard he finished last night. I cradle it in my hands, admiring the pale pink, baby blue, and gentle white. All I can manage is "thank you," even though I want to say, *This is the first time I've gotten to hold something with my colors.*

For some reason, a small laugh bubbles up from my chest. With my ruined mouth, it doesn't sound much like laughter at all, but Nick seems to know what it is because his face screws up and he says, "What?"

"Nothing, I just . . ."

I'm going to say it. I'm going to say it out loud. Fuck my betrothal, fuck Theo, fuck everything else.

I say, "I was just thinking about kissing you."

Nick says, slowly, "Why?"

Why? Because he's handsome, because we've been through things that make me feel like I've known him forever, because he's the most stable thing in my life right now. Because I want something *good* for once. Because the idea of leaving him terrifies me so much more than it ever did to leave Theo, and that has to mean something, right?

"Because I want to," I say.

Nick's throat bobs. "I don't think—"

"And I know it wouldn't work because, look at me, right? And you don't like being touched. I respect that. Kissing is really weird if you think about it too hard. I just thought you should know how I feel before all this happens. In case I don't get to see you again."

He doesn't meet my eyes.

I should have kept my mouth shut.

"I made it weird," I say. "Didn't I?"

"I don't like kissing," Nick says.

I'm going at this from the wrong angle. He's focusing on the kissing, not everything around it. Not what I actually need to say. "Nick, I'm using kissing you as shorthand. For the fact that I like you."

"Oh," Nick says. And then, *"Oh."* And then, "I don't know why you—" and a few other half-hearted, aborted protests that make an ache in my chest grow heavier and heavier before finally he lands on, "I don't know how this works."

I shake my head. "It's fine. We don't have to talk about it."

"No." He takes a half step away and taps the back of his neck with his palm like he's trying to knock his thoughts loose. He says, "I don't know how to tell if I like someone. I don't know how it works, and I don't want to be wrong." He says, "I don't know why you would like me, I don't understand." He says, "There are no rules for this. It scares me."

I never thought Nick could be scared of anything. "Really?"

"I don't want to be wrong. People get hurt when I'm wrong."

"Nick, that's not—"

"Salvador nearly died because of me," Nick says. "Because I made a mistake. Because I was wrong about something." I see the scars again—up and down xyr face, warping skin, painful—and the hurt in Nick's voice is enough to answer every question I've ever had about xe's old wounds. "So don't. Don't say that."

I swallow, hard. "I'm tough enough to handle it. I swear."

"But what if I lose you?"

Now I'm echoing him. Oh. *Oh.* What if he loses me. What if I lose him. What if all of this goes to hell, and we end up with bullets in our heads, and the Angels standing over our bodies. What if it all goes *right*, but I turn into a monster that isn't worth loving. What if all of it is for nothing?

"Then we can figure it out if I come back," I say. "When we don't have to worry about that anymore."

"Okay," he says. "Okay," and he reaches for me and pulls me in until our foreheads touch. Until our noses bump together, and his breath warms my cheek. God, he's so *warm*.

This is the last time I will be safe for days, but it might as well be forever. I'm terrified. I could stay here for the rest of time, if the world would just let me.

"When," Nick says. "When you come back."

When I come back, we can talk about it. We can face whatever the hell this is. We can figure it out.

When I come back.

"Okay."

"Are you ready?" he asks.

"Fuck no."

"Nobody in their right mind would be. Here." He takes a piece of paper out of his pocket and slips it into mine. "Promise you won't read this until later."

I wonder if it's the *I'm sorry* again. "I promise."

The door creaks open, and we step away from each other. Stale air rushes into the space between us. I have to keep myself from reaching for him, from pulling him back to me, because it feels so empty without him.

Erin steps into the room, face flushed and eyes wide.

"All right," she says. "It's now or never."

Nick offers me an awkward, perfect smile before he puts up his mask. I smile back, the best I can, and step out into the hall.

The three of us walk to the lobby. I swear the hall lasts forever. My mask is down. My sleeves rolled up. What's left of my heart beating *holy*, *holy*, *holy* in my throat.

We step inside.

John 8:32.

The truth will set you free.

"Uh," I say. "Hey, guys." People turn, confused to hear someone raise their voice in the quiet. Then they realize what they're seeing, all at once, and the silence could kill. "Hi again."

It's not enough. All the planning in the world, all of Erin's reassurance and Nick's control, and it's not enough.

The quiet goes on too long. The staring. The terror lodged in my lungs. It's long enough that I wonder if Seraph is playing tricks on me, more than the feathers at the edges of my sight and the tooth buried in the courtyard. It has frozen this moment and is forcing me to take it all in, to recognize the fear in my friends' eyes. Cormac reaching for a gun that isn't by his side anymore. Aisha's back pressed against the wall, trembling.

I promised I would be good. I should have known it wouldn't be enough.

It isn't until Carly audibly whimpers that I realize it isn't Seraph. It's just us, what's left of us, all terrified of one another. Nick puts a hand on my shoulder and squeezes. I can feel the tension in his fingers, like he's putting everything he has into this little touch.

"Easy," he says. I'm not sure if he's talking to me or everyone else. "Everything's okay. Benji, go ahead."

I don't know what to say. What is there to say at all?

"I, um." I am a monster standing among the living, a boy made of raw meat and dying flesh. "It's me."

Sadaf saves me.

She springs off the floor and runs to me, skirts billowing out in a pastel cloud. Aisha tries to grab her, then Faith, but she slips between their fingers and comes to a stop just inches away. Her soft hands clasp what's left of my cheeks. Her eyes *glimmer.*

"I knew it!" she cries in triumph. "I knew something was going on! I didn't think it could be the Flood, since it was moving too slowly, but I knew it had to be something—oh, are you contagious?" I shake my head. "Didn't think so. You wouldn't do that." My chest twists painfully. She has no idea. "Sarmat, Aisha, come look at this!"

That's what breaks the spell of terror. People come up, one by one, slowly. Faith whispers, "Does it hurt?" Salvador picks me up off the ground in a hug, saying, "You freaky bastard!" Erin leans against the wall, slumping with relief. Nick smiles down at his feet. One of his hands is going *tp tp tp*, but there's a happiness to it I've never seen before.

"So," Alex says, watching me cautiously from beside the radio. "Why are you telling us this now? What's wrong?"

"I'm, uh." Sadaf leans forward to watch how my mouth works when I speak. "I'm turning into an abomination. A Grace. I—I grew up in New Nazareth. I was an Angel." Cormac's eyes snap to Nick, but he does nothing. A few people glance away, like they can't bear to look at me while I speak. Like I'm something they have to reconcile now. "I ran away, but before I did, they infected me with a special strain of the Flood that's turning me into a Grace called Seraph. It, uh, I can actually control other Graces, talk to them, ask them to help. So Seraph is really, really important to the Angels. And they're not going to stop tearing apart the city until they get me back."

A deep breath. A steadying one, long and slow.

"So I'm going to go back to New Nazareth," I say, "and if you'll have me—if you'll help me—I'm going to burn it to the ground."

Quiet.

Look at these people, the silence says, *who have rejected you. You were wrong.*

But Sadaf's smile still gleams in her eyes. Aisha totters to her feet, pressing both hands to her mask. Salvador begins to laugh, and it is infectious. Cormac claps a hand on my shoulder, and Faith yanks me away to wrap me in her arms, and I am not alone, I am not alone.

"Looks like we can't get rid of you that easy," Alex sighs.

I will be good. I will make the Angels fucking suffer.

THEODORE

Chapter 26

Do you believe in God?

—I do, please stop, there's so much blood

Theo prays at the foot of the nest, and the words come out rotten; less *words* and more stomach acid or whatever terrible thing is forcing itself up this time. It's taken root in his organs, festering with maggots and eating him alive. No matter how hard he pulls, he just can't get the sick parts *out*.

He's ruined everything. Like he always does.

So many people have been sacrificed to get Benji back. Squad Rapture, cut down by the heretics days ago; Squad Dominion, who haven't returned from their hunt and probably never will; Squad Crucifix, who Sister Kipling says might still be out there, but there's no use in hoping.

The children, clergy, and everyone that day at Reformation. And all for what? For Theo to *fail*? Like he *always does*?

Theo presses his face into his dusty, torn-up palms. He'll be lucky if his punishment is just execution in the culling fields. He'll be hung from the gate. He'll choke on his own intestines. Or maybe his father will drown him in the river like an unwanted newborn, hold his head underwater until his lungs flood and he slowly, slowly stops struggling.

This was supposed to be something wonderful. No, more than wonderful. Something perfect. He spent so long praying for this—a chance to get Benji back, to get his father back, to get his dignity back—and it was finally in his hands, glimmering like a star plucked from Heaven just for him. Sister Kipling's own words: *We need your help*.

And he wasted it.

He has to make this right. He has no other choice. Reverend Mother Woodside made sure he knew, his father made sure he knew, every member of the death squads made sure he *knew*.

Make it right or die.

"O Lord," he starts again, because he has to, he has to, "my heart is rotten with sin. It is in every cell, and there is no part of me that is good. Yet You still love me." He has to keep saying it, or he'll forget. It's so easy to forget. "I have fallen short of Your infinite glory, but You are still here. I wash my soul in the blood of the Lamb and ask that You fill me with Your Spirit and guide me to where I need to be. Through Jesus Christ, I pray."

When the prayers slow to a trickle, the last strings of bile on a sick man's lips, finally, *finally*, Theo wipes his chin and faces Reformation Faith Evangelical Church.

Squad Absolution is falling apart at the seams. With two squads missing in as many days, they arrived last night on Mother Woodside's orders, and now the soldiers pace like trapped animals. They snap at one another, snarling over imagined slights. A few hours ago, a knife was drawn over a stolen cigarette. Their white robes are speckled with gentle spots of color, rainbow light filtering through stained glass windows, and the beauty of it makes Theo's breath catch for just a second—the Angels and their robes and the glory of God and everything—but one of the soldiers notices Theo is done praying and shoves him against the altar. The nest of Graces behind them keens, dozens of mouths wailing in unison.

"Don't *fucking* look at me," the soldier hisses. Brother Husock is twice Theo's size and almost twice his age, a truck driver who found God just weeks before Judgment Day.

"I wasn't," Theo whimpers, but he stops because if God sees fit to punish him this way, then he should keep his mouth shut and take it. He was the one who let Benji leave the church. He's the reason Heaven moves farther away every hour.

Forgive my unforgivable trespasses. Cleanse me from unrighteousness.

Benji was going to save them. Benji was going to make the world perfect again. Only then could the Angels come home to God's arms. Without Benji, there's nothing but a long, suffering existence in this world—and Hell in the next.

Make it right or die. He will be faced with flames. Every Angel will burn. God's wrath will come crashing down now and forever.

"Brother Husock. Please."

The softness of the voice shocks Theo for a moment. Every member of Absolution turns to find Sister Kipling emerging from the back of the church, the golden sash of her robe glimmering in the sun. Every mouth shuts, and every head dips in reverence, for there is a saint of saints among them.

The creator of the Flood. Seraph's godmother. The blacksmith of the sword of God.

"There's no need for this," she says.

"Of course, Sister," Brother Husock says, eyes downcast.

Sister Kipling, with the gentlest of smiles, holds out a hand, one with a cross carved into the back. Theo is at her side as quickly as he can make it. It's pitiful, but he can't stop himself.

She sits him down in one of the far pews and folds herself up beside him, watching as Squad Absolution goes back to its routine of pacing, checking weapons, staring blearily out the broken front door of the church.

"You must give them time," Sister Kipling says. Her voice is no louder than a whisper; her eyes focus on nothing in particular, staring thousands of feet away. "God's will finds a way."

She reminds Theo of his mother. They have the same mousy hair, the same shrewd face. The only difference is that Theo wonders if Sister Kipling purposefully avoids the sunlight or if her ghoul-pale skin is a coincidence.

"I know," Theo says. He's always known. He watched his mother walk away from their family to make the world right, knowing she would never come back. She and Father Clevenger went to the heart of the nonbelievers, unleashed the Flood unto them, and accepted that they would die to do what needed to be done. Theo had always accepted the same—but he had so much to do *before* that day. Benji was always a part of that.

The thing is, Benji has his priorities wrong. Benji puts people first. It makes him sweet, but it makes him weak. Theo puts the Angels first, puts righteousness first, puts *God* first. He always has. He always . . .

His fingers dig into his scalp. He can't even get that right. He loves Benji. They were supposed to save the world together. And somehow, they'd both managed to mess everything up.

Theo says, "It's my job to make it right."

"Theodore," Sister Kipling murmurs.

"It is." It *is* his job to make everything right. And he will. When he does, he will have Benji back by his side, his father will look him in the eye, and the death squads will realize the mistake they made when they cast him out. It will work out. It has to. God is good. "He'll come back eventually. He said he would. I can talk to him about how it's too dangerous out there, that it's better to come home—"

Another soldier, Brother Rowland, picks up his head. "There's not enough time."

"There's always time," Theo counters, because it's something his mother always said.

"Fuck that." Brother Rowland puts a cigarette between his lips and strikes a match. "We should just cut off her legs and be done with it. Let her try and run like *that*."

How dare he. That language in a holy place! "That is not how you treat a warrior of God!"

"That bitch took everything!" Brother Rowland's voice cracks through the atrium. Sister Kipling stares at nothing and does not say a word. "I'm not going to burn just because you can't put a heretic in her place!"

BANG.

Something hits the remnants of the door.

Brother Rowland drops his cigarette. Theo could choke on his heart climbing into his throat. The sound echoes, *bang-bang-bang*, bouncing off the rafters and deep into the cavity of Theo's chest.

A person steps into the sanctuary. Backlit by the sun. Hair turned copper, a halo.

Theo recognizes him immediately, and when his name

comes to him like a prayer, it is the first that has tasted sweet in days.

He whispers, "Benji?"

Benji crumples to the floor.

Theo is out of his seat, stumbling over his legs, catching himself on the pews. *Benji.* What happened to him? His face looks like it was put through a shredder. His clothes are torn. His arms are blistered and flayed.

Theo falls to his knees in front of him. "Benji," he says, "Benji, look at me." He pulls the tiny boy into his lap, gathering him against his chest, pressing his face to the ruined flesh of his cheek. "I'm right here. What happened? Are you okay?"

"They—" Benji chokes. The word sounds awful. Theo can't believe what the Flood has done to him, what Seraph has done. Sister Kipling will be so proud, Mother Woodside will be so proud, his father will be *so proud.*

Benji has come back to him.

"They found out." Benji is sobbing without tears, a painful hitch in his words. The nest howls. "They found out about Seraph, and they hate me."

"Oh, Ben," Theo murmurs. He had known they would eventually, but he doesn't say that. In a good relationship, there's no need for petty shit like, *I could have told you so.* Benji would realize Theo was right on his own, and they could talk about it then.

Weakly, his voice so small Theo can barely hear it, Benji says, "I want to go home."

Theo would hold him here forever if he could. The Angels are saved, and everyone in Reformation Faith Evangelical Church can feel it.

"I do too," Theo says. *Thank God, thank God, thank God.* "Let's go home."

BENJAMIN

Chapter 27

And so will I go in unto the king . . .
and if I perish, I perish.

—Esther 4:16

Before I left for Reformation Faith Evangelical Church, Nick told me that 99 percent of lying is just figuring out what the other person wants to hear. He said it's what the Angels have always done, and I laughed because otherwise it would have hurt too much to acknowledge. The other 1 percent is keeping your story straight, and if you read the Bible cover to cover, it's clear the Angels don't care about that, so feed them a steady diet of their own bullshit until they choke on it.

If Theo wants to hear I've been driven from my friends, then that's what I'll tell him. I'll tell him I want to go back to New Nazareth. I'll tell him anything.

But I can't call this home anymore.

It's been a month since I last saw New Nazareth, and it is the mouth of Hell. Death-squad soldiers stand at attention by the gate, their Graces wheezing and coughing. Snipers lurk behind curls of barbed wire at the top of the wall, some keeping an eye on the road from the shade of the stairs. Bodies of nonbelievers hang in various stages of rot. Between them, giant letters scream *GOD LOVES YOU, REPENT SINNERS, THE TIME HAS COME. TRUST IN THE LORD AND YOU WILL BE SAVED.* Flies buzz in an incessant cloud, and when the wind hits right, I smell it.

I hear it too; the crowd on the other side of the gate. Word must have gotten out that their savior is coming home. Through the narrow slats in the gate, an ocean of bodies presses forward, desperate for a look, a touch, a whisper, anything. A reverend on the other side preaches: "All our troubles have a part. Our groaning, our burden, they are His plan." Arms raise, fists beat on chests. "They shape us so we may see His truth. So that we may work, we may fight—and we have worked and we have fought, and today, today, our suffering will bear fruit."

My flesh is a single, perfect, God-given fig meant to feed all the hungry. I am their savior in Angel whites and skin peeling off the bone.

"Are you ready?" Theo asks.

I can't answer.

Sister Kipling looks over at us and says nothing. She's gilded like a saint, and I want to tear her apart. I want to ruin her, I want to make her hurt the same way she hurt me. *Vengeance is mine; I will repay, saith the Lord.*

A gate guard bellows, "Clear!" and it's met with the roar of motors and the rattle of chains.

The gates creak apart. Graces shake themselves and stamp their feet. I reach out to each, whispering that it's okay, to find solace because I'm going to buzz out of my skin with the strength of their emotions. The preaching turns to a cry: "We have sown seeds with our suffering, and now it is time to reap what we are due!"

I can do this. I trust the ALC to do this too.

CLANG.

The gates come to rest, and the mouth of Hell is open.

There are so many people waiting. A sea of white robes and white faces, painted with grass stains, dirt, and the gold and gray of the clergy; soldiers, children, and everyone I've ever known. The preaching stops, and the silence is a physical thing, crushing down on all of us, a vacuum left in the aftermath of hundreds of people sucking in a breath. There's no oxygen left. Or maybe that's just my lungs liquefying between my ribs, choking the air out of my chest.

This is all for me. Because I have come back. Because I have saved them.

The death squad escorting us starts toward the crowd, and they crush forward to meet us. A tide, a thousand prayers rising from the earth. The soldiers tighten around us, their bodies a wall, but hands still stick out between them. Someone snags my jacket. A nail hooks Sister Kipling's robes.

"Seraph!" a woman cries, cradling a baby to her chest. "Bless you! Bless you!"

Every face is one I left behind. Sister Faring, a young mother who helps teach Sunday school and smiles when Sister Mackenzie describes what it's like to burn in Hell. Brother Gailey, an old man who spends his days in the chapel atrium and critiques the apprentice reverends with a raspy growl. Sister Clare, who is my age, barely, clutching her mother's sleeve. We weren't friends, but sometimes we shared snacks, and that was good enough for us both.

There's a deep whining in my throat, animalistic and terrified, like the nest in Reformation. Theo pulls me closer, his body warm and solid against mine. A Grace tugs away from their handler, overwhelmed by the noise, and people surge back to avoid them. I whisper them back, begging them to be quiet, to not make things worse. *I'm scared, I'm scared too, I know.*

We reach the edge of the swarm of believers, a squadron of soldiers breaking away from the mob to follow while others bellow for them to disperse. We're in the middle of the final road to New Nazareth, the desiccated corpse of Pennsylvania Christian University, surrounded by parking lots turned to farmland and squinting against the sun glaring off Kincaid Chapel. The river, the same river I tried to cross to Acresfield County, loops around campus, trapping Acheson between water and this awful colony.

"Where to, sister?" the head soldier asks me.

"The dorms." I can't be out here any longer. "The dorms, please."

But before we can flee, a monster emerges from the crowd like the sun emerging from the clouds. She is wrapped in white and gold, a cross burned into her bare neck, a wedding ring glinting on her finger as if she didn't order a death squad to shoot her husband between the eyes. Tattoos crawl up her arms and jaw, demons and angels and Genesis and Armageddon, and every other beautiful and terrible thing.

I shrink back against Theo even as I hate myself for it, the way I always did when we were still together. He holds me close like nothing has changed at all.

The head soldier lowers his head in greeting. "Reverend Mother Woodside."

Mom is stunning. She is disgusting.

"Welcome home, Brother Millward," she says. "All of you."

Her eyes find mine—and she smiles, so soft and gentle.

A mother shouldn't be gentle when seeing her missing child for the first time in weeks. She should cry with relief and hold their cheeks tight to make sure it's them, that they're all right, that everything is okay now.

Isaiah 49:15—*Can a woman forget her sucking child, that she should not have compassion on the son of her womb?* If she had compassion for me once, I can't remember it. Mom doesn't hold me. She doesn't touch me. She just *smiles*. Like she knew I'd come crawling back to her eventually. Like everything had been set in stone long before I ever arrived on this earth, and she has just been waiting for it all to come to pass.

"And welcome home," she says, "Esther."

No.

The Graces *shriek*. It's a chorus of screams loud enough to drown out the ringing in my ears. A flock of ducks erupts from the Kincaid Chapel pond, their wings clapping in a rush of feathers. A string of saliva falls from the corner of my shredded mouth.

ESTHER.

I hadn't realized how much I hated that word until I'd spent so long free of it. As soon as I told Dad I was a boy, he'd never let it pass his lips. Nick and Erin saw the word on the document, but to them my name was Benjamin and would always be. The Watch and the ALC never knew me as anything else. Not Esther. Not Seraph. Nobody and nothing but *Benji*.

Something else is screaming too, and I realize it's me.

I should kill her. I should tear through the delicate arteries in her neck, and the taste of it would be sweet, ruining her white robes and the blinding paleness of her skin. This is Seraph burning me alive, the fury, the anger, this is *what I am*. This is what I need to do. It is an inferno, and I am meant to raze the Angels to the ground, and I am more than happy to start with this one person.

But I can't. Because if I kill her now, New Nazareth will fall into chaos, and I can't let that happen.

Not yet.

I need time for Nick to organize and get the ALC into position tomorrow. I need to buy the Angels' trust. I need New Nazareth to let its guard down. There are guns pointed at me again—at my legs, at my knees, right where it will be easiest to incapacitate me. They could still put a bullet in me to keep me down. Theo clings to my shoulders, whispering against my neck, begging me to stay calm the same way I begged the Graces.

I wrestle back the monster, even as I see feathers flitting in my vision, even though I can taste her blood. Not now. Not yet.

Mom says, "You made it just in time for Wednesday service, dear. Why don't we get you cleaned up?"

Chapter 28

NOW IS THE TIME FOR THE FAITHFUL TO COME TOGETHER. BRING ONLY WHAT YOU CAN CARRY. BRING ONLY WHO YOU WISH TO SAVE.

—The Cloister Order

"I can tell her you'll only wear robes," Theo says. I barely hear him over the rushing of blood in my ears, the static threatening to swallow me whole. He hovers by the door to what used to be, and is now again, my room—as if I'll break if he comes too close. "Get you out of that."

"Please stop talking."

"It isn't right. You shouldn't have to."

"Stop."

My voice shatters. That must be what finally gets the point across. Theo stares at the rough dormitory carpet so he doesn't have to look at me. I wish I didn't have to look at me, either. I wish I didn't have to look at anything. There is a mirror on my desk, and I'm going to shatter it if I spend one more second here.

I was supposed to be free of this room—with its blinds that never close all the way, the drawings I did with a stolen pen on the wall above my ugly Spartan bed. With the particleboard desk, shitty chair, and cross hanging by the door. I knew it would hurt to come back, but I want to slam my fist into the mirror until pieces of glass jut out of my knuckles. I want to tear myself apart so I don't have to see myself like this.

Breathe.

Dad told me that I am a man, and nobody can take that from me. I am a man no matter what Mom makes me wear. Besides, guys in the ALC wore skirts and dresses sometimes, and they were still men. *It doesn't make me a girl. It doesn't make me a girl.* Besides, nobody wears masks inside the walls of New Nazareth, so everyone will see my razor-sharp, jumbled mess of teeth and rotting flesh. I could pull out one of my fingernails and not feel a thing. When people look at me, the first thing they'll think is *monster*, is *Seraph*, not *girl*.

But I'm wearing the white dress from my engagement ceremony, from my unveiling as Seraph's host. It hugs my waist and lays embroidery across my chest as if demanding that you *look*. My hair is too long, reaching the nape of my neck, and my name is Esther again. Within the walls of

New Nazareth I am a girl, and God—God—I don't know if I can do this.

I deserve this. I have to repent for the mistakes I've made. I want to destroy everything I see, but it's just easier if I don't fight back. I need to save my strength for the absolution, and I deserve it, don't I? If it's happening, I must deserve it, right?

Repent ye therefore, that your sins may be blotted out . . .

"Just," I say. "Don't say anything to Mom."

"It isn't right," Theo whispers. "I love you."

No, he doesn't. He burned the ALC. He killed my people. He did this to me. I want to bludgeon his head against the cinderblock walls until his skull comes apart in my hands, seeping brain and shards of bone between my fingers.

I have to pretend I want to be home.

I say, "I love you too."

Since Mom is one of the most important people in New Nazareth, our family's apartment-style dormitory is a decent one. We're in one of the biggest residence halls, closest to the heart of campus, overlooking the courtyard nestled in the middle of our U-shaped building. I even get my own room. That's a blessing, because if this had been Mom and Dad's room too, I wouldn't be able to handle it. I'd keep seeing him over my shoulder. I'd keep screaming for him.

This is repentance.

Theo presses his face into the crook of my neck and stands there with me until Mom calls from the living room. It's time to go.

"She may not be the most accepting," Theo reminds me, "but she does care about you."

I nod like I believe him.

"We all love you," Theo says, and he holds out a hand for me to take. I accept, and my other hand touches the pocket of my dress, where I've hidden Nick's note.

Sister Nelson plays the piano since Sister Shoemaker, the usual church pianist, sprained a tendon in her wrist while I was gone. Every note rises to the towering ceiling of Kincaid Chapel, twinkling like invisible stars. I wasn't expecting to have a panicked reaction to an instrumental version of "When We All Get to Heaven," but here we are. Theo squeezes my hand as I fight to breathe, and Mom smiles as if she can make up for the gory mess of my body.

For the whisper of the boy she's tried to erase from me.

Kincaid Chapel is the centerpiece of New Nazareth, and it has been kept perfect even through the end of the world. The reception area is full of banners and murals, the sun beams through the glass walls, and there are so many people waiting for us that it feels like coming to the gates all over again. An apprentice reverend has left out a basin of water for us to wash our hands as we enter.

Sister May, one of Mom's friends, whispers "blessed Seraph" as we pass. The whisper starts a ripple, *blessed Seraph*, *blessed Seraph*, and Mom beams in the perfection of it all. She's smiling so wide, it shows every tooth, even the ones too far back in her mouth, like her lips are being stretched unnaturally. After so long in the ALC, it's unsettling to see everyone unmasked. They're all barefaced, showing their emotions to the world with nothing to hide them. Their smiles don't look right anymore. Or maybe they've always been this wrong.

"This is for you, Esther," Mom murmurs, resting a hand on the back of my neck. I want to grab it and break it. That or tear off the rest of my skin.

We're greeted at the sanctuary by Brother Hutch.

I stop in the middle of the room, accidentally jerking Theo's arm. Sister Nelson's playing has softened to something light and dainty, but every note still pounds in the back of my head.

No, this isn't the Brother Hutch I watched die in the street. This is a relative—his younger brother.

"Reverend Mother Woodside," the younger, living Brother Hutch says in greeting. "Brother Clairborne." That's Theo. "Oh, Sister Woodside. I'm so happy to see you've made it home. We prayed every day for your safe return."

When I don't respond, Mom pinches the back of my neck, but Brother Hutch continues anyway.

"Please, I'm forgetting myself. Let me show you to your seats."

The sanctuary is far too big, another belly swallowing me up just like at Reformation. Reverend Brother Ward, one of

Mom's closest friends in the clergy, stands at the pulpit, surrounded by curtains the color of fresh blood. Everything else is white—the robes, the hands, the faces. It's *wrong*. I want to smear everything with dirt and make it right again.

Brother Hutch takes us to the front row, where Sister Nelson's playing is so loud, I can't make out my own thoughts. Maybe it's better this way. I don't want to think about anything.

I just have to make it until tomorrow. This will all end, and I can see my friends again. That's it. That's the plan, that's what Nick promised. Just until tomorrow.

All of New Nazareth crams itself into the chapel. Even soldiers on duty lurk near the entrance, guns resting across their backs. Brother Hutch leads Sister Kipling to the seat next to Mom's, but the prophet refuses to make eye contact no matter how hard Mom tries. Sister Nelson moves on to a gentle rendition of "There Is a Fountain Filled with Blood"—*Lose all their guilty stains, and sinners plunged beneath the Flood lose all their guilty stains.* Theo hums along.

"Now," Mom murmurs, leaning her head to me. Her gaze doesn't move from the pulpit. "I hope you're prepared for what's coming tomorrow."

I nod. Her expression sours. I say, "Yes, Mom."

"Today is all about how happy we are to have you back," she says, "but tomorrow is when we make things right. I hope you understand that."

I remember my first absolution, the day we stepped foot in New Nazareth. My leg starts to shake. I have been out in the world of sin for too long. Theo went out in that world as a servant of God, but me? She knows I would take any opportunity to turn on my faith. It needs to be hammered back into me. I have to be cleansed again.

I say, "Yes, Mom."

"Good," Mom says.

The last note of the song slowly fades out. The doors to the sanctuary close. The only light comes in through the tall, high windows and the lanterns set on the stage, the candles flickering on the pulpit. The lack of electricity makes Kincaid Chapel feel like twilight, even at the height of day. Theo sits up straighter and lifts his chin, just like we were all raised to do.

"Good morning, all!" Reverend Brother Ward crows. "What a wonderful, glorious day we've had. Oh, what a blessing!"

Answering calls ripple through the congregation. I tug at the skirt of my dress to keep it from sticking to my thighs. I have to stop myself from ripping the fabric. I need to feel it tear. I hate it, I hate it.

"I want to begin our worship service by offering a prayer to our savior, our Lord, because He has answered our prayers."

"*Yes!*" someone cries. I want to burrow into the floor and never come up.

"He has brought our blessed Seraph back to us! Let us close our eyes and raise our hands." I squeeze my eyes shut as tight as I can get them and keep my hands clamped in my lap. Block out Mom, Reverend Brother Ward, Theo, and everything else. "Let us glorify Him in thanks! Thank you, God, for what You have done for us! First you sent your Son to save us, and now this daughter to lead us! We are honored to continue fighting the battle You have ordained for us."

With my eyes closed, I swear I could reach out and touch the red stream flowing through the culling fields. I can smell the bodies of the weak and the failures hanging from the trees. I can hear the rustling of feathers, the scrape of teeth, the wet heavy breathing of Seraph between Ward's cries.

I don't feel God. I don't even feel the peace I used to be able to snatch from the jaws of monsters.

Just the culling field and the beast.

"We will continue to do Your holy works, follow You in Your infinite majesty, Your goodness, Your mercy toward us sinners—those who fight for You, and even in those who have turned from You. In every way, You are glorious and perfect. In Jesus's name, Amen! Raise your eyes, faithful, and may we lay our gaze upon the one who will lead us in this struggle!" My eyes snap open. "Sister Woodside, blessed Seraph, if you would honor us!"

No. No, no, no.

Mom turns her perfect smile on me. Theo shines as bright as the stars.

"Go on," he whispers. "You can do it."

"I—"

"Go," Mom says.

One more day. One more day.

My leg shaking, my body turning to rot underneath me, I stand and climb the stairs to the pulpit. Reverend Brother Ward clasps my hands in his.

"Thank you," Ward murmurs, bringing his face too close to mine. "God has brought you back to us, Sister. I want to thank you for your bravery, your courage, your sacrifice. You are doing more for this world than you know."

I nod, unable to say a word, and he smiles because he thinks I am being modest when in fact I am teetering between terrified and wanting to tear out his fucking throat.

Reverend Brother Ward turns back to the congregation, one of my hands still held in his.

"When we first began our mission, there were almost nine billion people on this earth. Can you believe it? Earth creaking under the weight of nine billion souls. And as we watched that number climb higher, and we watched plagues sweep over our people, and summers got hotter, and unrest tore societies apart, our leader High Reverend Father Ian Clevenger received a message from God!" *Yes!* the chapel cries. "For the earth must be liberated of us once again for the world to be saved, for our souls to be saved, so we can reach the Kingdom of Heaven."

I stare across the congregation, at so many people who believe every word of this, who believe the only way forward is slaughter. Who want to wring every breath of life from the world and watch every person suffer. Who prayed for the creation of *me*.

"Our way forward has been returned," Ward says. "We will be washed in the blood. We will wash the *world* in the blood. We will cleanse the world for Christ's coming, and we will help the Lord bring His flock to deliverance. And you, Seraph—*you*, Sister Woodside! Are the one who will lead us! You will lead the Flood! You will lead the Graces! You will lead God's people!"

These people have lived their lives for murder. Their singular goal is genocide in the name of salvation, and they will not rest until every human on Earth is extinguished. We are nothing but vermin to them. I've watched attempts at reasoning be met with bullets and crucifixion, and now there is nothing else to be done but fight back. The only way to survive is to extinguish them first.

Tomorrow. I just have to make it until tomorrow.

Theo's father acknowledges him for exactly half a second after service ends, so Theo meekly returns to my mother to ask if he can stay with us.

"Of course, Theodore," she murmurs. The general disappears into the crowd with his men. "I'll make up the couch for you."

"Thank you, Reverend Mother."

We return to the dormitory, dodging people asking for blessings all the way, and Mom sends Theo to wash up for dinner before sitting across from me in the living room. I'm taking up the couch, staring at the empty entertainment center. There used to be a TV there, back when this was still a college dorm. Now there's a Bible opened to a random verse below a framed photograph of Mom, Dad, and me. It's the one thing we were allowed to keep when we arrived.

The two of them are beautiful. Mom in a sea-foam green dress, Dad with his grungy band shirt and dress shoes. They're both so young, so untouched by everything.

And then me, a newborn thing, cradled in their arms.

"You cut your hair," Mom says.

I grit my teeth. "Dad did."

"I loved him as much as you did, Esther."

The name sticks like a thorn, digging deeper and deeper. "You had him killed."

"I know his passing pained you," Mom says with a hint of disgust—*how dare you grieve what was always His to take*—"but you don't need to be cruel. He made a mistake that affected everyone, and what happened was God's will. Do you understand?"

I need to pretend I'm happy.

"I understand," I whisper.

"No matter what, I'm glad you're home." She comes over to press her lips to my temple. "Tomorrow is just the beginning. I hope we can put all this behind us."

Theo comes back. Even though the food is fresh and greener than anything I've had at the ALC—potatoes, kale, and hard bread, all grown and made within New Nazareth—the idea of dinner makes my stomach turn. I shut myself in my room and press my temple against the wall until Theo slips in.

"Hey," he murmurs, bringing me out of the groggy mess of my head. I've tried to pray but nothing's worked. All I can think of is the congregation watching me with awe, wondering when I'll bring hellfire raining down on the heretics. "How're you doing?"

"Fine." I want to rip out his stomach. It's right there, his guts under a thin layer of cloth and skin. It'd be so simple. Sink my teeth in and take out his intestines like too many worms stuffed into his abdominal cavity. "Keep the door open, or Mom will flip her shit."

"She just left, actually. Said she needed to prepare for tomorrow, and I should keep an eye on you." He sits down on the bed beside me. "Told her I could do that, no problem."

"She hates leaving us alone together."

"Well, we *are* engaged." Believe me, I haven't forgotten. "Must make it a little more palatable. Let's get you out of that dress."

I hate the way he says it, but I hate the dress more, so I let him untie the back. He pulls it down and presses a kiss to the side of my neck, right where the rot has started to reach, and I let him because I have to. I let him skim his fingers over me because I have to. I let him push my hair back from my face and hold me at the waist because I have to.

He lied to me. Fangs, feathers, and flesh shimmer at the edge of my vision. The red stream blooms on my tongue.

But he tries to pull off my underwear, and I make an inhuman noise, my jaw practically unhinging, my too-long tongue curling, saliva dripping over my teeth. No, *no*, he does not get to touch me, he does not get to touch me like *that*.

Theo stumbles back, eyes wide, hitting the bed. "Shit," he whispers, "I'm sorry, I thought—"

"Don't touch me," I snarl. "Don't you fucking think you can."

"Is everything okay?"

"Just give me some goddamn robes."

Theo hands me a set of plain civilian clothes and stands a few paces away while I wrap my arms around myself and try to steady my breathing. *Breathe, Benji. Keep it together.*

"I don't see you as a girl," he says, like that's the problem. Like a cis person would ever get it.

"Stop. Shut up."

"I'm sorry."

He's not.

Late that night, after Theo has left for the couch and I'm alone, I slip out of bed to the window. I pull Nick's note from the pocket of my dress and smooth it out, pressing down the folded corners, keeping the writing facedown.

Beside it goes the trans bead lizard. The one he gave me, the one I hid in my pillowcase when we arrived.

I turn over the note. There, in his scratchy handwriting, are two words:

Squad Calvary.

Nick was in Squad Calvary.

I wander out to the living room where Theo is sprawled out on the couch. His lips are parted gently in sleep.

Nick should have killed him.

Chapter 29

Lord, allow them injury so that they may turn to You. May they cry out to You. Let their blood mingle with Yours, so that they may be washed of their sins as they pass to You. Let them be judged. Give them what they deserve.

—Angel prayer for the unsaved

The river is monstrous this early in the morning. It's not as bad as the culling grounds on the other side of campus—in fact, it's beautiful, the rising sun gleaming gold on the water, the large oaks and maples creeping across the rocky bank. But something can be beautiful and monstrous at the same time. Like Mom. Like the Graces. There are teeth between the twigs only I can see, beside a black bird waiting for an execution. More holes in my head. More of myself eaten away by the virus.

I stand on the riverbank and steady my breathing to keep from collapsing to the stones. I pray, but nothing comes up except Revelation 13:1—*And I stood upon the sand of the sea, and saw a beast rise up out of the sea, having seven heads and ten horns, and upon his horns ten crowns, and upon his heads the name of blasphemy.*

Hide from the wrath of the Lamb.

Today is the day New Nazareth ends.

The ritual is a private one, meant only for those close to the one seeking absolution. Mom and Theo stand by me while Sister Kipling lingers under the shade of a towering oak. Reverend Brother Ward flips through his Bible, clustered with two other members of the clergy—Brother Tipton and Brother Abrams. I want to hold Theo's hand, and I hate myself for it.

My bare feet are already in the water, the current eddying around my ankles, and I'm watching where the New Nazareth wall meets the river. Past the wall lies Acheson's downtown district, with abandoned family shops, boutiques, and all sorts of little things. If you keep following the river downstream, eventually you'll find the only bridge leading out of the city. From there, Dad's body. Probably festered and eaten away by now.

Right across the street is the most important. Because Nick promised he'd be there, waiting, watching from the roof of a shop nearby. The Watch promised. That's the only thing that matters.

The plan is simple. I whisper to the Graces, I rip New

Nazareth apart with their claws, and the Watch keeps me safe until they can pull me out into Acheson. Back to them. Back to Nick.

But not yet.

I told Nick I would go along with the ritual until the very end, that we'd have to wait until I was pulled from the water because I'd be too scared to concentrate on calling the Graces until my absolution was over. Nick agreed. He'd been through it before. He understood.

I also told him to wait—though I didn't say it—because I *want* to do this.

I throw up into the river. Vomiting what's left of my organs is just a hassle now.

"Oh, baby," Mom murmurs, brushing my hair back from my forehead as I spit strings of black and red into the water. "It's all right. It won't take long."

Theo helps me upright, and Reverend Brother Ward reaches out a hand for me to follow him deeper into the river.

He's traded his Bible for a knife.

"Sister Woodside," he says, "come forward."

I don't have to pretend I want this. I wade farther into the water until it hits my shins, my knees, my thighs. It's cold. The current pulls at me, and I brace a foot in the smooth rocks to keep my balance. My dress hovers around my legs, pulled by the water as if trying to sweep me away from here.

"This is not baptism," Reverend Brother Ward says. "For you have already been baptized, and the heretical world beyond our walls cannot change that." The water has a dark tinge, brown and blue and gray and green and red. There shouldn't be blood yet, but there it is, appearing for just a moment every time the water whispers the right way. "This is absolution. You have left your original sin in the watery grave, but now these new sins must follow."

I am a man, and I fought for it, and nobody can take that from me. If these sons of bitches want to get their hands on me, I will make them suffer for it. And I will be good, I will be good, I will be good.

Seraph is a monster of fangs, feathers, and flesh. I have believed liars and brought suffering upon my people. I will absolve what I have done wrong in this river, I will wash away my past as an Angel and the future they planned for me, and then I will bring this cult down with all the fury of a wrathful God.

I won't be okay, but I will be better.

Reverend Brother Ward holds up the knife. "These sins must be purged from you."

Mom nods, hair twisting in the wind. Theo sees me watching him and smiles. Sister Kipling stares out across the riverbank, silent, her hands clasped as if trying to tear out her own fingers. Behind them all, Kincaid Chapel stands sentry, and New Nazareth spreads out like a feast.

Is Nick watching me now, the way I'm watching them? My heart, what's left of it, thrums pitifully in my chest. My knees threaten to give out. Please let him be. I can't spend any longer here.

That's when I see it.

Above the wall, a bit of light winking from a roof. And again. The glimmer of a scope.

Nick is there. The Watch. Oh God.

"Are you ready to be purged, Sister Woodside?"

I say, "Yes."

The first time this happened to me, I was eleven. I had been swept away from my home, from everything I had ever known, and dragged through the New Nazareth gate. Mom had been given absolution by the Angels long before we arrived, so I was forced to watch as a reverend did it to Dad. I don't know how he stayed quiet, but I do know that when Mom tried to bring me into the river after him, I started to scream.

I submit willingly now.

I undo the dress's button at my neck, and it comes apart in my hands, white cloth fluttering down to my waist. The early morning air is crisp against my bare spine. I hold the dress up at my chest to keep from being exposed.

I will be good, I will be good, I will be good, and I will feel far worse things than this.

The first cuts are on my back. The blade is sharp enough that it doesn't hurt when it slices through my skin, not at first. The pain waits for me to take a breath. That's when the wounds split further and hot blood rushes down my sides, right where my wings would go if I were a soldier. It pools in the fabric of my dress, wet and hot and dragging me down. Ward is talking. I barely hear it.

The next are at my hairline, the blade digging into the tender flesh of my forehead and scalp. I squeeze my eyes shut as it drips over my brows and down the bridge of my nose. I'm breathing hard, biting down on my tongue to keep from making noise because I have felt worse, and I will feel worse. The point is not the pain; it is the blood. Symbolic flagellation, symbolic crown of thorns, and now all I need is to wash the blood in the river, and it will all be over.

Reverend Brother Ward looks to Mom, as if asking her a question. What kind of answer does he need? He's done hundreds of these. *Please, just get it over with. Let this be over with.* I can't breathe. I'm shaking. Let this end.

Mom says, "Seraph will heal her. Do it."

Theo says, "Wait, what's happening?" and Ward grabs me by the left wrist and plunges the blade through my palm.

It doesn't hit all at once. At first, it's a crushing weight slamming down on my hand, like the world has been dropped onto it, then something wedging all the little bones apart, and then the pain of it finally snaps, and I *scream*.

"The sinful blood has been let!" Reverend Brother Ward cries, pulling out the blade, still shiny with my blood, and handing it off to Brother Tipton. *This wasn't supposed to happen, what is happening, what the fuck is happening*—"You have felt half the pain of Jesus just as you, blessed Seraph, will follow in His footsteps and continue our journey toward God."

I stare at the black hole in my hand, just like the black hole in Dad's head, streaming rot-tinged blood into the river.

I think I'm screaming, but I'm not sure because I can't hear a thing besides the howling of the river, the howling of the monster between the trees, and the howling of Reverend Brother Ward.

"Let the water wash away your sins; let yourself be cleansed by the blood of the Lamb!"

Ward grabs me by the shoulders and plunges me into the river.

The beast between the trees, monster of fangs, feathers, and flesh, *Seraph*—it chooses that moment to explode.

The agony is instant. White-hot burning from my hand to every inch of me, climbing up my spine to the spot behind my eyes. My vision cuts out under the murky water of the river, and my hearing comes rushing back all at once, shrieking. My body is being dragged to shore, and every bone creaks like branches in a storm. I fall to the river rocks and vomit up what looks like an organ, almost whole, a bundle of wet black flesh that washes away with the tide. Sister Kipling grabs one of my arms, and Theo grabs the other, and I scream and pull away but Sister Kipling grabs my hair and holds me to her chest.

She's barking orders, *"To the lab! Get the fuck out of here!"* Then Theo is on the ground, clutching a broken hand, and I think for a blurry moment, *Did I do that?* just as his index finger snaps on its own. Brother Abrams clutches his skull before it splits down the side, revealing a gaping maw of teeth. Reverend Brother Ward stares at the dark liquid trickling from his mouth, dripping off his chin.

Something moves underneath the bloody skin of my back before erupting—the raw, new flesh ripping me to shreds, then a second, then a third, unfurling and tearing me apart.

I realize, as Mom and Sister Kipling drag me into the grass, that they are wings.

And then, in the last second, even through the pain, another—I did not give the order. I did not whisper for the Graces to turn on their masters. My word will not spread from Grace to Grace like a plague, dragging this horrible place down into the flames.

Nick will not be coming for me.

Chapter 30

We have made so many mistakes. Am I the only one unable to sleep at night?

—Sister Kipling's notes

There are no bodies on the culling field today, so it can't be real. There's no buzzing of flies, no metronome dripping of blood. A crow hops from branch to branch in search of food that isn't there. The water flowing down the stream is fresh too, so clear I could drink from it.

The beast isn't here. No fangs, no feathers, no flesh. I touch my face, and my fingers meet smooth cheek instead of exposed teeth. There are no open sores on my legs, just plain white skin. I'm not in my dress, either. I'm in the clothes I'm supposed to be in—baggy shorts and a black jacket, sneakers instead of standing barefoot in the water.

New Nazareth is silent. Not a body exists except my own.

It isn't right.

I need to find the beast.

I leave the stream and go to the student union but find nothing on the roof. All I'm offered is a beautiful view of campus, with a bonfire of red and orange leaves lighting up in the gold of late afternoon.

Why am I still *this*? Why am I still no different than I was weeks ago? There's no tongue weighing down my jaw, no open wounds to feel the wind. I'm just a boy standing on a roof, alone. But I shouldn't think about it too hard. When I'm here, I'm not out there. Going out *there* means having to deal with the pain, and nothing hurts right now.

And there shall be no night there; and they need no candle, neither light of the sun; for the Lord God giveth them light.

For the world will burn under the weight of it.

I walk across campus until I make it to the old health center, Sister Kipling's building. The laboratory, the office, the examination room. I muscle aside the glass doors and follow the basement stairwell all the way down to a deep, oppressive hall.

At the end is the room I am being kept in.

A narrow sliver of glass cuts through the door, offering the only glimpse inside that isn't hidden tight behind laboratory walls.

I press my face to it. It's cold. It feels more real than anything ever has here.

A bulging white eye surrounded by rot stares back.

That's me.

Surely I come quickly. Amen. Even so, come, Lord Jesus.

Even through the hellfire, talking:

"How much longer?" Mom. Her voice is choked. I think. Choked? Over me? "It looks—"

Sister Kipling: "You don't have to watch if you don't want to, Reverend Mother."

"I do. Answer me."

Shuffling. "At least a day."

A day?

A day?

A day?

The pain is in an ebb now. It comes and goes like the tide, in and out. Big changes, then little ones to fill in the gaps.

I stretch my hands, and shattered-bone claws carve tracks in the floor of the isolation room. I want to stand, throw myself against the walls, tear the door off its hinges. But I am exhausted, and my wings weigh me down. Fleshy newborn things. Heavy and useless.

My neck and chest are sticky with black bile. My dress is stained and torn, and my unholy mess of a body has escaped it. It destroys the perfect whiteness of this room. Good.

Across from me, there's a two-way mirror halfway up one wall and a small hole for people to speak through. That's why I can hear voices, murmuring.

Mom says, "How's Brother Clairborne?"

"He's fine." Sister Kipling. "The effects were minor. Reverend Brother Ward and Brother Abrams are under observation now. Tipton wasn't so lucky."

"Poor souls. It happened so quickly."

That agony—was that me? Did I do that?

"It's fascinating, really, how even latent microdoses of the virus react in Seraph's presence. A side effect of the blooming, causing a mirror effect in nearby infected tissue. It should calm in time, once the virus settles, but—"

"As long as it happens quickly."

Please, God, if You prove Your existence by making this stop, I swear I'll follow You for the rest of my days.

Then, of course, proof that Mom has dug faith into me like thorns under my skin, like a tattoo I can't carve off, like trauma: Even when my chest splits open the next second, I think, *But He still might be real, and I'm just too broken to feel it. It's my fault.*

Another ebb, another pulling back, another breath. My hair falls out in clumps. Blood and Flood rot have mixed together on the floor into something wine colored.

My body is too big for itself. My limbs are long, like they've been stretched on a rack, bending in places they shouldn't and packed with muscle and tumors. Painful barbs jut from my shoulders and the curve of my wings, right where little spikes grow into feathers. I press my face against the tiles and gasp for air.

I wonder how Nick, Erin, the Watch, and the rest of the ALC are doing. There's an emptiness in my chest where something used to be, and I can't tell if it was another organ I can't keep track of anymore or the sinking feeling of failure. Nick and the Watch were *right there*, waiting for me, and my body tore itself to pieces before I could raise my hand and turn the Graces against the Angels.

That was my one job, and it fell apart because I waited for Reverend Brother Ward to make me bleed.

I failed. And now Nick and the rest probably have no idea what to do.

Neither do I.

The door opens. Sister Kipling comes in.

She's the opposite of saintly, with her hair unwashed and glasses sitting crookedly on her nose, though there's a look in her eyes like she's about to be martyred any second. Watching for arrows or burning stakes.

She created the Flood. She built Seraph. She killed so many people to make me, she turned me into a *monster*, and she can't look me in the eyes. The Angels have made her a living saint, and she doesn't even have the decency to take advantage of it. They'll let her do anything, and she spends that leniency staring into the middle distance, hardly ever blinking, her hands wracked with tremors. I have never once seen her pray. I have only ever heard her talk in whispers, except for the terrible moment on the riverbank.

She's going gray. Her glasses are held together with tape at the temples. The crosses on the back of her hands look like they were done weeks ago, not years, almost painful in how swollen and raised they are.

She says, "I wanted to talk to you. Without your mother."

Sister Kipling sits at my head, as if she's kneeling at the altar of my body. I have no sense of myself anymore besides the fact that I am not what I once was. I'm too tired to see my body from the eyes of others, in the terrible way transness demands—always existing both inside and outside myself, judging as an observer. Now, I am a pile of flesh on the floor, everything hurts, and I do not give a shit.

She says, "I just wanted to say I'm sorry," grabs one of the budding feathers sprouting at my shoulder, and tears it from me.

Pain rips through the delicate, dying skin, and I shriek, moving faster than I have in hours to slam into her tiny body and drive her to the floor. I'm hunched over her, *towering* over her, limp wings sagging and claws digging into the floor inches from her skull. My arms tremble under my own weight. I'm so, so much bigger than her. Her neck would tear so easily. A drop of saliva falls onto her collarbone, and she chokes down a whimper.

I should kill her for what she did. She deserves it. Dad told me to make them suffer.

"Please," she says.

Please . . . *what*?

A cold pit settles in my stomach, a horrible contrast to the fire still searing through me.

I step back, my wings dragging on the floor.

She wants me to kill her.

"No!" She reaches for me, snatching for my jaw the way soldiers hold their Graces. I rear back, and she grabs me by my half-broken arm. "Seraph, please. Please."

This is all her fault—everything she's ever done to me, to the people who came before me, every single person who suffered as the Flood broke them apart. I should tear her to shreds, drag her by the leg and bite it off, and crush her body under my claws.

"I know you hate me," she says, clinging to me, "and you have every right. I understand. If it's any consolation, we're all going to Hell for what we've done."

She—

Our living saint is saying the Angels are going to Hell.

Our living saint is . . . a heretic?

No. No, it doesn't work like that. She can't be. She created the Flood. She built Seraph from the ground up. She destroyed me, she destroyed *everything*. And now she's trying to repent her repentance? Now she feels bad? *Now?*

She's so close. Her face is so close to my fangs. I should just end her. End whatever bullshit she's trying to pull, end this pathetic attempt to trick me.

But I can't.

Even though my jaw is dislocated and my insides bubble up when I speak, I manage, "*Why?*"

"Why?" Her lip trembles. Her hands find my face, and she holds me close, like she's trying to cradle me, keep me away from the stained white walls and bloody floor. "We have made so many mistakes. I never should have wanted this." Her eyes are glassy—with terror, remorse, martyrdom. It scares me. "If I can't take it all back, I can do this. Please, let me do one thing right."

Mistakes. Let her do one thing right.

But why now? Why is she coming to me now, when I am this—not when she could have stopped this, when she could have never stepped into the Angels' arms in the first place? Why didn't she stop when I begged her to? Is it now that she can look me in the eyes and see what she's done?

I speak because I have to. "Mistakes."

Sister Kipling says, "Yes. A mistake."

"I could tell Mom," I say. "Have you killed."

"If you want me dead, you can do that now."

I snap my teeth at her. She squeezes her eyes shut and does not move.

She says, "Lord, just make it quick."

So I sit back and watch. Watch the heaving of her chest, the quiver to her lip, her fingers clutching her stained white coat.

A heretic. It's too good to be true.

Nobody who has caused this much suffering deserves an easy ending. She doesn't get to do one thing right to take even the smallest weight off her soul.

God will judge whether she has truly changed her ways in her heart, but I don't have the luxury of being *sure*. I'm fucked no matter what I do, so I might as well try.

She can let Nick know I'm still alive.

Chapter 31

O sacred head now wounded, with grief and shame weighed down, now scornfully surrounded with thorns, Thine only crown!

—Angel hymn

The pain eases eventually, like most pain does, and God has nothing to do with it. It's less the ebbing of a tide and more watching a tsunami wash back out to sea, taking everything with it except bones and exhaustion. It's the kind of exhaustion where even breathing is a struggle. Where you're almost asleep, but you barely have the presence of mind to close your eyes.

The door opens again. I pick my head up the best I can, expecting to see Sister Kipling, but standing in the threshold instead are Theo and Mom. Their eyes are wide like they've never seen a Grace before. Like they've never seen a monster or blood.

"Oh God," Theo whispers.

"Brother Clairborne," Mom chides. "Don't take His name in vain." Her voice isn't as sharp as it could be. It wavers, unsteady and small.

Good. Let her see what she's made of me.

"I'm not," Theo says. "God, look at you." He starts into the room, and Mom tries to follow, but Sister Kipling appears in the narrow space between them, murmuring that she should give us some space. Mom jerks back—"That's my child," she says—but Theo takes the opportunity and shuts the door behind him.

He smiles. "Hey."

He's carrying a pail of water and a towel over his shoulder, and there are two things about him that are different. One: His left hand is bandaged. Creeping out from under the gauze are cracks like mine, the edges of lumps and broken bones.

And two: There is a little spark inside him. Something that calls to me, one of my neurons wormed inside his brain. Milling around like ants, firefly sparks, feathers.

"Sorry," Theo says. "I know I'm staring. I just—*wow*. Look at you." He takes the towel off his shoulder and kneels beside me. "How are you feeling?"

I take my first words slowly, try to make my mouth and throat do what I've always done, just form the words and put them out there. Instead, I choke. My body worked when Kipling was here, so why won't it now? It doesn't come naturally anymore. I have to force it, the way you have to blink manually when you're reminded of your eyelids. And when I do make a single word, it sounds like something else, an animal putting together sounds in a rough mockery of human speech.

"*Better*," I say, and it is awful.

Theo dunks the towel in the water, picking up my head so he can clean the black sludge off my neck and chin. His fingers trace my jaw. "Good. Sister Kipling says it's all over. I swear, it looked like one of Dad's old zombie movies. Did you know he used to be a horror buff before all this? I think it's why he likes the Graces so much." He squeezes the towel, and gross water splatters onto the floor. "I think I'm starting to see the appeal."

He stretches out one of my wings. He has to step back a few paces to get its full length, huffing a little under its weight. Once it's laid along the floor, he starts working through the feathers: smoothing them out, picking at pieces of skin trapped between them, preening. The wings are white like everything else in the room, but the color doesn't make up for how ugly they are, like the rest of the white things I've ever known. There is nothing smooth or beautiful about them, the way angel's wings are in paintings. They're fleshy and twisted, the kind of wings a human body would make if forced to build them out of materials it wasn't meant to have. Six of them, giant and sickly and useless, only good for being tucked up against my sides.

And for being a symbol. From Mom's letter to the faithful: *For when Seraph spreads its six wings and screams, it strikes the fear of God into the hearts of all who witness.*

"You look tired," he says. I am. "But if it means anything, I'm proud of you."

He leans down to my face. He's so small now. I used to be a few inches shorter than him but even down here, curled up on the floor, I am *menacingly* large.

He kisses my forehead anyway.

"And your mom is too," he says. "Even if she's not good at showing it."

I rasp, having to force every word. "I don't want to hear it from her."

Theo sighs. "I know. I'm sorry."

I reach for his bandaged hand, my claws enveloping his entirely. He undoes the strips of gauze for me, letting them dangle to the floor.

It's still recognizable as a hand. Five fingers, a palm, a wrist. But it looks like it was run through a wood chipper and sewn back together. Pieces of bones jut out—some breaking the skin, some just pressing up against it like they're straining to escape—with muscle and discolored flesh holding it together.

I did that?

Me?

The spark inside him burns, an ember of Seraph's fire inside us both. So many little fires, scattered past these walls, past everything.

The Flood should have split his skull the way it did that brother, the way it did that little girl. It should have cracked him open too, Seraph's growing pains rippling outward with an uncontrollable roar. Grief is easier to fake when you're not allowed to show it in the first place. I'll be glad to be rid of him.

Not yet. *Not yet*, I keep saying, *not yet*, *not yet*.

I get one arm under me. The other. My feet. Theo steps back, holding out a hand as if he could steady me. I waver on all fours for a moment, breathing hard. This is where my body is meant to be—Graces often stay on all fours to steady themselves, and my proportions have shifted enough that this feels natural. But it isn't enough.

I stand.

My full height is immense. I loom over Theo, a snarled tree of flesh and bone, my wings blocking the light and shrouding us both in shadow. Theo stares up at me, eyes wide and glittering with awe. The bucket hits the ground. Water spills across the floor.

"God," he whispers. "God."

In the two-way mirror behind him stands the creature that lurked among the trees. The creature that slammed me through the skylight of the student union. The creature that peered at me through the window of this very room. A long tail made of sinew and spines curls at my feet. My face is unrecognizable, my eyes clouded white and the skin pulled tight against the skull. The only thing saying it's still *me* is the open-wound mouth full of fangs, each tooth a finger long. I am a charred corpse wreathed in wings, nothing but armor, sharp edges, and feathers.

Hell has followed us onto Earth, and I am the monster that has brought it forth.

"See?" Theo puts a hand on my stomach. "You're beautiful."

The rest of the week is a blur of exhaustion, tests, and wondering if I can have a panic attack in a body like this. White walls, Sister Kipling's office, exam rooms, over and over. The health center is on lockdown. Soldiers plaster massive sheets over the glass walls of the first floor. I have been cut off from the outside world, and the outside world has been cut off from me.

Every time the sheets flutter and I can see outside, I want to slam myself against the glass. Where is Nick? Is he okay? I don't want to be alone here.

I want them to be okay.

Throughout the tests, Sister Kipling does not say a word to me. She takes vitals, checks her notes, and won't even look at me.

"Meet me alone," I say to her. Her eyes widen, and she hurries off.

Theo barely leaves my side, and Mom is almost as clingy. The general comes around a few times, and Theo's excitement wavers when the man wanders too close. They have the same facial features except time has turned the general's cruel. The only solace Theo finds is in me and in the lab techs he follows around like a duckling. He hangs on their every word. They share notes on the intricacies of my power: how I can bend

Graces to my will, coax to life even the smallest viral load, and shatter a death-squad soldier or member of the clergy in an instant if I just put my mind to it.

"What do you mean?" Theo asks, leaning over the table as I watch.

"If you kissed the Grace at Reformation," the tech explains, "you've taken in enough of the Flood to make you sick, right? That's Flood our Seraph can control. That's Flood our Seraph can bring to life." The tech looks over at me with so much love. It makes my stomach, or what's left of it, turn. "We truly have been blessed." His voice lowers. "Now, if only we could get the prophet to see that . . ."

Theo wrinkles his nose. "Shush."

I want to bring New Nazareth *down*—but there are so many what-ifs. *What if* someone who isn't affected turns on me, *what if* my power isn't enough to incapacitate someone, *what if* I can't make it out in time? What if Sister Kipling's confession was just a ploy to get me to show my unfaithfulness, even after my absolution? To show my truth as the worst kind of sinner?

I still need Nick. Even God's perfect weapon is powerless without people backing it. Just because a soldier would be crucified for putting me down doesn't mean they couldn't still *do it*.

At one point, when Sister Kipling is taking a vitals test, the tech takes Theo into the lab proper to look at some of the processes, even leaning down to whisper conspiratorially in Theo's ear.

Theo comes back beaming.

"If the world was better, I think I'd have been a biologist," he says, eyes wide and somewhere far away from us. He is sinking his hands into the Flood again, chasing after his mother's death, chasing after his own. His eyes slide to Sister Kipling, a smile creeping over his face. "It's beautiful, isn't it, Sister?"

Her fingers slip off her instrument, and it hits the ground.

Then it's the general's turn. His tests are harder. He brings a small Grace into the lab, and I grab the Flood inside them and build them into something else, turning crumpled masses of flesh into terrifying things with teeth and claws.

He says that the heretics in Acheson don't have long. We'll start with the city and slowly, methodically, perfectly expand outward, washing the world clean as we go. And the sooner we finish these tests, the sooner my body settles, the sooner we can begin.

"You understand what's being asked of you," the general says, "don't you? Are you ready?"

I do, and I hate it. I don't want to think too hard about what I'm doing, turning scared little creatures into war machines, so I think about what happened with Nick in the rescue mission, or when the ALC burned—the way the Grace flowed to me, worked with me, a missing limb I'd been reunited with.

There's none of that here. There is no love. Just breaking and building. It's what I was made to do but not what

I'm *supposed* to do. As soon as the general turns his back, I pull the Grace into my arms and let them curl around me. Even as much as I've changed them, they're still so bright. They were a person once. I want to hold them here forever. They're purring, Jesus Christ, they're purring, I swear if I could cry, I'd be sobbing.

We are the same. Do they know? Can they tell?

"That's not part of the test," the general snaps, looking back toward me. I snarl. "You'll mess up the results. Get another one."

What would happen if I split the general in half too? If I took that bit of the Flood in his bones and tore him to pieces?

My brain recoils from the thought. If they could string up their own for speaking out of turn, if they could unleash a virus like the Flood, then they could do all kinds of things to me. Maybe they'd decide it would be better for me to be broken like the Graces they give to the death squads.

"I can handle this, brother," Sister Kipling says. "Aren't you late for a meeting?"

The general grunts. I see where Theo gets that look in his eyes from. "Don't fuck it up."

We're alone. Not even the lab techs are here, not even Theo. It's the most alone I've been since the isolation room. Sister Kipling's big eyes waver behind her glasses, her throat bobbing as if she's trying to draw my eyes to the delicate veins.

She says, so softly, "What?"

I start with, "I'm not going to kill you." She looks away. "If you really feel so terrible, make yourself useful. Do something for me."

"Yes," she says. "Of course."

I reach behind my wing, where an ugly pocket has formed in my skin, and I pull out the trans flag bead lizard. I gently clamp it between the teeth of the little Grace and draw them a mental map of Acheson—through the downtown district, through the government district, all the way to the ALC and the bank. I show them Nick's face, Erin's, everyone's. They stare at me with wide, beautiful eyes.

The clergy will want to bless me before my first march on the city. They will want to make a show—they have *always* made a show. They will make a worship out of it, a consecration.

I will make sure Nick does not miss it.

I hope.

"The day before the general sends me out into Acheson," I tell her, "you get this past the gates and into the city. Am I clear?"

"I don't know when that is."

"Then *find out*." I let the words snarl in my throat. She cringes. "These people would kill for you. Put your saintliness to some goddamn use."

"Of course," she says. "Of course."

Please let Nick know what it means. Please let the Watch come back for me. Please don't leave me alone. Because I don't know if I can stop this myself.

Days pass. I don't know how long it's been since my spine snapped in the river, but I do know that the days are getting longer, peaking hotter. It's the middle of the night, and I sit on the roof of the health center, wings spread out to soak up the moonlight. Graces walk the perimeter with their handlers. The river glimmers. Lanterns dot the landscape like fireflies. I squint as if I can see past the walls, into the city, to my friends.

I can't stand the waiting. I can't take it. I press my head to the gravel roof and pray, for the first time in a long time, for this to work.

The what-ifs come again. What if the Grace is killed before they can deliver their message? What if Nick doesn't understand it? What if they make it too late? What if they never make it at all? Even in the warmth of a February—is it still February? Maybe it's March—evening, I'm shivering. I just want this to be over with. I want to see Nick again. I'm so damn tired.

The door to the health center swings open below me. Sister Kipling steps out into the night, a heavy bag weighing down her shoulders. A guard at the door dips his head in reverence as she heads past the pond, through the field, to the road leading through campus. I pick myself up a bit, tucking my wings against my sides, and peer out over the edge. She keeps walking until she becomes nothing more than a little dot in the distance.

She's heading for the gates. She's keeping her promise. She *is* a heretic.

It must be tomorrow.

I can't breathe until I hear the distant hum of the gate. Tomorrow. It's tomorrow. Please, Nick, please.

I know Theo is expecting me—I've spent the past several nights in a renovated meeting room, where Theo sleeps on a mattress on the floor beside me—but I can't bring myself to move. I feel every single spark in the world. Every single Grace. I am there with every one of them.

When I was born, Mom named me after a woman in the Old Testament. She was a Jewish queen and one of the most beautiful women her kingdom had ever known. When her cousin offended the king's adviser, the adviser gained permission from the king to slaughter her people—but Esther foiled the plan and instead allowed her people to slaughter their enemies in turn. Mom thought she could name me *Esther* and not even consider the woman who saved those she loved? Or is the Angels' persecution complex so deep-rooted they think *they* are the ones who need saving?

Who am I kidding? I know damn well it is.

If Mom wanted to name me Esther, then fine. I'll live up to the name and lay it in an honored resting place at their graves. I won't be "blessed Seraph," I will not be *theirs*, and there is nothing they can do about it. I've taken what they've given me and turned it into a mockery of them. I will turn it into what destroys them.

If they want me to be a monster one step closer to God, that's fine.

In what world was their God ever a benevolent one?

Chapter 32

"Consecration" is the act of making or declaring something to be sacred; through the Flood, we consecrate the flesh as well as the spirit. Sanctify the blood, and make holy the bones.

—Reverend Mother Woodside's notes

Theo is taking a hell of a long time getting ready the next morning. Mom sits at the studying tables on the ground floor of the health center, legs crossed primly; Squad Devotion stands around, waiting for orders; and I'm eyeing the front door to figure out how I'm supposed to hold my wings to get through.

Sister Kipling, huddled across the hall, hasn't looked at me since she met my eyes this morning and mouthed, *It's done*. That's fine. That's all I need from her. The Grace is out in Acheson, the bead lizard between their teeth. My tail thumps excitedly against the floor. Anxiety thrums through my new body the way my heartbeat used to, replacing it as the thing keeping me upright and moving.

Mom says, "Sweetie?"

She never calls me that. I pick up my head to look at her.

"No matter what," she murmurs, "I cannot express how happy I am you're home." Her eyes are so, so full of love. I don't recognize it. She's never looked at me like this, especially not since she found out I was a boy. "We really are lucky to have you. I am so, so proud."

This is what it took for her to be proud of me?

The back door crashes open with an urgency that makes my wings fluff up like a startled cat. The soldiers have been using the back door to get in and out without drawing attention, but I thought they were all here. All of them, except—

Theo and the general.

The general stands aside, sneer lines permanently etched into his face, but Theo sprints across the lobby of the health center, grabs me by the neck, swings himself around, and *laughs*.

"Good morning!" he says. I wiggle out from his arms, rising up a bit on my hind legs so his grip loosens. I'm too stressed to play the good boyfriend. I don't want him to touch me. "It's a beautiful day, isn't it? God bless."

His head is shaved. His robe has all the room for armor underneath and a sash around his waist holds space for a knife and a pistol.

He's—

"Notice anything different?" he giggles.

He's been reinstated as a death-squad soldier.

I hate him. I hate him so much. Nick should have shot him when he had the chance. He should have killed him; he should have put his brains in the ground like the Angels did to Dad.

"This is for you," Theo says. "*Because* of you." He pulls my face down to kiss what's left of my nose. "I can't wait to show New Nazareth how much I love you."

I love you should never be so terrifying.

Please let the Watch be out there. Please.

"Are we ready?" Mom says, sweeping to her feet in a rush of silver.

"Ready as I'll ever be," Theo replies.

We fall into formation, Mom, Sister Kipling, and Squad Devotion all. Theo's hand rests on my arm as I step onto the lawn before the road to the gate, squinting against the brilliant light of late morning.

"How?" I ask Theo, because it's the only word I can get out of me that isn't a flurry of *fuck you fuck you fuck you.*

"You're home," he says. "I need to be by your side."

This is what he's always wanted. I came back, and he gets his dreams handed to him in a bundle of white fabric. They would look better stained with blood, the contents of his skull dripping down those perfect robes.

Keep it together.

We turn a corner, coming from the trees lining the path,

to face the gate. Three crosses draped in cloth have been erected beside the entrance. The entire population of New Nazareth has turned out to see me off, gathered desperately around Reverend Brother Ward's hastily constructed pulpit.

The hush is instant. The cloth of the crosses, red like Jesus's blood, flutters in the breeze coming off the river. The gate is cracked open the smallest bit, waiting for Mom's word, castinga shadow over the crosses complete with the silhouettes of barbed-wire coils and wall guards. It smells like the river, rotting bodies, and the sweat of hundreds of Angels pressed together in devotion.

I am a broken record, begging: *Please.*

And there are Graces. New Nazareth keeps at least a dozen beasts for war, and now they're here for me, shivering beside their handlers. Their emotions come in like the tide. Hunger. Anger. Pain. The things everyone would feel, really, if put in their places.

Look at the terrible, beautiful things the Flood has created. Three bodies lashed together, teetering on jagged stilts as ribs break through their skin. A grotesquely stretched thing with tentacles crawling out of their chest and throat. A tank made from dozens of the dead, eye sockets and wailing mouths opening like wounds. Old flesh, yellow fat, pink organs, torn edges, and broken bones.

I whisper to them, "*I am here,*" and they all swivel to look. They look, just like I made the Grace in the ambush look.

I whisper, "*I'm here.*" I whisper, "*I'm sorry.*"

Theo skims his fingers down my shoulder as we walk. "It's okay," he says. "Not much longer. And then we can begin." He laughs. "Our glorious work. Our God-given work. *Your* work."

He sounds like every other Angel. Holy words tumbling over his lips, rot coming up sick. How could I ever have thought he was different?

We reach the crowd.

We're swallowed whole. Squad Devotion is the only thing between us and the faithful. Reverend Brother Ward cries, "*Our blessed Seraph!*" and a cheer rises up like fire from Hell.

The long streams of cloth on the crosses snap in the breeze. I take my place in front of them, shaking myself out, spreading my wings. Theo laughs in awe. Sister Kipling keeps her head down, Reverend Brother Ward's jaw drops, and Mom just smiles as if the light of God is radiating from her.

I stare out over a crowd of murderers. Of slaughterers. Of people who think the only way to Heaven is *fucking genocide*. I want to burn this world to the ground, and I peek at the buildings beyond the wall for the telltale glint of a scope.

"Friends!" Reverend Brother Ward calls. "We are gathered here today in the presence of God to celebrate not only the blessing of our warrior, but also in a celebration of love and life!"

That—no. That doesn't make any sense. Theo watches Brother Ward with the expression of a little boy who's been told to wait patiently for his present but can hardly keep himself still. Mom clasps her hands, perfectly placid and calm.

I'm missing something. Something important.

Keep it together, Benji. Breathe. Everything is fine: Nick got the message, he understands it, he's going to make it in time. Everything will work out.

If it doesn't, I just have to tear this all down myself.

I don't think I can.

And suddenly I *know* I can't, because Reverend Brother Ward says, "We are here to celebrate the joining together of two people, two families, in holy matrimony."

WHAT THE FUCK.

"God brought Theodore and Esther together," Ward says. "They arrived just days after Father Clevenger gave the order to bring our Angels home, and God has raised them together into the wonderful young people you see before you today." *No, no, no; this isn't happening.* "They are warriors, and martyrs, and have made so many sacrifices for us. We should consider ourselves lucky to witness this here today."

A terrible feeling sinks into what's left of my guts. It takes me a moment to recognize it, but—it's dysphoria, worse than I've ever felt. Worse than when I was wearing that dress, worse than when Mom said my deadname. At least then I knew what people thought when they looked at me. Now my body is something else, something I don't understand, something I can't quite grasp. Do I have any part of me that still marks me as female? They have to be able to find it in something, so they can assure themselves that there's a woman under all this. Like there's a woman trapped in this flesh instead of a boy *being* this flesh.

"Let's bow our heads," Reverend Brother Ward says, "and pray together."

Did Mom know? Did Theo know? These motherfuckers. Mother*fuckers*.

"Oh Lord our God," Reverend Brother Ward begins, "we are thankful for the love You have given to Theodore and Esther's life—"

I say, "No."

Every head snaps up.

"What?" Mom gasps.

"No," I repeat. "No. I don't agree to this."

Theo reaches for me. "But we—"

I whirl on him and snap my teeth so close to his face that he falls on his ass into the dirt.

"*Fuck you*, Theo." I know I'm supposed to hold it together, I know, I *know*, but I can't *fucking* stand this. I rise to my full height with teeth bared and saliva dripping from my jaws, tinged black like the shit flowing through my veins. Soldiers raise their guns like I'm no better than a beast to be put down, and Mom screams at them to stop.

"Benji," Theo pleads. "Benji, please. Stop. Don't do this."

Did they even think about this for a second? Were they so ignorant that they thought I'd take this lying down? They know what they made! I'm done begging for a scrap of respect—I am done with those who enact suffering, and I am done with the sons of bitches who stand back and let it happen.

CRACK.

A gate guard screams. We look up just in time to see a man topple from the sniper perch and hit the road with a heavy, dull thud.

Thank God, thank God, thank God.

The Watch is here, the Watch is *here*.

Chapter 33

For in the book of Revelation, we see: We are God's chosen to break the seals, to bring forth holy war, to cleanse the earth and pave the way for Him. We shall do His will and bring the end times down upon the world, the end times, o LORD! The end times, o LORD!

—Sister Mackenzie's Sunday school lesson

This is how New Nazareth falls: in the wails of Graces and stench of blood, the same screams that must have come when Sodom and Gomorrah collapsed under the weight of their sins. Those lights stretching to the horizon, burning under my skin, they all blaze for me. The Graces standing guard at the gate brighten and erupt with fury. They surge forward like the *real* flood that God brought down in rage, grabbing limbs and heads, tearing flesh from bone. The taste of blood fills my mouth like it's my own.

This is your chance, I whisper. *They are the ones who hurt you.*

If they believe in judgment, let them feel it.

The people around me drop like the Lord has cut their strings. Watch snipers aim for the center mass of the soldiers standing around me, and the ones too far to get a clear shot at my body clutch their stomachs and skulls as I whisper, "*To me*," and coax the Flood out of their cells and into their bones. Reverend Brother Ward shatters the same way his brothers had at the riverbank. Brothers and sisters I grew up with crumble. Mom falls into the grass and blood streams over her delicate fingers.

And above me, on the walls of the New Nazareth gate, are the same black forms that saved me weeks ago. The Watch. *My people.*

Then Sister Kipling falls.

Two shots, high and hollow: different than the low chatter of rifles, a sudden *wrongness* that makes the Flood slip through my fingers. A pair of dark red spots bloom on her chest. She blinks, like she isn't quite sure what's happening, and she stumbles to her knees, grabbing one of the crosses on the way down. Her fingers snag the cloth, and it tears from the nails holding it in place.

That wasn't the Watch. That wasn't even an Angel soldier, it couldn't have been. That was—

That was—

Theo holds a pistol to my eye. His arm tightens around my giant neck and crushes our faces together, my whole body his shield from the Watch snipers, even as his broken Grace-hand squirms in every way it shouldn't.

My head is the only thing between a bullet and his skull.

My concentration shatters. The Flood escapes me. People scream, Graces howl, soldiers struggle through the pain of the virus to raise their rifles—but I am still.

"You told them," Theo wheezes. "You brought them here."

My voice catches in my throat. I can't speak.

"And she helped you, didn't she?" He pushes the gun closer. "I heard what the techs said about her. That you got into her head, made her weak. You did this to her, didn't you?"

The way he says *didn't you*, the way he trembles. He doesn't want to believe it. It's in the quiver of his hand, the way his eyes keep flicking to Ward's fallen body. There's a gold ring in the reverend's palm. Our engagement ring. What was supposed to be our wedding ring.

"Theo," I say. "Put that down."

"You're not saying you didn't."

My hesitation must be all he needs.

He takes a thick, ugly syringe from his pocket and plunges it through the tense muscle of his thigh, through robes and layers of white cloth. The gun trembles but doesn't drop as he slams down the plunger and the strange milky liquid inside pushes into his body.

The label on the syringe reads *HOST 12—DOMINION.*

He stole it from the lab.

"You know I'm smarter than that, babe." He pulls the syringe out of his leg and drops it, where it glints menacingly in the grass. "You think I wouldn't have a backup plan? You thought I wouldn't be *careful* with a heretic like you?"

Host 12—Dominion, a failed version of Seraph, moves like a breathing thing.

Theo's skin begins to boil, folding over on itself and expanding. His robes shred as twisted wings erupt in a spray of blood. An Angel stumbles too close and Theo grabs them by the arm and pulls them against him.

Into him.

His flesh melts into something *else*, consuming the body whole, bones snapping out from the skin and overflowing with tumors, eyes, and teeth. He grabs another Angel, slams them into himself, and explodes with organs and broken limbs.

He *smiles,* a mouthful of fangs, Flood rot weeping from open wounds.

Dominion is nothing like Seraph. Put together from spare parts, fingers reaching out from the skull, eyes opening across his neck and shoulders. His six wings melt into one another with shifting ropes of tissue, excess arms and legs dripping from his sides. Blond hair sticks out from bulging tumors and spikes of bone erupting from his jaw.

"You thought I'd let you mess this up?" Theo rasps. That's not his voice. It's nothing like it. "*I believed in you, Benji, but there are consequences for your actions. I had to be careful. I had to be* sure."

I grab for the Flood to stop him, but it slips through my fingers.

No, not slipped.

Pulled.

"Did you really think I was going to let you ruin this?"

With a scream like metal on metal, or maybe someone being torn apart, Dominion seizes me by the skull and drags me down into the culling fields.

Floating. *Drowning.*

My lungs burn. I can't open my eyes. I claw my way up toward air, but my body is so small, and my limbs are so weak. I kick and struggle, and when my lungs are about to collapse, I burst through the surface.

A warm wind blows through the trees, sending whirls of autumn leaves flying off twisted branches. I've surfaced in the red stream. It's so freakishly deep, it's flooded so much that the world is a flat plane of blood water. Trees and buildings jut out of the surface like the bones of the boy smeared into the road. Dozens of bodies hang from the trees. I recognize every single one. Sister Kipling, her face gray and bloated; Dad, a bloody mess; every single member of Squad Calvary. But how do I know their faces? I don't, I can't—

I struggle to shore, or what I think is shore, and find ground under my feet. My skin is stained, water dripping off my fingers and chin.

My hands are human. Not Seraph's. Not *mine.*

Behind me, a cough.

I turn. Theo drags himself onto shore, struggling for air on his hands and knees. He's just a boy. No Dominion, no Flood. Just a pale boy with pink lips and bright blue eyes.

Eventually, he gets his breath.

"You lied," he whimpers, and stands—Leviticus 20:27, *They shall be stoned with stones; their blood shall be upon them*—clutching a jagged rock.

NICHOLAS

CHAPTER 34

There is not much to say about the tragedy of Squad Calvary, except that we should have seen the sin in that boy from the start, and that it was an unfortunate failure that my son will not repeat again.

—The general of New Nazareth

"What the hell is that?"

Faith's elbow strikes Nick's ribs, and if she keeps moving like this, he's going to have to tie her down to get her off the wall. She's completely red with blood; head wounds bleed like a motherfucker, but the pain hasn't hit her yet. She's on the walkway with wild eyes, demanding, "*What the hell, what the hell.*"

"You good?" Aisha demands. She doesn't move from where she's keeping a steady stream of fire raining down on the lawn of New Nazareth. She's not allowed to be distracted, no matter how much she's shaking, no matter that she saw a bullet hit Faith in the head and now Faith is down and screaming. Her voice cracks when she says, "Nick, is she good?"

"She's fine." He holds Faith by the shoulders, by the jaw, trying to get her back to her senses. "Stop *moving*."

He's keeping it together. He saw Brother Clairborne down on the lawn, those blue eyes and terrifyingly handsome face, and he's keeping it together, so why can't they? She's supposed to be a goddamn soldier.

Nick bites down on his lip so hard it bleeds, and he drags Faith's arm across his shoulders. She's still making terrible noises. He draws down a shutter across the part of his mind that registers it as heartbreaking. Just because he can shut himself down—just because he can cram all the terror into a bottle, postpone the meltdown until he can explode without anyone getting hurt—doesn't mean others should be forced to do the same.

"All right," Nick whispers, pulling Faith close to him. The sweat, the skin on skin, the gunpowder, the ringing in his ears, and the weight of his rifle slamming against his back with every step, it will destroy him as soon as it is over, but right now he is holding it together. His job is to hold it together. "Up you go. Come on."

He pulls her down the stairs. The bottom, at the gate, is a terrifying opening—just a cramped space between the gate itself and the bloodbath—and Nick pauses there, waiting, until a Grace barrels past. Then he's pulling her through the gap, and she's crying into Nick's shoulder because the pain has hit, and it's clicked that she just got shot in the *head*. She collapses.

Sadaf catches her before she hits the ground. Sadaf's pink hijab is a mess of stains. Blood, sweat, dirt, God knows what else.

"It's shallow," he explains. Faith squeezes her eyes shut. Shiny bits of muscle stick out from her face. "Just a graze. Keep an eye on her arm." Sadaf nods and pulls Faith away from the slaughter.

The ALC set up base along the empty road, right across from the gate, as soon as the little creature brought him the bead lizard. Nick had known what it was immediately: a message. That Benji was still alive, that he was waiting for them. Across the street from this awful place, the place Nick had brought them back to, Erin yanks open the door of an abandoned florist shop to let in Sadaf.

Faith is okay. Erin is okay. That's his job.

Nick allows himself four seconds to feel the trans bead lizard in his pocket, resting right next to his own—to center himself, to get his heartbeat back to where it needs to be. Two seconds to breathe in, two seconds to breathe out. Two seconds to pack Brother Clairborne into the deep part of his mind where he won't come back; two seconds to reconcile the boy shivering against him with Seraph howling among monsters.

The four seconds end, and he snaps each thought off at the root and drowns them because if he doesn't, he'll melt down. Turns back to the bloodshed. Pulls the gun into his hands and goes through the gate.

Back to where the world is ending all over again.

One step into New Nazareth, and the crosses beside the gate are demolished in a screaming song of disintegrating wood. Nick stumbles back against the stairs, right inside the rough barrier. Twisted flesh and feathers shake off massive splinters, wailing with rage.

Benji. It's Benji. The creature Faith was crying about is Benji.

Seraph—Benji—is terrifying in his beauty, in his brutality. *That's* him? That's the boy who wanted to kiss him, who promised to come home, who made him face the broken fucking thing the Angels had turned them both into?

Nick realizes, horrifically, that he adores that boy with every ounce of himself, in a way that refuses to be packed down and ignored like everything else, and that is why he slams his fist into the stairs to shatter his train of thought. He pulls himself back onto the wall.

He slides into place beside Aisha. She's not going to last much longer. She looks like she's going to break with every breath she takes. On the other side of the gate, on the other wall, Cormac and Salvador struggle to keep up with the swarm of Angels between them and Benji. This has to end soon, or they're not going to make it. It's up to Benji now—all the Watch has to do is make sure he survives long enough to break this place apart.

But that thing. That fucking *thing*.

Brother Clairborne, or what's left of him.

The beast is a mockery of Benji, an unholy twin. It's what happens when the Seraph strain tears through its host too quickly for it to possibly stay intact, so desperate for meat it feeds on the corpses littering the ground. The soldiers still alive choke on their own vomit and shatter under the weight of the virus lying dormant in their bodies. One topples in the middle of the road as his head comes apart into a mush of brain matter. Benji and the beast smash together, ripping flesh and snapping bone, until the beast grabs Benji by the wing and twists him to the ground. Benji *screams* and barely tears out of its grasp, scuttling backward with his wing held awkwardly like an injured bird.

The battlefield begins to change.

The first error, and Nick registers it as an *error*: a Grace turns for the stairs on the opposite side of the gate, the ones that lead right to Salvador, and snaps its teeth inches from xyr leg. Xe only barely manages to put a bullet in the soft tissue of its eye as Cormac drags xem back. The second: a twisted hand reaching up from the stairs—*his* side of the stairs, *shit, he's been too focused on the lawn, he hasn't been watching his stairs*—and sinks its claws into his thigh. The Angel it's attached to wails, bloated skin marred with a too-wide mouth that explodes into gore.

Nick's response is an instinct—pull the knife from his pocket, flick the blade out, strike. The first hit breaks the nose and the Angel screams, and Nick yanks it out and slams it back in. This time it hits the eye and goes right through to the brain. It pops, and liquid streams down his hand. The Angel convulses, claws digging deeper, before finally going limp.

Nick muffles a cry. His thigh is a shredded mess of raw meat, wet and glimmering. The earth shakes as a Grace hits the ground, and he can't hear his own thoughts past the screaming of gunfire and the shouting of orders. His mind grabs for something to hold on to, but the pain snatches it away, taunting him, *mistake*, *mistake*, *mistake*.

This is what happens when he's wrong. People get hurt. The Angel didn't hit anything that's going to kill him fast. Just everything that's going to kill him slowly. God, the wound is *so big*.

He's so focused on his leg that he doesn't notice the Angel climbing over the wall behind him until something drips onto his forehead. He looks up to see a mass of flesh and organs grinning down at him.

And as soon as Aisha blows the Angel's head off, something in Nick's face shatters too.

Something trying to tear its way out of his skull. Something *has* torn out of his skull. The pain drives his vision to a single white point, and everything in his throat chokes on its way out. Bile floods his throat until he splutters for air, and it comes out his nose. He tears down his mask, and the same black shit falls out of his mouth, splattering his chest and pants.

The nest. The church. The Flood. Seraph is making the Flood bloom, the virus he took into his body when he kissed the nest at Reformation. No. No, Benji is too distracted, he's lost the Graces, it can't be him.

It's the beast. Taking Benji's powers and making a mockery of them.

Nick has been away from the Angels for too long. The virus has gotten weak in his head, away from other carriers, dormant and isolated all those months. And that means he has time.

He drags the Angel's broken body over his, wearing the mangled corpse like armor as he forces himself up to his knees—despite the pain, Jesus Christ the *pain*—just high enough to see over the edge of the wall. His hands tremble, little pieces of bone jutting out from under his skin. *Weakness can only be an excuse for so long.* Breathe, in, out. Pull the gun closer, settle the stock against his shoulder. Breathe.

On the lawn, Benji is on all fours, wings tucked in close, shoulders down like a cowed dog even as he gnashes his teeth at the beast towering over him. The twisted thing flaps its broken limbs and howls.

Nick was an Angel. He was made for war.

Breathe.

Benji lunges, tearing a bright streak from the Grace's stomach and exposing a pit of pulsing muscle. A string of what looks like intestines catches in his teeth, unraveling a nest of pink organs and yellow fat before the beast grabs Benji by the neck and smashes him into the broken tangle of crosses like a ragdoll.

The Flood sinks its claws into the empty space of Nick's skull. The wound on his face pulses with his heartbeat. He remembers how Benji talked to the Graces without ever speaking, how he could barely move his lips, and they would understand.

For the first time in a long time, Nick puts his faith in something and prays.

Benji. Can you hear me?

Benji makes an awful whimpering sound and pulls himself from the wreckage, splinters falling off his wings in a chorus. The Grace screams a war cry.

He prays, *I'm here. I'm ready.*

BENJAMIN

Chapter 35

Sometimes the martyrs speak of a place beyond us—beyond the understanding of those here on this Earth. As my faith wavers and wanes, most days, I wonder. Is it Heaven? Could it be?

—Sister Kipling's notes on the Flood

Red, bloody water drips off the sharp point of the stone, off Theo's fingers, falling in rivers down his pale cheeks. It's stained his robes pink, the same festering shade as infected gums. His head is still shaved, his robes still *soldier* robes, there's a hitch to his shoulders when he moves—and a curl to his lip, his cupid's bow twisted into a sneer.

He's crying.

I've never seen him cry before. He didn't cry when his mother martyred herself on Judgment Day. He didn't cry when his father flayed him alive. A teardrop traces its way through the slick water on his face, his eyes are red, and he's *crying.*

The blood water bubbles from my mouth. My normal human mouth, no fangs, no wounds. Without the Flood, I'm just a boy. No Graces to call, no Angels to shatter. I don't even have the testosterone to back me up on the *boy* part. And Theo has half a foot and fifty pounds on me—a cis boy who could shatter me if he put his mind to it. Who has done it before. Who is more than happy to do it again.

He raises the rock to point at me, his arm shaking.

"What," he gasps, "is *wrong* with you?"

I step back. My shoes sink into the slurry of mud and grass. "Theo, I—we—" Is this what I sounded like just days ago? How could anyone have seen me as a guy with a voice, a *body,* like this? "Put that down. Please."

"They gave you *everything*!" He closes the space between us and then some. He's almost within arm's reach, close enough that the rock could almost smash into my skull. "Do you even understand how much you're throwing away? How many people you're fucking over?"

His name comes out of me like a prayer, like reminding him he's human will snap him out of this. "Theo, please."

"All because you don't like it." He laughs, and his pale, pretty face twists into something more like Dominion than the boy I fell in love with. I take another step back and nearly trip over the submerged sidewalk. "You've never liked anything about yourself, have you? Always trying to *change* it. You've never accepted what you've been given by God."

He was the one who told me being trans wasn't a mistake, that God made me trans on purpose. Did he never actually believe it? "Shut up. Don't you dare."

"You'd burn the world down if you thought it'd finally make you happy with what you're supposed to be in this life. *This* life. You'd have a perfect one waiting for you if you just swallowed it like everyone else!"

But that would never work! Because—

Because I don't believe in Heaven.

The realization crashes down, sinks its claws into me, threatening to drag me to the water. I don't believe in it. I never have. I could tell myself that it all existed, I was just too wrong to feel it, that I had faith no matter how broken I was, but—oh God, I never believed.

That's it. That's what it comes down to. We exist in two entirely different versions of the world. Theo sees Heaven waiting for him when he dies, a life beyond this, something more. I see Dad's face and a fucking black hole. No matter how much I tell myself that there's a Heaven, I just can't believe it. My mind refuses to grasp it; it recognizes the idea, but as soon as I try to say it's true, I hit a wall. The same wall I'd hit if someone told me sewer water could be fresh and clean and clear if I swallowed and believed hard enough. It would be such a relief if I could just believe there was something after this, but I can't.

It's *terrifying.*

I say, "If you really think there's something after this, that still doesn't excuse what you're doing now."

"Don't say that like we're the bad guys."

"You *are*! Jesus Christ, you *are*! Nine billion people. You killed—"

Theo growls. "That's not the point."

"What, genociding the entire human race wasn't the *point*?" I fling my hand at the ghostly copies of New Nazareth buildings behind us, sticking up from the flood. "Like you haven't spent your whole life praying for this world to be wiped clean? Besides, you know, a bunch of rich white Christians and the handful of undesirables they decided were useful enough to man the guns?"

"Stop."

"I'm one of those undesirables, Theo. You are too."

"Don't."

"They just tolerate you because you *do what you're told*." The words come so easily, because I have seen what the Angels have done to the world and I *understand*. "They don't give a shit about you, and no amount of sucking up to God and your dad is going to change that!"

Theo lets out a low, guttural howl, just like Dominion, and lunges for me.

He brings the rock up wide to smash it down on my face—*bloody flower shattered skull*—but he's so much bigger than me, and I slip under his arm. Slam all my weight into his side.

We crash into the water together, splattering our faces. Theo scrambles to get himself upright. He's not holding the rock. He dropped it. I dig under the water to find it, but the blood is so thick I can't see, and my fingers push into mud.

Theo's elbow hits my ribs. I fall into the water.

He's on top of me.

He shoves me onto my back. His knees press into my stomach. I see his snarling face for just a second before he plunges my head underwater.

Don't breathe.

I grab for the Flood in his head, like I can pull it out of his body and leave an exit wound like the one they left in Dad. I reach out for a Grace that can snap their jaws shut and break him in half. But there's nothing. Just that girl's skull breaking with the force of the Flood, her hand reaching out for mine.

I want it back. I want Seraph back. I want it back not because of the power, but because it's who I am, and I am *done* being thrown among so many bodies.

Theo's arms tremble with the strain of holding me down. My nails find his cheek. His hand comes down on the side of my face, pressing my skull against the edge of the sidewalk.

He could bash my head into the concrete if he wanted.

I am part of the ALC. I am part of the Watch, the people who kill Angels, who fight back, who turned the extermination back on the exterminators. I am Seraph, and some boy isn't going to be the fucking death of me.

Wait—the Watch.

My head is going light from lack of oxygen, and the blood water is burning my eyes, and I reach into my pocket to find the knife.

This is the knife Nick gave me. The one he gave me because he saw a warrior, because a person like Seraph would be able to walk through the flames of Hell and come out snarling and burned—but alive.

The knife I haven't *had* since I gave it back to Nick in his room.

But I haven't had these clothes, either. I haven't had this body.

And I'm not going to be afraid of some boy.

Click.

The knife hits once, but that's all it has to do. It sinks right into the soft flesh beneath Theo's ribs, and I rip it out as hard as I can. A hot cascade of blood erupts across my hand, and Theo screams and stumbles away, his weight suddenly disappearing from my chest.

I sit up, water rushing over my face. It falls into my mouth as I struggle for air. Fresh red swirls around my arms, bright against the dark, browning pink. I shove myself to my feet, head swimming, trying to focus my vision.

Theo stands half bent in the water, robes pooling around his shins, clutching his side. Blood trickles through his fingers. His robes have fallen off his shoulder—he never bulked up as much as he claimed he would—and there are bandages sprawling the expanse of his back, peeking from his underclothes.

Bandages? For what? What kind of injury would follow Theo into the culling fields?

. . . A tattoo.

I'm wearing cargo shorts and a jacket. I haven't worn these clothes or held this knife in *days*. Theo hasn't had death-squad tattoos in months, let alone fresh ones that hurt.

He lets out a small, pained noise, barely holding himself upright. His shoulders hitch. He's dressed like he's always wanted to be, the way he's always seen himself: a soldier. And I'm dressed the way I've seen myself lately: a kid only playing soldier behind enemy lines. The bodies hanging from the trees are the deaths that have followed *us*. The stream shifts and changes with the bodies above it and the boys in it.

This place is what we make it.

I drop the knife into the water. It hits the surface with a hollow sound and sinks.

"Theo," I murmur.

His glassy eyes focus on me.

"You have no idea what you're doing," he says. "You're going to hurt so many people."

Slowly, I reach him. My hand curves to his cheek. He flinches away, more blood streaming through his fingers. He's sheet white, lungs laboring for breath.

My hand is so much bigger than his. His baby-blue eyes widen as he looks up, cracked lips parted just enough for me to kiss him.

"*Benji.*" Nick's voice. As if through the water, warped into something Grace-like. "*Can you hear me?*"

My teeth sink into Theo's bottom lip. My wings drag in the blood water. The warm spring sun beats down hard between glittering glass buildings and the New Nazareth wall, and I know the world has returned because I would know that voice anywhere.

Nick says, "*I'm here.*" He says, "*I'm ready.*"

My claws dig into the thick mass of tumors swallowing Theo's neck, and I tear back, rearing my head like I'm taking out a soldier's throat. Dominion's bottom jaw snaps between my teeth, tongue and muscle ripping with a rush of black sludge.

I reply, "*Look.*"

Nick hears me.

The air explodes.

Theo's head caves around the bullet, his warped skull crumpling in on itself like it's been bashed in, his left eye swallowed up into a deep, dark hole.

Chapter 36

And be ye kind one to another, tenderhearted . . .

—Ephesians 4:32

The carnage.

God. The carnage.

As I stare at the body of a father who had broken the neck of his infant as soon as the Graces set upon the crowd, I remind myself of the babies drowned in the river. These are the people who would cheer to see my friend's bodies hanging from the gates. These are the people who prayed for me to slaughter what little remains of the human race.

They did this to the world. This is their own fault. They brought this upon themselves.

But that doesn't make me feel better. Nick told me it's

okay to be scared, and looking out over a field of corpses, I am terrified.

Dominion—Theo—lies in the grass at my feet. His brain is dead, but the virus hasn't gotten the message, snaking through his suffering body. The Graces, the ones still alive, flee to the far corners of New Nazareth, unsure of where to go but understanding that the safest place to be is *away*.

Is this what the martyrs of Judgment Day witnessed before the Flood took them too? Was this the smell? Was this the silence?

No. Not silence. Someone is shouting.

"Stand down! Don't shoot!" Nick. *Nick.* Oh God. *"That's Benji! Put your guns DOWN!"*

I turn just in time to see Nick collapse into Erin's embrace; a shivering, blood-soaked ball with his arms clamped over his head.

Those who need help are taken back to the ALC. The rest stay in New Nazareth to deal with what we've done.

Sarmat and another large boy, Rich, build a stretcher for Nick since he can't walk on his own. He refuses to take a big scrap of cloth away from his face. At first, Nick shoves Erin away when she tries to coax him onto it. She gently points out that we didn't lose anybody, we didn't lose *anybody*, we're all okay, it's over. That's enough to get him to agree to leave, but not enough to get him onto the stretcher.

He stares at it like it's the greatest form of humiliation he's ever seen. Erin tries to reason him on, but Cormac shakes his head and says, "All right, go then," and Nick tries to get to his feet but falls. "That's what I thought. C'mon, boss."

Faith goes; the wound on her arm is too bad, the one on her face too painful. Salvador goes too, because xe walks out onto the lawn and sees the expressions of the dead and can't stop sob-laughing long enough to breathe. Sadaf goes with them, wiping blood off her hands and telling Lila to deal with the rest. Aisha lets out one long, muffled wail, but after Cormac helps her to her feet, she's shockingly okay.

"I'll lose my shit in a few," Cormac says, glassy-eyed while Aisha clings to his arm, trying to regain her balance. "Give me some time."

Erin leans against my gnarled arm and stares past the bodies toward the towering buildings of New Nazareth—Kincaid Chapel, the health center, the student union, the dormitories.

There are no questions about my body. We all heard Nick well enough.

"So," Erin says. "What do we do first?"

I don't know where to start. "The ears, I guess?"

Aisha says, "We don't need them anymore." She flings a hand at the landscape as if it'll hide her shaking. "We've got—we've got all this. Fuck the Vanguard. Condescending, cowardly pieces of *shit*!"

It's a glorious roar, and it sets off every living soul standing in the wasteland of blood and mess. We're screaming at the

Vanguard, at the Angels, at every motherfucker who has done anything to us. Erin flings her arms around my neck and staggers, squeezing her eyes shut. Across campus, Graces wail in so much pent-up anger that I can feel it flowing through my veins, a flood, a *real* flood, and we are *alive.*

We are alive, we are alive, holy shit, we are alive.

We decide we'll search a few buildings for supplies to bring back to the ALC, to tide us over until we decide what to do. Everyone but me, that is. I said I'd deal with the bodies alone. Nobody argues, because nobody wants to deal with the blood, organs, and limbs. I don't either, but I'm the one who can stomach it.

I need to see the dead.

Reverend Brother Ward and my engagement ring are stamped into the dirt. Sister Kipling's corpse curls around the wound in her chest as if she could survive if she held it tight enough. I find every soul I know and then some, and I press my face into the dirt and breathe in, breathe out the stench of Judgment Day.

I find Mom.

She bled out from a hole in her face. The bullet went in by her nose and came out by her ear, but she's recognizable the same way Dad was. How fitting that she went out like her husband did. To lose both of my parents to the same senseless war. *We will return to the earth for out of it we were taken; for from dust we were made and to dust we will return.*

Maybe it would be better if I did believe in God, in Heaven, in Hell. If I could believe she's going somewhere that will punish her for what she's done. But I can't. When I pick up her body—a sad, limp bundle of meat and bones—I can't believe that. Maybe I'll change my mind eventually, maybe something will happen, and I will finally feel that *push*, that call to faith, but until then, I'm okay not believing in anything at all.

I find Theo.

His body is the one that makes me stop. He looks like me, kind of, but what my corpse would look like after days of decomposition. A version of me long dead.

. . . Is that what he was? A queer boy like me who rotted under the weight of what happened to him?

How easy would it have been for me to end up just like him?

My eyes burn. My vision dissolves into blurry smears of color.

I plunge my hand into his flesh.

I pull together the Flood from his body, what lingers in his corpse, and build. I take out pieces, draw from his organs and bones, and sew it together with sinew. I cut apart his skin and pull out a little creature, eyes squeezed shut and shivering, wet from the blood and pus.

Theo loved me. I loved Theo. He was wrong and he was a monster, but I did. I do. Maybe I'm just a stupid boy, but

I don't know. Maybe in another world, one that didn't ruin him, he could have been better.

I hold the tiny creature to my chest. There is no other world. Just the one we have here. And in this one, I am alive.

I pull my engagement ring from the dirt and fit it in the creature's little palm—and I set them down. I wave my hand and whisper, "*This world is yours. What do you want?*"

They stay by me.

We come back to the bank late in the evening. Erin and Aisha and Cormac, Sarmat and Lila and Carly, all of us, have been talking the whole way—about the future, about what will happen to the Angels across the world, about how Acheson will change. By the time we make it back to the courtyard, though, we are quiet. The realization of what we've done and what's going to happen swirl into a blurry mass of past, present, and future, of fatigue and occasional fits of disbelieving laughter. One erupts when Faith picks up the little Grace that's followed us home and spins them around, saying, "Hello! You're an ugly little thing, yes you are!" The people who didn't come to New Nazareth, who stayed back to hold down the fort, gawk at me, touch my face, and ask if it's me, if it's really me. Does it hurt, am I okay? Are the Angels really dead?

Not all of them, I say, but enough.

I think it hits us all at the same time that maybe we'll live long enough to grow up.

But as soon as I find a place to breathe, Sadaf comes up to me and says, "Nick wants to see you. He's in the copy room."

I run to him.

The copy room has been set up as a miniature version of Nick's room in the ALC: a mattress, his beads, dim lighting, and not much else. I squeeze my massive body through the door, wincing when my wing catches on the threshold. It's just the two of us here, alone.

Nick tries to smile. It doesn't work.

He looks like hell. He's sitting up on the mattress, supported by the wall, surrounded by stained bandages and shreds of clothing. Part of his pants leg has been cut away to reveal jagged wounds packed with gauze. His mask is down, but he's holding the same ruined cloth to his face, and I realize with growing horror that he's just as much of a death-squad soldier as the Angels who were torn to shreds by the Flood at New Nazareth.

He takes the cloth down.

A fault line has opened across his face, from the left side of his forehead down across his eye all the way to his chin. Teeth sprout from odd parts of his cheek. The affected eye sits low in its socket, the bone holding it up shattered.

"I could—" *I could fix that.* I know I could. But before I can finish the thought, Nick squeezes his eyes shut.

Too loud.

Okay. He's here, and he's alive. That's what matters.

I lie down beside him, the only way to get down to his level, and my head settles against his knee. Not touching it, no, but close enough. His gaze sweeps over the broad forest of spikes, exposed bone, and feathers of my back and shoulders; the kink in my wing; the wounds, welts, and cracks in my skin.

We can talk about it all later. We don't have to speak right now. We promised we'd speak after I came back from New Nazareth, and now we have all the time in the world.

Nick reaches for me. His fingers press against my weird, broken excuse for a nose, the ridge of my brows, the soft spot under my eye, the edge of my jaw. The rough skin smothering my skull, the sores on my neck, all the things the Flood has done to me.

And he grabs the back of my head and pulls me up, arms trembling with the strain. I scramble up to follow him. He pulls me in until our foreheads are pressed together again, and I don't realize how much I'm shaking until he holds me tighter just to keep me still.

This is home. I am alive, these are my friends, this is my *family*.

Wherever the Watch is, I'm home.

ACKNOWLEDGMENTS

Hell Followed with Us began life as a fit of rage. It was written by a bitter, terrified boy barely out of his teens and came into the world an unrecognizable mess of viscera. I am forever grateful to the people who saw the beautiful thing inside and helped coax it into the open.

First, my agent—Zabé Ellor took me under his wing when I gave him a stack of half-finished drafts and a promise, and he helped shape it into something to be proud of. And then Ashley Hearn—my editor at Peachtree Teen and real-life literary genius, a whirlwind of brilliant ideas and unconditional support. As for the masterpece of a cover, Melia Parsloe and Evangeline Gallagher came together to make something that absolutely took my breath away. Peachtree Teen built an amazing team for this book, and I couldn't be more honored.

I can't forget my friends; the ones who gave me the strength to write the bloody trans horror of my dreams. H.E. Edgmon, Alina, M.J., Raviv, and all the others who have supported me while I found my way, I adore you. And the folks in my MFA, students and professors alike, who have put up with my work from the get-go, I've been so lucky to have you.

Mom, Dad, Mamaw, Papaw—we've come a long way together, haven't we? I swear this book isn't about you. (This time.) And Alice—of course, you. Always you. I'd burn anything down if you so much as asked, even on the days you have to talk for me because I can't. Especially on those days.

I couldn't have done this without you.

About *THE AUTHOR*

Andrew Joseph White is a queer, trans author from Virginia, where he grew up falling in love with monsters and wishing he could be one too. He earned his MFA in creative writing from George Mason University in 2022 and has a habit of cuddling random street cats. Andrew writes about trans kids with claws and fangs, and what happens when they bite back. Find him at ***www.andrewjosephwhite.com*** or on Twitter **@AJWhiteAuthor.**